THE SHADOWY SECRETS

THE SHADOWY SECRETS

TZANGEL

CONTENTS

DEDICATION

To the Magick within us all, the star seeds among us, and to those who dare to believe in the extraordinary power of love,

This story is dedicated

May it serve as a beacon of light in the darkness, igniting the flames of possibility and inspiring all who journey through its pages to embrace the boundless wonders of the universe within and around us.

ACKNOWLEDGMENT

I am deeply grateful to the following individuals, whose support has been invaluable in my journey:

- My mother, the remarkable woman who taught me that I could achieve anything I set my mind to. Her unwavering belief in me instilled the confidence I carry today.
- My husband, Anthony, my steadfast partner through life's ups and downs. Your patience and unwavering support during the creation of this book have been a pillar of strength. You are truly my king and soulmate.
- My children and extended family, whose endless support for my varied and ever-evolving projects has never waned. Your

belief in me, no matter how wild my ideas, means everything.

- My daughters, Summer and Jessica, who inspired the character of Saturn Eridanus. The beauty, love, and magic you embody sparked the creation of this magical being.
- My sisters from other mothers, Ashley Johnson-Stovall, Laura Reyes, and Patricia Benares, thank you for your constant encouragement, invaluable feedback on numerous drafts, and unconditional love.
- Everyone else who has touched my life, whether by teaching me something, offering words of encouragement, or simply believing in me. Your support and kindness have been magical, and I am thankful for our shared vibrations.
- Lastly, I thank the Goddess for the abundance and blessings in my life. Without your divine influence, none of this would have been possible.

Thank you all for being part of this journey. I cherish and love each one of you and send back all my blessings and purest love.

ABOUT THE AUTHOR

Tzangel, a Northern California native and a third-degree witch, intricately blends her deep connection to magick into her artistic, crafting, and writing endeavors. Her creative spark for The Shadowy Secrets series was ignited one night after being awakened by a beam of light from her Lemurian Crystal and a sighting of Achenar, the brightest star in the Eridanus Constellation, prompting her to tell the story of Saturn Eridanus. Her narratives, rich in magickal beings and paranormal adventures, spring from a vivid imagination to captivate readers with tales of quests, magick, and love.

With over 20 years of experience in marketing, along with crafting enchanted items, drawing fairies and angels, and celebrating the pagan Wheel of the Year, Tzangel now dedicates herself to sharing the magickal escapades from her mind. Married for 23 years and a mother to seven children, now enjoying her role as a grandmother to seven, she cherishes time spent with family, communing with nature, and delighting her grandchildren.

PREFACE

In the celestial expanse, where the fabric of the cosmos stretches infinitely, lies the Eridanus Constellation. Known as the celestial River, it meanders through the dark sky, a sprawling constellation that links star systems in a cosmic flow reminiscent of earthly rivers. This river of stars, one of the largest constellations, guides the journey of light and shadows, embodying the essence of both creation and the unknown.

Within this cosmic river, sister star systems flourish, each a guardian of mysteries untold and worlds unexplored. These systems, bound by the silken threads of gravitational harmony, share more than space; they share ancient tales of guardianship over the universe's magick, weaving the destiny of countless worlds into the fabric of Eridanus.

Amidst this celestial tapestry, a strand named Saturn

Eridanus shines with a light that transcends the ordinary. Named after the planet that mirrors her enigmatic and radiant essence, Saturn's story unfolds not in the vastness of space but within the serene landscapes of Massachusetts. Here, an extraordinary legacy awaits —hidden beneath the veil of an ordinary life lies a power inherited from the Eridanus Coven, star seeds of the Eridanus Constellation.

These star seeds, born from the cosmic river hundreds of years ago, were destined to blend the magick of the universe with the earthly realm, maintaining a balance that has protected both the witching world and the cosmic order. Saturn, a direct descendant of these celestial guardians, embarks on a journey through life's tapestry, encountering love, betrayal, enlightenment, and the unveiling of her dormant magickal abilities.

Miles, a witch torn between the worlds of loyalty and love, finds his destiny irrevocably intertwined with Saturn's. Together, they navigate the complexities of their shared fate, unraveling the mysteries of Saturn's heritage and the powers that lie within.

The revelation of Saturn's connection to the Eridanus Constellation and the legacy of the star seeds marks the beginning of a saga that transcends the bounds of time and space. Her journey through the shadows into the light of understanding and magickal awakening heralds a tale of discovery, heritage, and destiny—a tale that resonates with the essence of the Eridanus Constellation itself.

As Saturn's luminous path weaves through the darkness, it illuminates the potential for greatness that lies within even the most seemingly ordinary lives, watched over by the ancient celestial guardians of Eridanus. Her awakening is a call to those brave enough to explore the unknown, a testament to the enduring power of ancestry and fate.

Join Saturn Eridanus as her story unfolds, inviting you into a realm where the magickal and the mundane are intricately intertwined, guided by the ancient lineage of star seeds from the celestial River, Eridanus.

PROLOGUE

As twilight gently unfurls its velvety cloak across our quaint Massachusetts town, I find myself enwrapped in the delicate dance between the magical and the mundane. I am Saturn Eridanus, a name whispered by the cosmos through my mother at birth, binding me to the mysteries of the stars and the boundless universe.

Under the celestial canopy, the stars ancient sentinels of the sky, narrate tales of timeless voyages and cosmic lore. My nightly wanderings beneath their luminescent gaze transform into a sacred ritual, a silent homage to the vast, unending tapestry of the universe stretching infinitely beyond our reach.

Come morning, the world shifts into a vibrant tableau painted by Mother Earth's own hand. The forest near our home becomes a sanctuary brimming with life, where the emerald leaves form a lush canopy overhead, filtering beams of sunlight that dance merrily on the mossy floor. The air, fragrant with the earthy scent of pine and fresh soil, envelops me in a symphony of tranquility. Here, guided by my beloved Aunt Sage, I delve deep into the ancient wisdom of herbal lore and the sacred connections of our earthly realm.

Together, Aunt Sage and I meander through the verdant woods, each step resonating with the heartbeat of the earth. The morning light, now a kaleidoscope of golden rays, pierces through the leaves, casting playful shadows that dance to the tune of the gentle wind. The forest breathes around us; it exhales a whisper among the trees.

"Do you ever feel as though the trees are listening to us, Aunt Sage?" I venture, my voice a hushed murmur blending with the rustling leaves.

With a knowing smile, she replies, "Oh, my dear, they do more than listen. They speak. If only we know how to hear them." Her gaze drifts to the ancient oaks, their bark gnarled and wise.

Our path leads us deeper into the forest's embrace, each step a deeper communion with the verdant world. Aunt Sage pauses by a fern, its fronds arching grace-fully toward the earth. "This one," she murmurs, caressing the leaves gently, "has been a healer since time immemorial. Can you feel its vitality?"

I reach out, fingertips brushing against the cool,

damp foliage, and a subtle energy pulses against my skin. "It's like a heartbeat... a slow, rhythmic thrum of life."

We continue our journey, the forest slowly unveiling its secrets. By a babbling brook, we kneel, the water clear and laughing as it trips over stones and roots. We gather its gifts: stones smoothed by centuries of water's embrace and wild mushrooms nestled in the damp earth, each a testament to nature's quiet perseverance.

As the day wanes, painting the sky in hues of fiery orange and soft lavender, we find ourselves in a clearing. The meadow before us bursts with wildflowers, their colors a riotous celebration of life—vivid blues, radiant yellows, and passionate purples. The air is thick with their sweet perfume, weaving a tapestry of scent that lingers on the breeze.

"Do you feel it, Saturn? The delicate dance of sky and earth?" Aunt Sage's voice is soft, reverent.

I nod, overwhelmed by the profound unity of it all. "I do," I reply, my heart swelling. "It's as if we're part of a grander dialogue, a cosmic unveiling."

We sit, the earth firm and comforting beneath us, and talk of Daniel, my soulmate, whose love is as pervasive and essential as the starlight. Aunt Sage's words weave through the complexities of love and destiny, her wisdom a guiding beacon.

Then, our thoughts turn to Dianna, my childhood

best friend. Aunt Sage's brow furrows with concern. "Have you heard from her recently?"

I shake my head, trying to infuse my voice with optimism. "Not yet, but I'm sure she's just caught up with her studies. She'll reach out soon."

Night descends fully now, the first stars twinkling in the deepening blue of the sky. Together, we gaze upward, lost in the unfathomable mysteries that stretch above us. Our connection, rooted in a shared reverence for all life, gains poignancy under the watchful eyes of the cosmos.

"This journey, Saturn, is merely a whisper in the grand symphony of life," Aunt Sage whispers, her voice blending with the night. "But what a beautiful melody we contribute."

Here, where magic weaves seamlessly with the fabric of daily life, we dance in an endless interplay with the elements, continually reaching into the heart of the cosmos—a journey filled with love, learning, and legacy beneath the eternal gaze of the universe.

CHAPTER 1

"MYSTIC BEGINNINGS: THE SANCTUARY OF AUNT SAGE"

In our cozy little community, Aunt Sage shines as a beacon of wisdom, her wild, gravity-defying hair and vibrant outfits capturing the essence of her spirit. Her crystal shop remains a magickal haven, brimming with the enchanting scent of herbs, the gentle whispers of the wind, and the mystical aura of crystals that hold the secrets of the universe. Ever since I was a child, I have sensed the deep connection between my life and the metaphysical realm.

Entering Aunt Sage's shop is like stepping into another world. The air is filled with the comforting scent of incense and earthy dried plants while wind chimes play a gentle melody that seems to soothe the soul.

Behind the counter, Aunt Sage gracefully runs her hands over various stones, and her eyes meet mine with a warm smile that holds untold knowledge. Her presence has always drawn me in, like a magnet for curious souls.

"Saturn... I've been looking for you," she says softly as I approach, and I feel a shift in the energy around us, as if unseen forces are at play. "Aunt Sage, what's new in the world of crystals today?" I ask, taking a seat in front of her.

She chuckles, her laughter resembling wind chimes in a soft breeze. "Each crystal has a story to tell, and today, they whisper of transformation, my dear." She hands me a sparkling ametrine with delicate grace. Ametrine, a stone for balance, courage, and strength, is known as a stone of harmony because it combines the energies of both Amethyst and Citrine. This enchanting ametrine helps bring balance to all areas of your life. It can assist you in finding your inner strength and courage, keeping you grounded in times of stress. Furthermore, ametrine is also known as a stone of manifestation, capable of helping you manifest your desires and create abundance in your life. Its purple and gold hues dance in the light, feeling cool and smooth to the touch. Holding it, I feel a wave of clarity and peace wash over me.

"Ametrine," Aunt Sage says with a touch of mischief. "A stone of balance, courage, and strength, is known as a stone of harmony. Carrying it will help balance you, and enhance your courage and strength." I nod, admiring her talent for conveying information through stories and symbols. Aunt Sage doesn't just tell you; she allows you to experience the marvels of the universe firsthand.

And on that note, Aunt Sage used to spin the most spellbinding bedtime stories for me as a child, always beginning with a mystical prelude, "Let me recount to you the wonders of the cosmos, my dear."

Her tales would commence with, "Long ago, in a galaxy quite within our reach, there dwelled a young girl much like yourself. Accompanied by her protective older brother, they traversed through stars and planets, seeking kinship with other beings of light."

On a particular excursion to a neighboring celestial body, the young girl turned to her brother with a question burning bright in her heart. "Of all the realms we've ventured through; which holds the title of the most marvelous?" she inquired with wide-eyed curiosity.

Her brother, with a knowing smile and a sparkle in his eyes, replied without hesitation, "That's simple, it's Earth."

The young girl's eyes widened in sheer awe. "Earth? You've been to Earth?" she gasped.

He nodded affirmatively, "Indeed, I have."

Her astonishment only deepened. "Truly? Were you once human?"

With a soft chuckle, he confessed, "Yes, for a time, I was."

Captivated, she pressed on, "Are the legends of Earth true then? Were they all really trapped?"

He began to explain, "Some stories hold truth. I swear, I was among those who chose to serve."

Her curiosity peaked, and she probed further, "Hold on, you willingly chose to journey to Earth?"

He affirmed once again, "I did, out of necessity. Our kin were bound there."

She puzzled over this, "But how were you trapped on Earth?"

Patiently, he explained, "It's something you must experience to grasp fully. On Earth, remembrance escapes you."

She gasped, stunned, "What? How could that be possible?"

He explained with a touch of admiration for the design, "It was ingeniously crafted to immerse oneself deeply in oblivion, to traverse through the veil of darkness, and yet rediscover your true essence—that was the real mastery."

Intrigued, she urged him, "Incredible! I can hardly believe it. Please, go on."

He continued, "Earth operated under its own set of cosmic laws—gravity, where what ascends must descend, and linear time, where days succumb to nights."

Puzzled, she queried, "What is time?"

He illustrated, "Imagine it this way; here, our thoughts manifest instantaneously. On Earth, there was a lapse, a delay, which rendered the experience particularly difficult."

Finding the concept fascinating, she said, "That's intriguing, this 'time.' Tell me more."

He elaborated further, "Prior to your Earthly sojourn, you'd select your family, decide your gender, choose your ethnicity, pick a geographic setting, among other life variables."

Realization dawned on her, "Ah, so you got to choose your personality."

He concurred, "Precisely. You'd incarnate as an infant, entirely dependent on others to indoctrinate the rules. Yet, since none retained their memory, the rules were often fear-based, leading to a relinquishment of personal power."

She concluded, "That sounds less than delightful."

He agreed, "It wasn't for everyone."

Driven by her curiosity, she inquired, "What did you do while everyone was so entangled on Earth?"

He chuckled lightly, "I observed, and admittedly, it was quite entertaining."

She wondered, "What was so entertaining?

Reflecting, he shared, "Here we were, magnificent beings engaged in the universe's most avant-garde experience, yet completely oblivious. I endeavored to guide them as best I could."

She asked, "Could you communicate with them?"

He nodded, "Yes, but they couldn't hear me. I could only offer signs or promptings to aid them, yet they remained oblivious to the guidance."

She asked, perplexed, "Why so?"

He detailed, "They lacked self-trust and twisted the messages sent by volunteers, which only propagated more fear."

Confused, she queried, "What do you mean, more fear?"

He elaborated, "Messages intended to empower, like 'The Divine resides within you,' were changed to 'You are separate from the Divine,' and 'All answers lie within' became 'You cannot trust your own intuition.'"

Shaking her head, she lamented, "And they accepted these falsehoods?"

He sighed deeply, "It spiraled beyond control."

She inquired further, "How could they accept such delusions?"

He replied thoughtfully, "One must live it to understand fully. They even believed themselves to be the cosmos' sole beings."

Laughing, she exclaimed, "That's just crazy."

Agreeing, he affirmed, "Quite ridiculous, indeed."

Curious about the outcome, she probed,

"Then what happened?"

He continued, "The architects knew Earth was approaching a galactic phase unlike any prior, filled with a frequency that could reforge their genetic connection; their DNA."

Intrigued, she questioned, "What was amiss with their DNA?"

He explained, "It ceased to function properly. Their DNA was crucial for connecting with their higher selves, which is why our incarnations communicate so clearly with us. However, the new initiative required physical presence to resonate with these frequencies."

Understanding the gravity, she realized, "Ah, so more volunteers were needed."

He confirmed, "Indeed, but this time, precautions were in place. It required millions in physical form, attuned and ready."

She recognized, "These must be the 21st-century humans from the legends?"

He affirmed, "Precisely, volunteers from every cosmic corner converged to awaken humanity."

Eager to understand their role, she asked, "And what was required of the volunteers once there?"

He concluded, "We needed to awaken ourselves, harmonize with these frequencies, and proliferate them across the globe."

Awed by the enormity, she marveled, "That sounds nearly impossible.

He admitted, "Many observers doubted our success."

As their dialogue drew to a close, her eyes alight with wonder, she looked up at her brother and exclaimed, "But we are making it happen, aren't we?"

And I would always affirm with enthusiasm, "Indeed, we are!"

Aunt Sage would smile warmly and chuckle, adding, "Yes, my love, we certainly are. And you, one day, will realize that you are the living testament to this truth!"

Reflecting on these stories, I smile.

Surveying the variety of crystals on display, I wonder how Aunt Sage had chosen which one to offer to each visitor. Each seemed to pulse with a unique energy.

Suddenly, her voice pierces the air, and I snap out of my reverie. "Saturn," she whispered, her eyes bright behind the counter. "I have a special demonstration for you today."

My curiosity piques, and I move closer to her. She is holding a crystal I have never seen before, its deep blue patterns shimmering and changing as I gaze upon it.

"This," Aunt Sage explains, "is lapis lazuli. It's a stone of inner insight, wisdom, and truth. It can help you connect with your inner self and reveal hidden talents."

Reaching out to touch it, my fingertips brushed its slick surface, and I felt a surge of vitality. It was as if the crystal spoke directly to my soul, awakening a part of me I never knew existed.

Aunt Sage grins slyly. "Saturn, you have a natural

affinity for crystals. They respond to your energy, and you can harness their power."

The realization leaves me amazed and overwhelmed. I feel like a door to a secret universe has swung open, and I stand at the threshold, eager to explore what lies beyond.

Aunt Sage sits across from me, her eyes filled with satisfaction as the sun sets, casting a warm glow from the candles. "Saturn," she says, "You're a born mystic. The metaphysical world is your birthright."

I grin, expressing my heartfelt gratitude to the woman who had introduced me to a magickal and wondrous realm. "Thank you, Aunt Sage. I don't know where I'd be without you."

As we hold each other in a warm embrace, I sense a connection that transcends the physical. It is a link formed in the metaphysical realms, destined to shape the course of my life.

Sitting in Aunt Sage's crystal shop, surrounded by ancient knowledge and the radiant beauty of crystals, I can't help but feel I am exactly where I belong. The journey of self-discovery has just begun, and with Aunt Sage's guidance and the mysticism of the metaphysical world, I eagerly await its unfolding. Little did I know that Aunt Sage harbored secrets about my birthright— the Eridanus Coven from San Francisco but rooted in the Universe. Soon, I will uncover my legacy and all that will come with it.

CHAPTER 2

"STORM OF HEARTS: BETRAYAL IN THE SHADOWS"

Daniel entered my life like an unexpected storm back in high school. Now, a banker, just like his father and great-grandfather, he possesses sympathetic brown eyes and a subtle charisma that seems to seep into the very fiber of who I am.

Our relationship starts off with a fiery passion, promising excitement, and adventure. But as time passes, that fire grows out of control, burning everything in its path, including the fragile trust that once bound us together.

Every morning, memories of our private moments flood my mind, the laughter echoing throughout the days, and his glance making me feel like the most cherished star in the night sky.

But as the sun sets and the world falls silent, the night envelops us in darkness, and heartbreaking truths surface.

Once a star in my sky, our connection starts to fade, leaving me with an uncontrollable feeling of dread as I watch it slip through my fingertips. I can't deny the mounting unease in my heart; something isn't right.

One evening, as we sit in a dimly lit area of our favorite cafe, I finally muster the courage to express my feelings.

"Is everything alright?" I ask, my voice quivering under the weight of apprehension. He raises his head from his coffee, his dark eyes meeting mine, yet there's a distance in his stare that makes my skin tingle.

"Of course, Saturn," he says with a smile that doesn't quite reach his eyes. "Why do you ask?"

I pause, my heart hammering in my chest. "You've been very distant lately," I say, the words tumbling out. "And I can't help but feel like you're keeping something from me."

When his eyes briefly dart to the side, I know I've hit a nerve. But in an instant, his expression is perfectly controlled.

"Saturn, you have an overactive imagination," he says, shaking his head. "Everything is perfectly fine."

I want to believe him. I want to hold onto the life we've built and the magickal moments we've shared.

But the uncertainty gnaws at me, leaving me unable to trust.

Weeks pass, and tension between us builds like a storm on the horizon.

The unspoken secrets that linger between us poison our moments of laughter and desire.

Then, one evening, I overhear a phone conversation that shatters my world. Standing in our apartment's dimly lit hallway, I hear Daniel's voice, low and full of compassion, speaking words that slice through my heart like a knife.

"Yes, Dianna," he says, his voice a cruel echo of the love he once professed for me. "I want to get a divorce and be with you. I love you, and I'm going to tell her soon. I promise."

Those words shock me to my core. My heart, once full and overflowing with love, feels as though it's been torn apart, piece by agonizing piece.

I wait until he hangs up before confronting him, my voice shaking with a blend of hurt, rage, and disbelief. "How could you, Daniel?!" I exclaim, the words tumbling out in a torrent of emotion. "With my fucking best friend? When everything seemed to be going so damn well, why now? Why would you wish to sabotage it?! Us?!"

He looks into my eyes, and for the first time, I see a glimmer of regret.

"Saturn," he whispers, his voice heavy with an

unbearable burden. "I've fallen in love with Dianna, and I can't keep living this lie. I want to be with her, but I can't do that unless we split up and get a divorce."

I stumble back as his words hit me, my world spinning out of control. In that moment, all my hopes and dreams for our future fade away, leaving behind only the bitter taste of betrayal.

As I grapple with the aftermath of Daniel and Dianna's affair, I'm consumed by a tumultuous mix of emotions—betrayal, anger, and an insatiable need for answers.

After confronting Daniel about his infidelity, I feel compelled to talk to Dianna, my lifelong now ex-best friend.

Dianna was my best friend since elementary school —our once-strong bond, forged through years of friendship, now lies shattered at my feet.

This betrayal destroys my trust and faith in her, leaving me reeling from the pain of her betrayal. As I sit with Dianna, the weight of our conversation hangs heavily between us, a palpable tension that neither of us can ignore.

I need closure, so I ask three simple questions, "Why did you do this? How could you do this? You knew how much Daniel meant to me." At first, she's stunned by the straightforward questions, unable to express her thoughts. But slowly, she begins to open up, revealing the complexity of her emotions and the tangled web of deceit that led to her betrayal.

During our conversation, there's a sarcastic undertone to Dianna's responses, as if she's using it as a defense mechanism to protect herself from the emotional turmoil that's about to consume her.

As I listen to her words, a mix of hurt and anger washes over me, leaving behind only the bitter taste of betrayal.

After our conversation, I realize that I'm at a crossroads—I need to explore the depths of this agonizing predicament, but I also need to confront the sorrow and rage that have consumed me.

As I stand up to leave, I turn to Dianna one last time, my voice shaking with emotion.

"I don't ever want to see or speak to you again, Dianna," I say my words a final condemnation of her betrayal. "You've betrayed me in the worst possible way, and I'll never forgive you for that."

With those words hanging in the air, I walk away, leaving behind the shattered remains of a friendship that was once the cornerstone of my life. In the aftermath of Daniel and Dianna's affair, I find solace in the embrace of a new city, the night sky a canvas of endless possibilities, no longer a reminder of lost love but a promise of new beginnings.

Following the tumultuous end of both my marriage and a significant friendship, I sought refuge at Aunt

Sage's residence, where I stumbled upon an intriguing opportunity on Craigslist. It was an advertisement for a photographer position at an independent newspaper group in San Francisco. Seizing the moment, I promptly submitted my resume and portfolio before retiring for the evening.

The prospect of residing in San Francisco had long captivated my imagination; I always felt an inexplicable certainty about my connection to the city—a profound "knowing," as Aunt Sage would often remark, which she believed might one day prove crucial to my survival.

To my astonishment, I received a response the following day from William Tuttlebaum, the editor-in-chief at "In the Cut," an urban-focused publication. William expressed considerable admiration for my portfolio. "You possess a unique talent, Ms. Eridanus," he declared, offering me a competitive salary, expense coverage, and a corporate apartment in the city.

Throughout our conversation, which lasted nearly forty-five minutes, he detailed the newspaper's history and success, along with the expectations associated with the role. Feeling a warm and enthusiastic connection during our discussion, I accepted the position, committed to relocating within three weeks, and expressed my gratitude for the remarkable opportunity. "I won't let you down, William," I affirmed before ending the call. Reflecting on the swift turn of events, I thought to myself, "What an incredible stroke of fortune." Elated, I hurried to inform Aunt Sage of my impending move to California. The prospects ahead seemed exceptionally bright.

Six months later, as I sat in my well-appointed flat, I reflected on the seamless transition into my new job and life in San Francisco. The ease with which everything had fallen into place was almost disconcerting.

CHAPTER 3

"SAN FRANCISCO SERENADE: ECHOES OF A NEW DAWN"

San Francisco unfolds before me as a kaleidoscopic tapestry of hues and sounds, alive with boundless possibilities and energy. The decision to relocate here comes at a time when the scars of a betrayed love still linger in my heart, marking an unexpected twist in the story of my life.

The final days of my previous life are filled with a myriad of emotions. Each item packed into boxes evokes memories, from pictures capturing special moments with Daniel to mementos collected during our travels. Yet, these relics now seem like distant echoes of a bygone era as I watch the past slip away.

Six months have passed since my divorce from Daniel Darkwood, a name now relegated to a distant memory. Though the wounds remain, they no longer bleed. Determined to move forward, I leave the past where it belongs—behind me.

A ray of optimism suddenly materializes when I need it most, offering a chance to emerge from the shadows of the past and embrace a bright future filled with potential and fulfillment.

Venturing towards the old Eridanus Mansion nestled in a secluded, woodsy enclave of San Francisco, a whirlwind of emotion engulfs me. "Why now, Aunt Sage? Why tell me I have a family home in San Francisco now? Why keep this from me all these years?" I ponder aloud, keys to this ancestral marvel in hand. Claiming the mansion, with its Chateauesque elegance and Venetian Gothic nuances, feels like stepping into a storybook. "Well, isn't this unexpected?" I muse to myself, gazing at the architectural marvel now under my ownership. The city, with its endless possibilities, beckons me from the quaintness of Massachusetts to the grand adventure awaiting in California.

The mansion, a testament to architectural grandeur, stands proudly amidst an oasis of green, its silhouette a stark contrast to the urban landscape of San Francisco. With each step up the ornate, ivy-clad staircase, anticipation washes over me, drawing me closer to what feels like a predestined refuge.

The mansion's façade takes my breath away with its exquisite detail: pristine white walls complemented by sophisticated teal trim, towering spires, and arched windows whispering tales of yesteryears. "This isn't just a house; it's a piece of history," I note, stepping into the embrace of my newfound home.

The interior unfolds like a scene from a period drama; the foyer alone is a spectacle of opulence. A dazzling chandelier casts prismatic patterns across the room, illuminating the grand staircase and promising mysteries on the upper levels. "Wow, talk about making an entrance," I remark, my voice echoing in the vast space. Each room of the mansion reveals its own character, frozen in time yet alive with stories.

The blend of Chateauesque elegance and Venetian Gothic flair is evident in the ornate fireplaces, intricate woodwork, and stained-glass windows that filter light into a spectrum of colors. "These walls have tales to tell," I whisper, half-expecting the house to respond. The mansion's scale is both daunting and thrilling, a labyrinth of rooms and corridors unveiling pieces of the Eridanus legacy. The library, with its towering bookshelves and hidden nooks, feels like a sanctuary of knowledge, while the drawing room, adorned with velvet drapes and antique furnishings, beckons for evenings of introspection or grand gatherings. "Who knew my life would take such a Gothic turn?" I chuckle, admiring a portrait with a knowing gaze. The mansion, for all its grandiosity and ancient charm, feels strangely welcoming—as if it had been waiting for me all along.

Exploring the Eridanus Mansion is like walking

through a living museum; each artifact and piece of décor is a bridge to the past. Yet, amidst the echoes of history, there is room for me—a space to carve out my own story in this grand setting. "Alright, Eridanus Mansion, let's see what secrets you and I can uncover together," I declare, ready to embrace the mystery and magick of my family's home.

After delving into my newfound inheritance, I return to my flat, the stark contrast between the mansion's opulence and my modest living space striking me. The flat now feels smaller, its walls enclosing me within their bare, lifeless embrace.

The city's energy is infectious, each neighborhood a distinct piece of San Francisco's vibrant tapestry. My new job immerses me in a world of innovation, surrounded by creative souls driven to redefine the boundaries of possibility.

San Francisco's nightlife is a kaleidoscope of experiences, from chic bars in SOMA (South of Market) to eclectic venues in the Mission. Each night promises new adventures, and I embrace them all, eager to weave my own story into the city's fabric. Yet, amidst the excitement, a sense of anticipation lingers, a feeling that something extraordinary is on the horizon. It is as if the city itself holds a secret, a whisper of destiny waiting to unfold.

Meeting people from all walks of life, I realize I am part of a larger narrative, a diverse mosaic that makes

San Francisco unique. Standing on my balcony, over-looking the Golden Gate Bridge, I feel a profound sense of gratitude. This city offers me a chance to redefine myself and pursue my dreams with relentless passion.

One evening, as the sun casts its golden light over the bay, I catch a glimpse of a shadow across the street. Leaning out for a closer look, it vanishes, leaving me to question my own senses. "That's weird," I murmur, brushing off the fleeting image as a trick of the light, a remnant of childhood fears long since passed.

Embracing the opportunities that San Francisco presents, I find new communities, pursue my passions, and allow myself to dream bigger than ever before. The city becomes my canvas, a place where I can paint a new beginning, rich with possibility and promise. The wounds of my past, though still visible, no longer define me. San Francisco has become more than a city; it is a rebirth, a place where I can discover who I am meant to be, find my voice, and forge my path.

Gazing at the city skyline, lights twinkling against the night like distant stars, I realize that the extraordinary something I felt is now my reality. San Francisco welcomes me with open arms, and together, we craft a story uniquely our own.

CHAPTER 4

"ENIGMATIC ENCOUNTERS: A DAY IN HAIGHT/ASHBURY"

On a whimsical Saturday morning, the sun casts a golden hue over the famed Haight/Ashbury district, infusing the streets with an air of nostalgia and adventure. As I stepped onto the vibrant sidewalks, I was greeted by a kaleidoscope of colors and sounds, the echoes of a bygone era mingling with the hustle and bustle of modern life.

The streets hum with the energy of history, each building a testament to the district's storied past. Colorful storefronts beckon with their eclectic displays, offering a glimpse into the vibrant culture that thrives within. From vintage boutiques to quirky souvenir shops, every corner seems to hold a treasure waiting to be discovered.

Dressed comfortably in my go-to jeans and snug

black turtleneck, I feel like a part of the fabric of the city, ready to immerse myself in its rich tapestry. My trusty Converse All-Stars padded along the pavement, their familiar rhythm a comforting presence as I navigated the bustling streets.

As I make my way through the district, my camera slung over my shoulder. I feel a sense of anticipation building within me. San Francisco's streets are calling, promising hidden gems and untold stories waiting to be captured through my lens.

The panhandle greets me with open arms; its streets transform into a lively marketplace of sights and sounds. People from all walks of life mingle together, their laughter and chatter filling the air with a sense of camaraderie. Stalls line the sidewalks, offering an array of handmade crafts and exotic treasures, while street performers entertain the crowds with their music and antics.

"Looks like I've found the city's heartbeat," I muse, my camera clicking away as I try to encapsulate the spirit of the community through my lens. Faces blur past me, each one a story waiting to be told, each one a piece of the puzzle that made up the rich tapestry of the district.

Continuing on my journey, I pass through the majestic expanse of Golden Gate Park, where the air is alive with the symphony of nature and the vibrant energy of city life. Towering trees stretch their leafy branches toward the sky, creating a lush canopy that filters the sunlight into dappled patterns on the ground below.

As I stroll along the winding pathways, the scent of fresh flowers envelopes me in a fragrant embrace, each bloom adding its own unique perfume to the air. Vibrant beds of colorful blossoms lined the walkways, their petals dancing in the gentle breeze like a kaleidoscope of hues.

The park is alive with activity, the sound of laughter and conversation mingling with the chirping of birds and the rustle of leaves. Families picnic on the grassy lawns, their children playing tag and flying kites against the backdrop of the park's iconic landmarks.

Skateboarders carve graceful arcs through the air, their wheels gliding effortlessly over the smooth pavement as they perform tricks and stunts for the gathered crowds. With each flip and twist, they seem to defy gravity, their movements a testament to the spirit of freedom and creativity that permeate the park. As I wander deeper into the park's heart, I stumble upon hidden gems tucked away amidst the greenery. A tranquil pond shimmers in the sunlight, its surface rippling with the movements of ducks and swans gliding gracefully across the water. Nearby, a quaint bridge spans a babbling brook, its weathered stones telling tales of bygone days.

With each step, I feel a sense of wonder awash over

me as if I were stepping into a magickal realm where time stands still and the worries of the world melt away. Golden Gate Park is not just a place of natural beauty; it's a sanctuary for the soul, a refuge from the chaos of city life where one can find peace and tranquility amidst the hustle and bustle of urban living.

Despite the bustling scene, my stomach's insistent rumbling reminds me of my neglected breakfast routine. Spotting a quaint café nestled among the trees, I decide it is the perfect spot for a much-needed break. The aroma of freshly brewed coffee wafts through the air, drawing me in like a siren's call as I settle into a cozy corner, ready to refuel before continuing my exploration of the city. Seated with my tea, the café's ambiance enveloped me, offering a front-row seat to the city's lively tableau. It is moments like these that remind me why my camera is more than just a tool—it is my anchor, helping me navigate through life's storms.

Lost in thought, I suddenly find myself transported to a vision so vivid that it feels like another reality. I am standing before a majestic Chateauesque Victorian mansion, its Venetian Gothic details merging seamlessly with the surrounding forest. It looks like the Eridanus Mansion. The beauty of the scene is overwhelming, a stark contrast to the city's hustle.

But this daydream took a dark turn as an ominous shadow approached, sending adrenaline coursing through my veins. My escape from the shadow is abruptly cut short, not by the root of a tree but by the unexpected interruption of a real-life enigma.

Miles, as I eventually come to know him, stands before me, a figure so striking he seems to have stepped out of my wildest dreams. His presence alone shifts the café's atmosphere, drawing every gaze toward him because of his unearthly magnetism. His emerald-green eyes appear to draw me into their depths as though they are hiding something, like undiscovered treasure. He has beautiful olive-colored skin, and his back is covered in a waterfall of long, wavy, dark silky hair. There's an ethereal quality to him because of his pale skin, like a fictional figure emerging from the pages and entering the actual world. He's about 6 ft tall and has an athletic build. He's wearing jeans, an Abercrombie & Fitch tee shirt, and black Converse All-Stars. During that brief initial contact, our eyes meet. Albeit the otherwise ordinary get-up, something in his eyes hints at a world beyond the ordinary and a promise of undiscovered tales, and to me, he is a living, breathing piece of art, exuding an allure that is impossible to ignore.

"Mind if I join you?" His voice, smooth and inviting, asks, "Of course," I find myself responding, intrigued by the mystery he embodies.

He sits down, extends his hand, and says, "Miles. Miles Nightshade." I find myself drawn to his magnetic presence as my hand answers his, "Saturn, Saturn

Eridanus," I introduce myself, adding a playful nod to the grandiosity of our names.

His eyes fixate on mine. Miles leans forward, his gaze intense and captivating. There's an unspoken connection between us, a silent invitation to delve deeper into each other's worlds.

"Saturn, what a celestial name," Miles remarks with a charming smile, his voice carrying a hint of admiration. "And here I thought I had a unique name."

I smile and slightly chuckle, feeling a sense of camaraderie, and respond by saying, "well, Miles, your name certainly carries an air of mystery and adventure. "

Our conversation flows effortlessly, weaving through topics ranging from art to favorite travel destinations. With each exchange, the air between us crackles with energy, igniting a spark of curiosity and anticipation. It's as if we're embarking on our own journey, exploring the depths of our passions and the mysteries of the world together.

His stories weave a spell around me, drawing me deeper into his world of exploration and discovery. Eager for more, I press him to share his favorite destination.

Curious to know what he does for a living that would take him to the places he's speaking of, I ask, "What do you do that takes you to so many different places?"

"Oh, I am in antiquities and run my family business,

with our headquarters being in New York, but I spend most of my time here in San Francisco." He responds.

I lean in, eager to hear more about his globetrotting escapades. "Tokyo must have been incredible. What was your favorite part?"

A reminiscent smile tugs at the corners of Miles' lips. "The energy, Saturn. It's like nowhere else on Earth. The neon lights, the bustling crowds, the juxtaposition of tradition and modernity—it's truly mesmerizing."

I nod in agreement, envisioning the vibrant streets of Tokyo in my mind's eye. "It sounds like a sensory overload in the best possible way. And what about Scotland? The Highlands have always held a special allure for me."

Miles' gaze turns wistful as he recalls his time in the rugged landscapes of Scotland. "Ah, the Highlands; my favorite out of all of them. It's like stepping into a fairy-tale. Rolling hills, mist-covered moors, ancient castles— it feels like you've been transported to another time."

I listen intently, captivated by his vivid descriptions. "It sounds enchanting," I murmur, a sense of wanderlust stirring within me. "I've always dreamed of visiting the Highlands and experiencing that timeless beauty firsthand."

Our conversation drifts to art, a shared passion that brings us even closer together. Miles speaks passionately about his love for classical paintings, his eyes alight with enthusiasm as he describes his visits to renowned museums around the globe. "Have you ever visited the Louvre?" he asks, his excitement infectious.

I nod, a smile playing on my lips. "Yes, it's a remarkable place. The Winged Victory of Samothrace, the Mona Lisa... each visit feels like stepping back in time." Miles leans back in his chair, his gaze drifting upwards as he reflects on the timeless allure of art. "Art has a way of transcending time and space," he muses. "It allows us to connect with the past and glimpse the future." As our conversation continues, we share our favorite hidden gems in the city, each revelation drawing us closer together. Miles tells me about a secluded bookstore where rare first editions can be found while I divulge my favorite spot overlooking the bay, where the setting sun paints the sky in shades of gold and pink.

But beneath the surface of our lighthearted banter, there's a palpable tension building between us. It's as if we both sense that this meeting is more than mere chance, that there are depths to our connection yet to be explored.

As the afternoon sun bathes the café in a warm, golden glow, Miles opens up about his hopes and dreams with an intensity that leaves me breathless. His gaze meets mine, and I can feel the weight of his words echoing in the air between us.

"There is something I've been searching for," he confesses, his voice barely above a whisper.

I lean in, drawn to his vulnerability. "What is it?" I ask, my heart pounding in my chest.

For a moment, Miles hesitates as if weighing his words carefully. Then, with a quiet determination, he speaks. "Something real, you know? Like I run one of the most successful antiquities companies in the world, but I've yet to find anything that is out of the ordinary, not mundane. I'm not sure what it is exactly, but I just feel like I'm destined for more, you know?"

"Hmmm, I agree with you on that. I'm a photographer, and even though I capture images of the world, I feel there is something more to find in my future, something meant just for me." I respond.

I'm captivated by the mystery in his eyes, the promise of adventure and discovery that hangs in the air between us. As Miles and I delve deeper into our conversation, the cacophony of the café begins to dim, transforming the space around us. It's as if the world outside our bubble of dialogue has ceased to exist, leaving us ensconced in a private universe of our own creation.

The clinking of cups, the murmur of other patrons, and the occasional hiss of the espresso machine fade into a distant, unnoticeable hum. It's in this secluded cocoon that our words find deeper meaning, flowing freely and without reservation.

The bustling atmosphere that once enveloped us now seems a world away, making it feel as though we're the only two souls in existence, sharing moments and thoughts that transcend the ordinary.

Before we realize it, the sun is dipping below the horizon, casting long shadows across the empty tables. My stomach growls in protest, reminding me of the neglected meal.

As if sensing my hunger, Miles suggests, "Would you like to grab a bite to eat? There's a fantastic Italian restaurant near my favorite art gallery." I pause for a moment, contemplating. Despite the pleasant day we've spent together and his charming demeanor, I'm hesitant to accept. After all, I've only just met him. But rather than rejecting outright, I offer him my cell number and suggest we take a rain check. Though disappointed, Miles graciously agrees and offers me a ride home.

I decline his offer, insisting that I can walk the short distance. However, he's persistent, citing the darkness and safety concerns for a woman alone. With a coy smile, I acquiesce, accepting the ride. His sleek black Lexus is parked nearby, and Miles gallantly walks me to the passenger side, holding the door open for me. We ride in comfortable silence, punctuated only by my directions to my apartment. When we arrive, he exits the car and walks around to let me out.

As I step out, Miles gently takes my hand, his touch sending a flutter through my stomach. "Promise me we'll see each other again," he says, his eyes holding mine with an intensity that sets my pulse racing.

I meet his gaze, feeling a sense of anticipation and excitement building within me. "Until we meet again," I reply, my voice barely above a whisper.

With a final smile, I turn and make my way into my building, feeling a curious mixture of exhilaration and uncertainty. As I settle into my apartment, I reflect on the day's events, my thoughts drifting back to Miles. Retrieving my camera and laptop, I upload the day's photos, all the while unable to shake the image of his handsome face from my mind.

"Dam, what a handsome man," I murmur to myself, a smile tugging at the corners of my lips as I lose myself in the memories of our encounter.

CHAPTER 5

"TANGLED DESTINIES: THE TEMPEST WITHIN"

Caught in a tempest of reflection, here I am at a crossroads, reeling from the recent, unexpected twists that have upended my life. The mission was straightforward from the start: shadow her, earn her trust, and then, at the perfect moment, snuff out her life to claim her powers for my coven.

But since that accidental meeting with Saturn Eridanus in that quaint café—which now feels like the prelude to an uncommitted crime—time has slipped away like sand through my fingers.

"A tempest of the heart," I muse, grappling with the storm Saturn unknowingly unleashed within me. Her effortless grace has shattered my life's delicate balance, binding my fate to hers in a complex tapestry I'm still unraveling.

Each day, the burden of my mission grows, not because of its weight but due to an unexpected affection rooting deep within—a sentiment whispering treason against my vows.

As I observe her from afar, a quiet voice inside dares to ask, "How can you extinguish a light that shines so brightly?" For the first time, dressed in my convictions, I find myself disarmed and without answers.

With every covert glance and each word cloaked in innocence, the harsh reality of my mission turns unbearable. Saturn, with her unwitting smile and vibrant laughter, has evolved from a mere target to an integral part of me—a part I cannot, dare not cut away. As loyalty to my coven blurs with this growing affection, I find myself questioning not only my commands but the core of my existence.

What was once a clear path has twisted into a journey of self-discovery and forbidden longing. The stakes are higher than ever, affecting not just Saturn's fate but the redemption or damnation of my own soul, now irreversibly intertwined with hers.

In this dance of shadows and light, I fear I'm no longer the hunter but a man ensnared by a love that could doom us both.

I'm captivated by her—the way her long, brown hair dances in the breeze, outlining her perfect features. Her petite frame moves with the grace of a ballerina, captivating time itself. Her lips, naturally pouty, and her smooth, light-coffee skin beckon for a gentle touch. But it's her eyes, a mesmerizing mix of brown and green with hints of sunlit yellow, that draw me in, revealing a world of surprises and secrets waiting within.

As she peers over her balcony, stretching on tiptoes, her beauty and curiosity meld into a vision that leaves a lasting imprint on me. She's become the center of my inner turmoil—a war between duty and desire that escalates daily.

My once-secretive gaze now betrays my agony, flitting between the world I knew and the one my heart yearns for—a path intimately linked to Saturn. Every moment we share, every glance strengthens her hold over me.

The full extent of my torment surfaces in those brief, stolen moments. My carefully maintained composure is fragile, easily shattered by a shared smile, a touch, or the sound of her laughter. Beneath my composed exterior rages a storm of obligation and desire I cannot navigate, relentlessly driving me down a path of forbidden yearning. I yearn to confess the turmoil to Saturn, but such an admission could unravel everything. Our coven's survival hinges on secrecy, and any breach could have dire consequences.

The persona I've crafted obscures Saturn's view of me, complicating how she perceives me with each curious glance.

No matter how hard I try to maintain distance, the

barriers between our worlds thin daily. This bond we share defies logic and threatens the ties to my past.

The anguish deepens as our connection strengthens, pulling me into a vortex of emotions, each more turbulent than the last. One evening, as we discuss destiny over a candlelit dinner, Saturn's perspective on life—her belief in the paranormal and our cosmic roles—resonates deeply.

"Imagine if changing one action a second ago could alter our lives," she muses.

I love her outlook on life. She believes in anything and everything that is paranormal. She also believes that we are all star seeds who came to Earth to help humanity. We all volunteered and planned out exactly how our lives would be. Little did she know just about how much of that was true. 'At least the paranormal part is!' I laugh to myself.

"Don't laugh at me, Miles! I am serious," she says, a little annoyed, but I can tell she is enjoying the banter. "Trust me, I know. I told you that I am Claircognizant; I just KNOW things!" She continues laughing and semi-rolling her beautiful eyes at me. A Claircognizant, someone possessing the ability of Claircognizance, also called "clear knowing," is someone who can know something without understanding how they know it. Winking, I respond, "Oh, I wasn't laughing at you; I was admiring you and all that energy bottled up inside of that beautiful body. I believe you. Keep going, please."

She locks eyes with mine, her gaze intense. "Sometimes we're drawn to something—or someone—without understanding why. It's as if the universe has its plans."

Moved by her words, I feel the gravity of their significance. The universe does seem to have a plan, though comprehending it escapes me.

As I look into Saturn's eyes, I know the struggle for my soul has only begun. This enigmatic force in my life is both the source of my deepest pain and the beacon that might lead me out of the shadows.

The choices I make now will determine not only my destiny but also the fate of this mysterious woman who has unwittingly captured my loyalty, trust, and heart. This is driving me to the brink of insanity. I've never felt this way about anyone. Before Saturn, it was all about me. But her energy, her pure, vibrant vigor, compels me to aspire to be as good as she is—she naturally uplifts everyone around her.

As we sit in the dimly lit nook of a classic Italian restaurant, discussing life's intricate paths, I realize just how profoundly Saturn has changed me and how impossible it seems now to follow through with my original mission.

CHAPTER 6

"UNVEILING SECRETS: EXPLORING THE CITY OF HIDDEN GEMS"

San Francisco spreads out in front of us like a vast painting just waiting to be explored. Together, Saturn and I started spending a lot more time exploring through meaningful day trips that she always calls road trips to check out places new to both of us. Our expeditions take us to secluded locations in the city that are only known to a small group of people, and each new find strengthens the bond that has already developed between us.

As the city shimmers with possibility, I can't stop feeling grateful; no, humble, watching my world merge with Saturn's. It feels almost like a veil has been lifted, revealing the natural beauty of life that has always been there but has been concealed from view.

Saturn is a fascinating companion because of her distinct viewpoint and unwavering interest. It's exciting to observe the world through her eyes because she elicits an air of adventure at every turn. She continues to be blissfully ignorant of the many layers of secrecy and the complicated details of my life that I have concealed.

We go to places together that have the air of being hidden and just waiting to be discovered. We dine at eateries that are only known to the locals, roam through secret gardens, and discover abandoned book-shops nestled away in little passageways. Saturn's enthusiasm as she talks about the hidden treasures of the city always makes me smile, and each time, I feel a ping in my heart. I recall one night when we were sitting on the balcony at Saturn's place, admiring the city's skyline; Saturn's voice disturbed the silence. Pondering, her eyes reflecting the lights decorating the buildings, "Ya know, there's something truly magickal about this place," she says. "We are but a strand in the DNA of this city that has a heartbeat of its own."

She never ceases to surprise me with the words that come out of her mouth. I am moved by what she says, and I can't help but sense that there is more depth to her remark. Saturn is the key that has allowed me to unlock the mysteries of the city, which does appear to have a heartbeat and a rhythm of its own, beating with life.

She and I continue our "road trip" as the sun falls below the horizon, spreading a warm, golden glow over the city. Our trips have become a testimony of the closeness that has grown between us, and we have come to cherish all of these opportunities for exploration.

As Saturn and I weave our way through the vibrant tapestry of San Francisco's Chinatown, the atmosphere is alive with a symphony of sights, sounds, and scents. The air is thick with the heady aroma of incense mingling with the tantalizing scent of sizzling street food, enticing us further into the heart of this bustling enclave.

The narrow alleyways are a riot of color, each storefront adorned with intricate lanterns and ornate decorations that seem to dance in the dappled sunlight. Saturn's eyes sparkle with excitement as she takes in the kaleidoscope of sights around her, her camera poised and ready to capture the magick of the moment. "I love the energy here!" she exclaims, her voice barely audible over the lively hum of the crowd. "It's like stepping into another world." I nod in agreement, a smile tugging at the corners of my lips as I watch her navigate the throng with effortless grace. "It's one of my favorite places in the city," I confess, my gaze lingering on her with admiration. "There's always something new to discover."

As we meander through the labyrinth of streets, Saturn's camera is never far from her side, a silent companion capturing the essence of Chinatown with each click of the shutter. She pauses every so often to frame the perfect shot, her eyes alight with passion and purpose as she seeks out the hidden beauty in the everyday.

"You have such a keen eye for detail," I remark, my admiration evident in my voice as I watch her work. "It's like you have the ability to freeze time."

Saturn grins, adjusting the settings on her camera with practiced precision. "Photography is my way of preserving the beauty of the moment," she explains, her voice soft yet determined. "Each photo tells a story, a glimpse into the world as I see it."

As we continue our journey through Chinatown, Saturn's enthusiasm is contagious, infecting me with a newfound appreciation for the vibrant culture that surrounds us. We sample exotic fruits from market stalls, exchange smiles with locals, and lose ourselves in the rhythm of the bustling streets. Our meandering journey unexpectedly guides us to the doorstep of a quaint bookstore tucked away in a serene part of the neighborhood. Stepping inside, the atmosphere shifts dramatically from the lively streets to a realm of hushed tones and the rustle of pages. The soft illumination from overhead lamps bathes the labyrinth of bookshelves in a golden hue, inviting us into its embrace.

We find ourselves gravitating towards a secluded nook within this haven of literature, surrounded by the musky scent of old books that speak of untold stories waiting to be discovered.

Saturn settles comfortably against a pile of over-stuffed pillows, her eyes sparkling with an unspoken joy as she takes in the walls lined with books. "This place is magickal," she breathes out, her voice barely a whisper in the sacred silence of the bookstore. "It's like we've stepped into a different realm altogether."

I can't help but agree; the tranquility of our surroundings envelops me in a calm I've rarely known. "It's moments like these that really make life worth living," I find myself saying, reaching across the small space between us to take Saturn's hand. Our fingers lace together naturally, forming a connection that goes beyond words, a tacit vow of togetherness and shared discoveries.

Saturn's eyes sparkle with excitement as she steps through the threshold, her gaze immediately drawn to the towering shelves that line the walls like sentinels of knowledge. The air is heavy with the scent of old paper and ink, a nostalgic perfume that transports us to another time. The shelves are a treasure trove of literary delights, each one crammed with well-loved classics and hidden gems. Saturn's fingers trail over the spines with reverence, her touch is gentle yet purposeful as she seeks out the perfect addition to her growing collection. The soft murmur of voices drifts through the air, mingling with the occasional rustle of pages and the creak of wooden floorboards beneath our feet. There's a sense of hushed reverence in the bookstore as if each book holds a secret waiting to be unlocked.

Saturn's excitement is palpable as she loses herself in the maze of shelves, her eyes alight with the thrill of discovery. Every corner reveals new treasures, from weathered tomes of ancient lore to meticulously preserved first editions that gleam like rare jewels in the dim light.

As we wander deeper into the heart of the bookstore, we stumble upon a cozy reading nook tucked away in a secluded alcove. The air is thick with the scent of leather and dust, a comforting embrace that invites us to linger a while longer.

Saturn settles into an overstuffed armchair, her eyes dancing with anticipation as she flips through the pages of a weathered tome. I join her, my own fingers tracing the embossed letters on the cover as we lose ourselves in the timeless magick of storytelling.

For a moment, time stands still as we immerse ourselves in the world of words, each page a portal to new adventures and untold wonders. In the quiet sanctuary of the bookstore, surrounded by the whispers of literary history, Saturn and I find solace in the shared love of books and the boundless possibilities they hold. "I could spend hours here," she says, her voice filled with wonder.

I smile at her enthusiasm, feeling a sense of peace settle over me in the quiet of the bookstore. "Me too," I agree, reaching out to take her hand in mine. "It's like stepping into another world."

The owner of the bookstore is kind enough to allow us access to some rare first editions, so we get up and head over to the private room. As we enter, my gaze strays over the warm room, looking for the minute details that give the setting life.

I've become more conscious of Saturn's constant companion, her camera, and her unabashed passion for taking pictures over the last few days. I finally asked her, "Why do you love photography so much? I mean, I love how you bring your camera everywhere you go; I'm just interested in knowing what possessed you to follow this path."

With a reflective undertone, she responds, "I started taking pictures in the rural, rustic settings of my little hometown, Bernardston, Massachusetts. I've always had an instinctive connection with nature growing up. I was fascinated by the ever-changing interplay of light and shadow, the minute intricacies of a single leaf, or the stunning colors of a dawn when I found myself wandering through the woods. I craved to seize those moments and hold onto the energy and beauty they possessed as if I could see all of its hidden beauty."

She's so animated; it brings a tender smile to my

face. "Saturn, you have a talent for seeing beauty in the ordinary. It's quite a gift."

Saturn's tone becomes thoughtful as she explores what, to her, are the fundamentals of photography. "For me, photography is my haven as much as my career. It's a means of understanding my surroundings and preserving their transient beauty. Every picture I take is more than a simple image; it's a piece of my soul, a reminder of the beauty that endures through the lowest points of life. During times of vulnerability, I chose to turn my love into a career, to share with people the world as I see it, full of emotions and stories. Also, it is an excellent tool for meditation! You know, like I always tell you, quiet your mind – quiet your soul."

How she always ends a serious conversation with something lighthearted and funny makes me fall in love with her even more than I already am and reinforces the fact that I want to be more than just friends.

Her responses reveal more about her journey as she goes on. "My deep-seated love of photography is what convinced me to accept the job here. It was exactly what I needed, and it seemed promising.

The city's backdrop has provided me with a brand-new canvas for me to create moments in time and save them. It was a chance for me to change my perspective and find fresh stories to tell with my camera. I was drawn to capturing the spirit of this city and incorporating its distinct hues and textures into my artwork."

She makes a warm turn and looks at me. "You know, I believe that each person has a special story to share. It's simply finding someone who will take the time to listen."

Her words strike a chord with me, and I'm terrified by the thought of telling Saturn my story while we sit in the little bookstore, surrounded by the echoes of the past.

I constantly feel nervous as the burden of my secrets continues to rest heavily on my shoulders. I'm not sure if Saturn will be ready for the truths that will be revealed to her because the hidden truths I carry have the potential to change the course of our lives.

As we continue to the next place to discover, we find a secret garden tucked away in the middle of the city. We stroll through winding roads as the aroma of blossoming flowers fills the air. As Saturn savors the golden light, kissing the bright rose petals, she takes a moment to linger.

She comments, her fingertips caressing the delicate petals, "They say that every flower has a meaning. They have their language, a way to express feelings without using words."

Watching her, I'm mesmerized by how she seems to see significance in everything. "Perhaps," I retort, raising an eyebrow and adding a note of mystery to my voice. "But sometimes, the most important things go unspoken."

Saturn turns to face me and peers into my eyes. "Miles, is there something you're not telling me??" she counters back with her raised eyebrow.

"I'm taken aback for a moment, then regain composure. "No, Saturn," I respond, trying to mask the nervousness bubbling within me. After all, I've witnessed her uncanny ability to just know things all the time when she's around. Her Claircognizance always makes me a bit uneasy, but I push aside those thoughts, focusing on the task at hand. My hand is in hers when she poses the question, and she gives it a comforting squeeze. "Miles, I'm here for you. The Universe sent me. You can tell me anything, and we will deal with whatever it is together." I wonder how much longer I can keep up this façade as we continue our quest for hidden gems in the city and delve deeper into its hidden corners. The mysterious aspects of my existence start to come into focus, and I realize at that moment that the time to tell Saturn the truth is drawing near.

The future sparkles with possibilities, but it also carries unseen perils, which I have made a vow to myself to shield her from. My commitment to my coven and the life I have chosen to live with Saturn is most certainly in conflict.

Her story has an unearthly dimension to it due to the mystery surrounding her existence and her extraordinary point of view of the world around her. I worry the revelation that lies ahead of us will drastically alter the course of our lives in ways we couldn't have imagined as the layers of all that are hidden start to fall away.

San Francisco may be a city of hidden secrets and buried truths, but with Saturn by my side, I know that together, we can conquer anything that stands in our way. The journey ahead may be uncertain, but one thing is clear: with her unwavering trust and boundless spirit, Saturn has become the beacon of light that guides me through the darkness.

CHAPTER 7

"WHISPERS OF AWAKENING "

In the heart of San Francisco, beneath the city's bustling veneer, I find myself at the center of a personal awakening, a revelation of dormant powers stirring within me, guided by an unseen force. Miles, ever the curious explorer beside me, marvels at our serendipitous excursions, not realizing they are whispered directions from a universe that is slowly unveiling itself to me. The air around us seems to thrum with a vibrant energy, especially as we navigate the crowded metro areas, where the pulse of the city beats the strongest.

It begins subtly, with moments of keen intuition that seem to direct my steps down alleys and paths less trodden, an increasing awareness that the world is much more than it seems. But it is at a bustling farmer's market, under the radiant glow of the sun, that the true extent of my awakening is revealed. As my fingers graze a ripe apple, it levitates as if buoyed by an invisible force, a clear manifestation of a power I hadn't known resided within me.

The market crowd's astonished gazes become the backdrop to my realization: I am a conduit of something extraordinary. Gently guiding the apple back into my hand, I feel a connection to something ancient and profound, a lineage of dormant powers passed down from my mother.

Each new discovery, each unveiled ability, fuels my resolve to unearth the secrets of my family's past and my place within the cosmos. The unknown force that nudges me towards hidden corners of the city seems to echo my inner transformation. With Miles by my side, we uncover secluded spots that feel like they are waiting just for us. Our adventures take on a deeper significance, each shared laugh and playful jest weaving us closer together, even as I grapple with the burgeoning mysteries of my abilities.

One evening, as we sit watching the city unfold below my balcony, I muse about the magick that seems to permeate San Francisco. "This city," I say, "is like a living, breathing entity, a testament to the interconnectedness of all things." It is a revelation seeing my journey reflected in the city's endless maze, a journey that is leading me back to my celestial origins in the stars, specifically to the constellation of Eridanus, which whispers to me of home.

My newfound abilities are a gateway to understanding the universe in ways I had never imagined. In Golden Gate Park, I feel the whispers of the earth, the dance of the trees responding to my silent call, revealing the symphony of life that resonates through every leaf and blade of grass. This connection to nature is exhilarating, a reminder of my role as a steward of this earth and of the delicate balance that I must maintain.

Animals, too, become my companions in this new world. A squirrel's playful leap into my hand is a testament to the universal language we share, a language of trust and mutual respect that transcends species.

It is a humbling reminder of the interconnectedness of all life and of the responsibilities that come with my awakening powers. But it isn't just the natural world that responds to my touch. The elements themselves seem to bend to my will. By the ocean's edge, I marvel at the water's intricate ballet at my command, a display of power that both thrills and terrifies me. The ocean, vast and untamed, is a mirror to the untapped depths within me, a reminder of the immense potential and danger that my powers hold.

In the solitude of my exploration, without Miles' guiding presence, I delve into the mysteries of my heritage. Each discovery is a step closer to understanding the legacy of the Eridanus Coven to unravel the cosmic tapestry that is my birthright.

My journey is solitary but not lonely, for the city itself becomes my companion, revealing its secrets in the quiet moments we share. In a secluded grove, I whisper my fears and hopes to the ancient trees, finding solace in their silent wisdom. It is there, amidst the gentle sway of branches, that I admit my love for Miles, a confession that the universe seems to embrace with a gentle breeze.

This path of discovery is not without its challenges. The weight of my newfound powers is a constant companion, a reminder of the delicate balance I must strike between embracing my abilities and safeguarding the world around me. The allure of the unknown is tempered by the responsibility that comes with my awakening, a responsibility to use my powers with care and compassion.

San Francisco, with its hidden groves and bustling streets, is the backdrop to my transformation. From a bystander in my own life to an active participant in a universe brimming with magick and mystery, I have stepped into a role that is both exhilarating and daunting. As I navigate this new world, the realization that my journey is just beginning fills me with anticipation. The constellation of Eridanus, a celestial guide, beckons me toward a future where the limits of reality are just the starting point.

CHAPTER 8
"SHADOWS OF DECEPTION"

Returning to New York from my time with Saturn feels like stepping into a whole new world. The towering skyscrapers and busy streets of the city are a stark contrast to the places we've explored together. Even amidst all the concrete and steel, I can't help but notice that the city holds its secrets, whispered in quiet corners.

This penthouse in New York serves as my second home when I have to travel from San Francisco to our corporate headquarters here. It has an added advantage – it's located in the same building where the mysterious Conclave of Shadows holds their meetings, though they occupy the highest floor, and I'm just one floor below them.

This penthouse, situated at 53 West 53 in midtown, just a few blocks south of Central Park, stands tall above the Museum of Modern Art. Perched on the 76th floor, it's an impressive four-bedroom duplex that covers nearly 8,000 square feet. The penthouse features a spacious double-height lounge and a private dining room, both offering breathtaking views of Central Park.

What's more, there's a massive 15,000-square-foot wellness center equipped with a state-of-the-art fitness center, a 65-foot lap pool, a golf simulator, a regulation squash court, spa treatment rooms, and much more. The penthouse even has its wine room and private wine vaults. As I stand here, miles away from the incredible adventures Saturn and I have shared, I can't help but wonder how she would feel in this entirely different world. "Bringing Saturn here... will she feel comfortable in this extravagant setting? Or will it all overwhelm her? She grew up living a simpler life in Massachusetts. But she knows about my wealth... Maybe amidst all this opulence, she'll still feel the same connection we've cherished together," I say to myself, my thoughts swirling with uncertainty. Would the grandeur impress her, or would it only serve as a reminder of the stark differences between our worlds?

Leaving the safety of my penthouse, I step into the elevator, bound for The Conclave's headquarters, my mind swirling with strategies to thwart their sinister plans against the woman who holds my heart. "Come on, Miles, think!" I mutter to myself, frustration bubbling up as I tap impatiently on the elevator door before it opens. As I approach the imposing doors of the Conclave, I remind myself, "Keep up the act; can't let them catch a whiff of my true intentions to protect Saturn."

The Conclave, fueled by their dark ambitions, seeks to seize all of Saturn's innate power, molding it into a malevolent force with aims to dominate not just the universe but every star seed witch on Earth.

Their covetous gaze is fixed upon the Eridanus Coven, the foremost group of star-seed witches entrusted with maintaining the delicate balance of the universe and every star seed on our planet. Saturn remains oblivious to her royal and influential lineage, a significant threat to the Conclave's relentless pursuit of absolute control. Thus, they conspire to eliminate Saturn in their quest for supremacy and dominance. "I can't let this happen," I murmur, the weight of the situation bearing down on me. The knowledge that Saturn is unaware of the danger surrounding her fills me with urgency. She's a beacon of light in a world overshadowed by darkness, and I refuse to stand idly by as the Conclave schemes against her. Our bond compels me to act, to protect her at any cost.

Approaching the foreboding door of The Conclave's headquarters, I'm met with only a sigil, devoid of any apartment number. It stands as a grim testament to their dark ambitions and hunger for power. The sigil's design is hauntingly intricate, and its imagery is a chilling reflection of the Conclave's malevolent nature.

At its center lies a menacing eye, radiating an aura of watchfulness and control. Surrounding it are jagged lines intertwined, a visual representation of the Conclave's manipulative and deceitful tactics. Behind the eye, a swirling vortex of darkness speaks to their insatiable thirst for power and their willingness to delve into the depths of darkness to achieve their goals.

Thorny vines encircle the entire sigil, a stark reminder of the Conclave's ability to ensnare and entangle anyone who dares to oppose them, leaving no avenue for escape. It's a potent symbol of their malevolent influence and the dangers they pose to all who cross their path. As I take in the sight, a surge of resentment courses through me. 'I hate this sigil,' I think to myself, steeling my resolve as I prepare to enter.

Opening the door, I'm met with Seraphina's soft yet commanding voice. "Ah, so you decided to grace us with your presence," she says, throwing me an icy glare. As the room settles into a contemplative silence, Seraphina's voice cuts through the stillness like a sharp blade. "Where's Lysandra? She's supposed to be here for this meeting," she inquires, her tone laced with thinly veiled impatience.

With a smirk playing at the corners of my lips, I offer a nonchalant response tinged with just the right amount of sass. "I'm her brother, not her keeper,

Seraphina. She'll show up when she shows up," I quip, earning a raised eyebrow from Seraphina.

But behind the playful banter lies a deeper truth. Lysandra's presence, or lack thereof, is a reminder of the complexities and loyalties that bind us to the Conclave. As we await her arrival, I can't help but wonder what role she'll play in the events that lie ahead and how her decisions will shape the outcome of our shared destiny.

"As I was saying before, I was so rudely interrupted..." Seraphina pauses, her gaze lingering on me before continuing, "Our clandestine assembly brings together a convergence of formidable abilities, with each member a master of their own dark craft."

I respond, my tone measured but with a tinge of unease, "Indeed, it's an impressive display of our collective power. Seraphina, your illusions are unmatched, and they will undoubtedly play a crucial role in our plan." Yet, even as I speak, a gnawing ache twists within me, knowing that deceiving Saturn tears at my soul.

"Thank you, Miles. With your support, we can sway Saturn's trust and ensure our victory," Seraphina says, her gaze unwavering.

As her words linger in the air, Seraphina gestures subtly, and suddenly, the space around us shimmers and distorts. Illusions begin to take form, twisting and weaving through the air like ephemeral specters. It's a mesmerizing display, showcasing the full extent of her power. I can't help but marvel at the intricacy and realism of her illusions, even as a sense of unease settles in the pit of my stomach. This is the kind of magick that can sway minds and bend reality to the user's will. And with Seraphina's mastery, there's no telling what illusions she could conjure to deceive even the most discerning eye.

"Agreed. We must do whatever it takes to achieve our goals, even if it means bending the rules. Saturn's influence must be brought under the Conclave's control," I reply, my words ringing hollow, weighed down by the guilt that threatens to consume me.

"Precisely. With your strategic insight and my illusionary prowess, we will be unstoppable," Seraphina asserts confidently.

"Let us proceed with caution, Seraphina. We must ensure that our plan remains undetected until the moment of fruition," I caution, masking my inner turmoil behind a facade of composure. After voicing this caution, I silently reaffirm to myself, "Yes, caution indeed, for I refuse to allow any harm to befall Saturn."

Seraphina responds with a nod, her confidence unwavering, but within me, a storm brews, torn between loyalty to the Conclave and the desire to protect Saturn at any cost.

Lucius steps forward, his voice resonating with a primal elemental resonance, "Her powers, combined with ours, can forge an unparalleled force."

"Indeed, Lucius. Saturn's elemental affinity presents a unique opportunity for us to strengthen our collective might. With her abilities, we could reshape the very fabric of existence itself," I reply, trying to maintain a facade of agreement while my mind races with conflicting emotions.

As if to underscore his point, Lucius extends his hand, and the air around us crackles with energy. Flames dance at his fingertips, water swirls in intricate patterns, the earth trembles beneath our feet, and gusts of wind swirl around us. It's a breathtaking display of elemental mastery, a reminder of the raw power at our disposal.

"Precisely. Imagine the possibilities, Miles. With Saturn gone, her powers would be ours. We could wield forces beyond comprehension, ensuring our dominance over all who oppose us," Lucius continues, his eyes gleaming with ambition.

"Agreed. Saturn's potential is limitless, and harnessing her powers is key to achieving our goals. Together, we will become unstoppable," I respond, my voice steady despite the turmoil within. Beneath the surface, however, I'm conflicted. My loyalty lies with Saturn, and I'll do whatever it takes to protect her from the Conclave's grasp.

Isolde steps forward next, her presence shrouded in shadows, "In the depths of night, our intentions shall remain hidden," she whispers, her words as ephemeral as the shadows she commands.

As if summoned by her words, the darkness around us seems to deepen, enveloping us in its velvety embrace. Isolde's form wavers, blending seamlessly into the obsidian cloak surrounding her. It's a mesmerizing display of her mastery over the shadows, a reminder of her prodigious skill in the art of stealth and deceit.

"Indeed, Isolde. Your mastery of stealth is unparalleled. Keeping our intentions concealed is crucial to our success," I reply, nodding along outwardly while my heart aches with the weight of deception. The thought of betraying Saturn gnaws at me, but for now, I must play my part in this intricate dance of shadows.

Finally, Malachi speaks, his words laden with caution, "Saturn's mind is a celestial fortress, shielded by cosmic might. We must tread lightly, weaving our intricate web with precision."

His voice carries a weight of wisdom, resonating with the authority of one who delves into the depths of consciousness. I can almost feel the probing tendrils of his telepathic abilities reaching out, delving into the minds of those around us, uncovering their deepest motives and secrets. Instinctively, I subtly weave a protective time loop around my thoughts, ensuring that Malachi's psychic probes cannot penetrate my psyche.

"Indeed, Malachi, your insight is invaluable. Saturn's mind is indeed formidable, and we must approach with caution," I reply, maintaining the facade of loyalty to the Conclave. Yet, internally, I struggle with the notion of exploiting Saturn's trust. How can I betray her when my heart is sworn to protect her at all costs?

As the sinister plans unfurl, a creeping dread envelops me. The path ahead is one of betrayal, a sharp deviation from the awe and wonder that Saturn and I share. The notion of weaponizing her trust against her poisons my very soul.

Yet, as the allure of power and the binding oaths to the Conclave have kept me ensnared within their nefarious designs, the sumptuous meeting place, perched high above the bustling city below, serves as a constant reminder of the life I lead—a life now standing at a crossroads.

Saturn, with her burgeoning powers and her celestial heritage calling from the stars, remains blissfully unaware of the tempest brewing around her. The Conclave's meticulously crafted plans, woven within the shadows, are poised to entangle her in a web from which escape appears futile.

While the city below us bustles with life, blissfully ignorant of the cosmic battle unfurling in its midst, I wrestle with the monumental decision looming before me. Protecting Saturn means challenging the very essence of my existence, defying the Conclave, and reshaping a destiny etched across centuries.

The Conclave's opulent meeting place, with its

panoramic views of Central Park, now feels like a gilded prison. The realization that Saturn's fate, and perhaps the very balance of the universe, rests upon my shoulders is a heavy burden and a clarion call to action.

In the looming shadow of the Conclave's ambitions, I understand that a decision must be made. The battle for Saturn's soul and the destiny of all covens is about to commence—a battle not merely for power but for the heart of the cosmos itself, with Saturn, an unwitting star seed from Eridanus, at its epicenter. The night air on the 77th-floor brims with anticipation and the weight of centuries-old machinations. As I gaze upon the sprawling expanse of New York, the city that never sleeps, I know that the path ahead will be treacherous. Deep within me, a resolve begins to take shape. The time has come to stand in the light to protect Saturn and the legacy she carries.

As I make my way back to San Francisco, I come to a realization: the Conclave of Shadows has underestimated the power of loyalty and love as they set their sights on cosmic dominion. I swear to myself, as the stars above whisper of past battles and the destiny awaiting, I will defy the darkness and inscribe a new chapter in the saga that has unfolded over centuries. A chapter where the light will confront shadow, where the fate of the universe hangs in the balance.

CHAPTER 9

"WHISPERED MYSTERIES UNVEILED"

I am desperately trying to contact Aunt Sage because I need to share something extraordinary. These newfound powers are like a riddle in my life, and I believe Aunt Sage could be the guiding light to unlock the mysteries. Her wisdom has always been my North Star, and her enigmatic aura has shaped my view of the supernatural and the extraordinary.

But despite my relentless attempts to reach her, there is only silence. Aunt Sage vanishing like this is unusual, and it stirs up an anxious storm within me. I turn to Miles, pleading for his support yet hesitating to reveal the specifics of my newfound abilities, which have been my secret treasure.

As Miles and I embark on our journey to Aunt Sage's cozy cottage in a quaint East Coast town, it is a long flight filled with turbulence due to the rain. Once we land at the airport, we grab a car rental and head to Aunt Sage's. The air in the car feels heavy with unspoken tension. Miles breaks the silence, sensing the weight of doubt that hangs over me.

"Saturn, we'll track down your aunt," he reassures me in a soothing voice, his hand resting gently on my knee. "From what you've told me, she's no stranger to challenges, and there might be a simple explanation for her absence. Let's keep our hopes high." I nod, finding solace in his presence by my side. "I get it, Miles, but it's been too long for her to be off the grid. I've got something I've been wanting to share with her. I need her insight and advice."

He looks at me with empathy. "Are you alright, Saturn? You can confide in me. We're in this together."

I pause, carefully selecting my words to unveil the mystery of my newfound abilities. "It's about these powers I've stumbled upon, Miles," I begin cautiously. "I can commune with animals and nature, manipulate elements like fire and water, and I feel an innate connection to energy. It's all incredibly weird to me, and I believe it's tied to my ancestry somehow. I wanted to discuss it with Aunt Sage."

Miles nods thoughtfully, his expression turning serious. "Those powers sound truly amazing, Saturn. Wow! Well, sounds not only scary but exciting at the same time. I hope your aunt can help you through all of this and can give you some answers."

I wasn't expecting Miles to be so understanding, with him being a mortal and all, but I felt a weight lift from my shoulders. His unwavering support is welcome and very sweet, I think to myself as we continue our journey. Sharing my secret with him lightens the burden, and despite the uncertain path ahead, I am confident that with his help, we will catch up with Aunt Sage and figure out these enigmatic powers shaping my life.

The familiar "Welcome to Bernardston" sign stands timeless ahead of us. The town where Aunt Sage's cottage and crystal shop are nestled is like something out of a storybook. It is a serene and idyllic New England town nestled in the heart of Franklin County. Here, time seems to slow down, and the air carries the sweet scent of pine trees. As we drive from the Massachusetts airport towards Bernardston, I can't help but be reminiscent of its charm.

Our drive leads us past Kringle Candle Store, where the scent of vanilla and cinnamon fills the air, and rows of handmade candles await. The Farm Table restaurant serves farm-to-table delights, and locals gather there for Sunday brunch. Two pizza spots, Antonio's II Pizza & Grinders, and Hillside Pizza, are cozy spots where townspeople enjoy delicious meals.

But our destination is Aunt Sage's Crystal Shop and Cottage, which lies on the edge of town. The lavender-colored cottage stands as a beacon of mysticism in this picturesque setting. I feel a sense of longing as we arrive at the wooden gate.

Unlocking the gate and stepping onto the gravel path, I marvel at the beauty of Aunt Sage's home, memories of my childhood and life flooding my mind. The cottage stands at the edge of a lush forest, its weathered cedar shingles blending seamlessly with the surrounding landscape. The exterior is painted a very light lavender, almost white, with hints of purple and deep purple trim.

The front porch, bathed in the warm glow of the setting sun, beckons with a wooden swing swaying gently in the breeze. Tall oaks, maples, and pines embrace the cottage, their leaves rustling softly in the wind. The gravel path leads us to the front door, an invitation to explore further.

When we open the door and enter Aunt Sage's charming cottage, everything seems perfect except for the absence of Aunt Sage herself. We decide to stay there for a few days, hoping she'll return or we'll receive any lead on her whereabouts. Stepping inside, I feel an immediate sense of comfort and belonging. The walls are painted in soft earth tones—sage green, warm beige, and hints of burnt sienna. Sunlight filters through lace curtains, casting delicate patterns on the hardwood floors. In the living room, a stone fireplace takes center stage, its mantle adorned with family photos and a vase of wildflowers. A worn leather armchair and a hand-knit Afghan on the sofa promise cozy evenings. The kitchen, with its vintage stove and the lingering scent of incense, is the heart of the cottage. A wooden table with mismatched chairs invites you to sit down for a hearty meal, while pantry shelves are stocked with Aunt Sage's lovingly made preserves.

Upstairs, the bedroom awaits with a sloping ceiling that adds character. A four-poster bed with a patchwork quilt promises restful nights, and a window overlooking the forest allows the gentle rustle of leaves to serenade you. A vintage writing desk sits by the window, adorned with ink bottles, quills, and a leatherbound journal.

As we settle into Aunt Sage's enchanting cottage, it truly becomes a sanctuary amid the uncertainty that has taken hold of our lives. Each room holds memories of her, and I can almost feel her presence in every corner, a reassuring ghost of comfort and wisdom. Miles and I find ourselves exploring the cottage's nooks and crannies, discovering hidden trinkets, and sharing stories about Aunt Sage.

Our days in Bernardston stretch out before us like an open book, each page filled with hope and, sometimes, despair. The sunlit mornings are spent sipping tea on the porch, the gentle rustling of leaves above us forming the soundtrack to our contemplative conversations. Miles and I often share knowing glances, our connection deepening with every passing day.

In the afternoons, we take long walks through the forest, hand in hand, our fingers intertwined like our fates. The woods seem to embrace us, whispering secrets of ancient magick and untold tales. Our footsteps are soft against the carpet of fallen leaves, a sound that is both comforting and eerie in its solitude.

Evenings are a time for reflection and planning in Aunt Sage's cozy cottage. After our daily search for Aunt Sage, Miles and I sit by the crackling fireplace, its warm flames casting a soft, comforting glow on our faces. We discussed the conversations we had with everyone in town as to her whereabouts, dissecting every word spoken and looking for some sort of lead as to where she could have gone, but we always hit a dead end. Nobody has a clue, and it's very disheartening, but amidst the seriousness of our quest, there are also moments of tenderness and laughter.

Miles has a hidden talent that adds magick to our evenings – he is an excellent cook. He loves preparing meals for us, and his culinary skills are a delightful surprise. We take turns setting the dining table, the aroma of his dishes wafting through the cottage, making our stomachs rumble with anticipation.

One evening, as we share stories of our past and dreams of our future, Miles leans in, his eyes locked onto mine, and places a gentle kiss on my forehead. It is a simple yet heartwarming gesture, a testament to the deepening love between us.

"Saturn," he whispers, his voice a soft, comforting secret, "no matter where this journey takes us, I want you to know that I'm here for you, and I love you more than words can express."

Tears well up in my eyes, and I can't help but smile through them. "I love you too, Miles," I reply, my heart swelling with affection.

Our nights are filled with tender moments and shared dreams. We sit on the porch under the moonlight, telling each other stories that make us laugh and forget the weight of our journey. Our laughter echoes through the forest, and it feels like the trees are listening, their rustling leaves providing a soothing background to our conversations.

Miles often steals innocent kisses, each one a promise of a future filled with love and hope. We sleep in separate rooms, respecting the boundaries of our relationship, but our hearts are inseparable, beating in perfect harmony with each other's dreams. These evenings, filled with love and warmth, become our sanctuary in the midst of uncertainty.

However, as the days turn into weeks, Aunt Sage remains elusive, and the weight of uncertainty presses upon us. One evening, as we sit in her cozy living room surrounded by her eclectic belongings, Miles turns to me, his expression g rave.

"Saturn, we should brace ourselves for the possibility that Aunt Sage may not return," he says, his voice steady but determined. "Days have gone by without any clues."

My heart feels heavy with uncertainty as I nod in agreement. "I know, Miles, but she wouldn't just vanish without a trace. I can't help but fear the worst."

Miles offers a reassuring hand on my shoulder. "We'll employ every resource at our disposal to find her. And while we wait, let's keep our spirits up and keep searching."

Our relentless search for Aunt Sage leaves us both emotionally drained, each day blending into the next without a trace of her. The cottage, once a haven of warmth and cherished memories, now echoes with her absence. Amidst our growing despair, Miles suggests taking a formal step in our search. "Saturn," he says one morning, breaking the silence that has settled between us, "we should report her disappearance to the police. We need additional help."

I hesitate, knowing that involving the police will bring a sense of finality I'm not ready to face. "Yes, you're right, Miles. I've been avoiding it, hoping she'd walk through the door at any moment," I admit, the harsh reality pressing down on me.

Miles and I head down to South Street to the Bernardston Police Department to file the missing person's report. The police department itself is this sturdy brick building located at 256 South Street in Bernardston, Massachusetts. It's got that no-nonsense, functional look from the outside, evoking significance and purposefulness. There are big windows that let in tons of natural light into the reception area, and you could just feel the authority and dependability emanating from the place.

When we get closer, there's this prominent sign by the entrance that proudly displays the department's name and emblem. It's like a beacon for anyone who needs help or wants to report something. Right next to that, they have a whole parking area just for police vehicles, including cruisers and other specialized units. Seeing those cars around would make anyone feel safer, I guess.

The whole building is surrounded by well-kept landscaping, with greenery and flowers that add a bit of beauty to the practicality of the place. It kind of creates this sense of calm amidst all the hustle and bustle of police work.

Inside is where things get really interesting. The reception area is our first stop, and it has this secure setup with a bulletproof glass window where you can talk to the front desk officer. They have comfy seats for visitors, just in case you have to wait around for a bit.

Next door, I can see what looks like administrative offices; they are like a beehive of activity. That's where officers handle all the paperwork, do their investigations, and keep things running smoothly day-to-day. It shocks me how everything is super organized.

The dispatch center is a big deal, with lots of work-stations where dispatchers coordinate emergency responses and keep in touch with officers out in the field. The place is buzzing with activity, and you can feel the dedication to public safety all around.

Then, there's the briefing room, at least it looks like one to me; that's where officers gather before their shifts to get updates, talk strategies, and get ready for their duties. You can feel the camaraderie in there; it's like they're a tight-knit team.

They have bulletin boards all over the place with community alerts, safety tips, and info for residents. It shows that the police department is really committed to keeping the community informed and safe.

The reception desk is manned by an officer who greets us with curiosity and professionalism.

"Can I assist you?" he asks, his voice carrying in the busy lobby.

"We need to report a missing person," Miles states firmly, his presence offering strength as we're directed to a small, somewhat cramped office to file the report.

The officer who interviews us exudes seriousness and sympathy. "Tell me about the person you're report-ing," he begins, his pen poised over the paperwork.

As Miles recounts the situation, memories of Aunt Sage flood my thoughts, from the day of my birth, where she had been present, to the countless after-noons spent in her crystal shop, learning about the power of stones and incense. Aunt Sage had been more than just an aunt; she had been my guardian, my mentor, and, in many ways, my mother.

"Saturn was raised by her Aunt Sage after her mother, Willow, passed away during childbirth," Miles shares, casting a supportive glance in my direction. "Aunt Sage promised to raise her as her own."

The officer nods, recording every detail with care. "We'll do everything we can to locate her," he assures us, his words resonating with genuine concern.

As we leave the police department, the weight of our situation presses upon us. Yet, within that weight, a glimmer of hope remains. Miles takes my hand as we walk back to the car, his touch grounding and reassuring.

"Saturn, no matter what's waiting for us out here, we're in it together," he says, his voice cutting through the chaos swirling inside my head. "Your aunt loved you more than anything, and she's a part of who you are. We'll find her, or at least, we'll figure out what really happened."

"And that's the thing, isn't it?" I reply. "My aunt was just the lady who ran a crystal shop, another familiar face in our tiny community. The idea that she's just... gone and that there's some mystery we need to solve about her disappearance—it's surreal. She wasn't some undercover spy or anything; she was just this wonderful, beautiful, small woman who belonged to this equally wonderful, small town, keeping to herself for the most part."

I lift my gaze to Miles, finding solace in his steady presence. "Thank you, Miles. For everything. For standing by me through this and for your unwavering support... I can't imagine facing any of this without you."

The visit to the police department, though daunting, has deepened our connection. Our bond, already strong, has become unbreakable, our love boundless. As we drive away, the path ahead remains uncertain, but I know that together, we will figure it out.

CHAPTER 10

"SHATTERED BONDS"

Weeks of agonizing silence from Aunt Sage culminate in a devastating revelation that leaves me shattered. After enduring days filled with anxious waiting and futile attempts to contact her through calls, texts, and even reaching out to her circle of friends, the harsh reality crashed down upon me. The police have discovered a body, identified as Aunt Sage's, through personal documents found at the scene—a brutal confirmation of my worst fears. The details are grim, her face unrecognizable, a stark testament to the violence she has suffered.

This revelation breaks me, and I find myself crying uncontrollably, grieving the loss of the woman who has been more than family—she has been my mentor, my protector, and the guardian of our ancestral secrets.

The funeral procession itself is a solemn affair. Most

of the townsfolk, all dressed in black, attend because they all love Aunt Sage. The cemetery in Bernardston, Massachusetts, is where it all happens, and it is a beautiful yet solemn place.

The day is clear, with a bright blue sky and gentle breeze, as if even the weather understands the gravity of the occasion. The cemetery is a peaceful and serene spot, surrounded by towering trees that rustle softly in the wind. It feels like a place where time stands still, and the only sounds are the chirping of birds and the distant murmur of the town. As we make our way through the cemetery gates, I can't help but notice the eclectic group of mourners. There are neighbors who have known Aunt Sage for years, shop owners from the town who have visited her crystal store, and even some folks who have only heard about her mystical wisdom. It is a diverse gathering, a testament to the impact she has had on everyone.

Nestled among rolling hills and ancient trees, Center Cemetery in Bernardston, Massachusetts, is unlike any other place. When you drive through its wrought-iron gates, it feels like time itself slows down. You can almost hear the whispers of generations past in the air. The gravestones stand like silent sentinels, each one holding countless stories of the people who have come before.

As you enter, there is this path flanked by wildflowers that leads you deeper into the heart of the cemetery. When you walk on the gravel, it's like the sound echoes the footsteps of everyone who has ever visited. Tall oak trees stretch their branches overhead, casting dappled shadows on the ground. It feels like a place of reflection and reverence.

To the left, there is a cluster of ancient pine trees. Those trees have seen it all. Their needles rustle in the breeze, and if you listen closely, you might catch fragments of conversations carried by the wind. It's like they hold the secrets of the cemetery, the laughter, the tears, and the quiet contemplation of countless souls.

In the heart of the cemetery, you'll find the Serenity Garden. This place is special because it has marble benches where people can sit and rest. The garden itself blooms with roses, their petals soft as memories. It's a place of peace and solace. Now, if you want a view that seems to reach beyond the earthly boundaries, you can climb Sunset Hill. From there, you can see the entire cemetery, and when the sun starts to set, it bathes the tombstones in golden hues. Many folks choose this spot to say their final goodbyes to their loved ones, watching as day turns into night.

In one far corner, there is an ancient oak tree. Its roots are all gnarled up, gripping the earth like it's holding onto its own stories. Families often gather under its sheltering branches during memorial services. The oak's leaves rustle like old parchment, as if it's recording the stories whispered to it over centuries.

And when night falls, Starry Hollow comes alive. The sky above is like a canvas of constellations, and fireflies dance among the tombstones. This is where poets, dreamers, and stargazers are laid to rest—those who find solace in the vastness of the universe.

Near the oldest gravestone, there is a single rose-bush that thrives. Its crimson blooms defy the passage of time, symbolizing love that never fades. Visitors often leave small tokens among the petals, like hand-written notes, feathers, or polished stones.

And there is a narrow brook that winds through the cemetery, its gentle babble soothing to the soul. Some believe it carries messages between the living and the departed, like a bridge connecting both worlds. Along its banks, forget-me-nots bloom, promising never to forget. Aunt Sage's grave is in this extraordinary place, surrounded by the beauty of nature and the stories of those who have come before. I chose a special tomb-stone for her, a gray stone with an Ametrine Crystal that sparkles in the sunlight. The inscription reads, "Sage Agnes Eridanus—Sister, Aunt, Mentor," and it feels like a perfect tribute to her. The quote I picked for her tombstone is, "Like a star in the night sky, your light will always guide us." It reflects her fascination with the stars and the universe, something she has passed on to me.

The funeral service itself is touching. There are heartfelt eulogies from friends and family, each sharing their own cherished memories of Aunt Sage. The whole town comes together to say their final goodbyes, and it's a bittersweet moment. The presence of Daniel and Dianna adds an extra layer of tension to the atmosphere, their arrival unwelcome yet inescapable.

I confront Daniel and Dianna with a mixture of anger and heartache. "I can't believe the two of you had the audacity to show up," I hiss, the pain of their betrayal evident in my voice.

Daniel's attempt at an apology falls short. "Saturn, I'm so sorry," he mumbles, but I cut him off, my patience for his excuses has worn thin.

"Your apologies mean nothing, Daniel. After everything, you expect me to just simply accept them?" My words drip with scorn.

Dianna, ever smug, tries to defuse the situation. "We're here to pay our respects, Saturn. Let's not make this any more difficult."

My response is terse, my disdain for her thinly veiled. "Respects? After your betrayal, you dare speak of respect, Dianna?"

The small town has a close-knit community, and her presence has touched so many lives. However much-loved Aunt Sage is, the funeral is charged with unspoken accusations, and the townspeople's speculative murmurs only add to the tension. Their curiosity about Aunt Sage's life and the secrets they suspect she holds are now openly discussed, albeit in hushed tones.

Miles stands steadfast beside me, a pillar of support amidst the emotional storm brewing around us. His timely intervention when Dianna attempts to provoke me further is a testament to his unwavering loyalty and quick wit.

"Really, Dianna, your presence here feels as welcome as a storm cloud on a clear day. Quite bold of you to drop in uninvited," Miles quips, his sarcasm slicing through the air like a sharp knife. I can't help but let out a stifled laugh at his words, a brief moment of lightness in the midst of all this turmoil.

"Who the hell are you? You don't know us or our past with Saturn!" Dianna retorts sharply, her voice laced with venom as she turns her glare to Miles.

I step forward, meeting Dianna's gaze with a steely resolve. "Regardless of our past, your presence here is unwelcome and disrespectful," I declare firmly, refusing to back down in the face of her hostility.

Miles, ever the voice of reason, adds his own brand of sarcasm to the mix. "Ah, but isn't it just like a dark storm cloud to show up uninvited and make a nuisance of itself?" he remarks dryly, his tone dripping with sarcasm.

Miles' sharp retort leaves Dianna momentarily stunned, her usual confidence faltering in the face of his cutting sarcasm. The look of embarrassment on her face speaks volumes, her usual retorts silenced by his biting words. Seeing his wife's discomfort, Daniel intervenes, his voice tinged with frustration. "Come on, honey, let's go," he says, his tone a mixture of resignation and irritation as he attempts to diffuse the tense situation.

With a final glare directed at us, Dianna follows Daniel, her pride wounded and her plans for provocation thwarted. As they retreat, the tension in the air eases slightly, leaving behind a sense of relief mingled with lingering resentment.

As we leave the funeral, the intricate tapestry of my past and present has never felt more intertwined. The presence of Daniel and Dianna, alongside the whispered speculations of the townsfolk, underscores the constant division between my mystical heritage and the ordinary world.

Miles and I lean on each other, our bond deepening through shared hardship. "We'll get through this, Saturn. Together," he assures me, his voice a constant presence amidst the chaos of my thoughts.

The funeral isn't just a farewell to Aunt Sage; it's a stark reminder of the complex web of my life. Amidst the grief and the presence of those from my past, I stand at a crossroads, with the secrets of my heritage and an uncertain future stretching out before me.

CHAPTER 11
"ENCOUNTER OF INTENSITY"

While waiting for Saturn to finish her conversation with some of the mourners, Daniel Darkwood approaches, and an uneasy feeling crept over me, a primal instinct warning me of his presence. Despite his outward appearance of normalcy, there is an undeniable intensity emanating from him, something that stirred a sense of caution within me. Our handshake, a mere formality, carries an unspoken tension, like two opposing forces meeting in silence.

"I'm Daniel," he introduces himself, his voice smooth yet edged with a sharpness that cut through the polite facade.

Responding cautiously, I mirror his wariness in my tone. "Miles Nightshade."

The pleasantries we exchange feel superficial, a thin

veil over the underlying animosity simmering between us. Behind his attempt at a friendly smile, Daniel's eyes betray a storm of emotions, hinting at a complexity beyond the ordinary.

Then, he makes an announcement intended to unsettle me. "I believe you've heard of me, Saturn's ex-husband."

His words hang in the air, heavy with unspoken accusations. Unable to resist a touch of sarcasm, I reply, "Ah, the prodigal husband. The one who went astray."

Daniel smirks, a defiant look masking the turmoil in his eyes. "Every story has its shadows, Miles. Not everything is as Saturn may have portrayed it."

With a smirk playing on my lips, I can't resist a witty retort. "So, you didn't cheat on her with her best friend Dianna? Is that what Saturn got wrong?"

Daniel's smirk doesn't wane, but there's a flicker of stormy defiance in his eyes before he manages to mask it with his usual composure. "Miles, every story has its darker sides, its own narrative complexity. It's not as straightforward as Saturn might have made it out to be," he retorts, his tone casual yet tinged with a note of defensiveness.

I can't help but let my smirk broaden, intrigued by the tension and unbothered by the undercurrents. "Oh, so the whole saga with you and Dianna is just one of those 'complex narratives'? Saturn got her wires crossed, is that it?"

That's when I see it—a brief falter in Daniel's polished façade, a sign of discomfort he quickly masks. It's a fleeting moment but unmistakably revealing. The air thickens with unsaid words, and I lean in, eager for his reply.

Daniel pauses, then his voice sharpens, albeit maintaining a hint of his earlier nonchalance. "Look, Miles, every tale has its layers, its own set of complications. As for what happened with Dianna, let's just say it's intricate. It wasn't some clear-cut betrayal like you're suggesting. It was more about a series of choices, events... not a simple moment." He sidesteps the core issue with a finesse that's almost admirable, deftly navigating the conversation without fully disclosing anything.

Then, with a slight edge of irritation, he adds, "And frankly, it's none of your business."

I lean back, my interest piqued but my stance firm. "Actually, Daniel, anything that involves Saturn becomes 100% my business. She's more than just a part of this story; she's someone I care deeply about. So, yeah, it is my business." My response is measured but clear, underlining my unwavering support for Saturn and my intent to understand the full scope of what's at play here.

His lips twist into a semblance of a smile, though the air between us is charged with an unmistakable tension. "And what about you, Mr. Nightshade? You and Saturn seem to have grown quite close rather swiftly," Daniel probes, his gaze sharp and inquisitive.

I pause for a moment, weighing my words carefully. "Well, that's none of your business, is it?" I retort with my response curt and leaving no room for further intrusion. The standoff that follows is dense with the things left unsaid, a silent contest of wills playing out beneath the guise of our casual exchange.

There's something about Daniel that sets my instincts on edge, a feeling I can't quite shake off. It's like there's this eerie, almost paranormal vibe around him, whispering secrets the air itself seems hesitant to share. It's a sensation that teeters on the edge of the supernatural, challenging everything I've come to trust about my own senses. Logic tells me he's mortal—Saturn, with her finely tuned perception, would have definitely picked up on any hint of power, and she hasn't said a word. Yet, there's this nagging doubt, a shadow that casts our every interaction in a more intriguing, somewhat ominous light. It's almost as if there's something Conclave-like about him, a darkness that's hard to pinpoint but impossible to ignore.

Our conversation veers toward the earlier altercation between Saturn and Dianna, and Daniel's calm facade cracks, revealing a simmering anger beneath the surface. "Your words to Dianna earlier were less than polite. Is that how you treat all your guests?"

Meeting Daniel's gaze head-on, the tension between

us crackles with unspoken challenges. My resolve hardens, my eyes silently affirming my stance. "My remarks reflected the respect—or lack thereof—Dianna showed. Civility, Daniel, should be mutual," I assert, the weight of my words hanging in the air. "We don't treat our guests like that, but let's be clear—you and your wife are not invited guests; you just showed up." My tone, firm and unequivocal, leaves no room for misinterpretation, drawing a clear line in the sand between courteous hospitality and the uninvited intrusion they've imposed upon us.

As we make our way to the car, Saturn's curiosity breaks through the lingering tension. "What were you and Daniel talking about back there?" she asks, her tone light but probing.

With a smirk, I reply, "Oh, nothing much. Daniel was just being nosy, but I squashed it," and I throw her a wink, hinting that there was a bit more to the story than I'm letting on.

Saturn pauses for a moment, then asks, "Oh, ok; should I be concerned?"

I shake my head, trying to keep the mood light. "No, baby, but let me ask you something. Do you think Daniel has powers like you do?" The question slips out, coated in my casual tone, but it's anything but casual.

She looks at me, puzzled by the sudden shift. "That's a strange question. No, not at all. Why?" Her brows furrow slightly, a mix of confusion and curiosity painting her features.

I shrug, trying to shake off the heavy feeling settling in my chest. "It's just a feeling I have," I say, keeping my gaze on the path ahead. The moment hangs between us, thick with implications and unspoken thoughts, before we slide into the car and drive away, leaving the question and the day behind us.

In the wake of Aunt Sage's farewell and back at Aunt Sage's cottage, Saturn and I dive into the solemn task of sifting through her treasures. Aunt Sage's absence weighs heavily on Saturn, but amidst the memories, there's a resolve to honor her legacy. After meticulously organizing her possessions, we decided to bring practical items back to San Francisco, cherishing sentimental objects that hold no tangible value but are priceless in sentiment.

As we uncover Aunt Sage's life through her belongings, her essence seems to linger in the air. Each book, crystal, and herb tells a story of her enduring legacy. When Saturn stumbles upon an old tome filled with mysterious symbols and arcane writings, it's as if destiny itself is guiding our hands. "The Book of Shadows," Saturn murmurs, cradling the volume with reverence. The moment I see it, I recognize its significance. It's not just a book; it's a key to unlocking Saturn's potential.

Contemplation washes over me as I ponder the

possibilities. Could this ancient manuscript be the catalyst for Saturn's awakening? I have no doubt. The journey ahead may be fraught with challenges, but I am determined to stand by Saturn's side, protecting her from any threat that may arise.

As we delve into the mysteries within The Book of Shadows and explore Saturn's latent talents, our bond deepens with each passing day. There's no uncertainty in my heart or mind. I will defy the Conclave, if necessary, to protect Saturn and help her realize her true potential.

Despite the shadows that may attempt to tear us apart, I know that together, we are stronger. Saturn's unwavering determination, her thirst for knowledge, and the bond that binds us are unbreakable.

As our journey unfolds, I find myself drawn closer to Saturn, captivated by her strength and resilience. The challenges we face only serve to strengthen our resolve. With each obstacle we overcome, we grow stronger and more determined to defy the forces that seek to control us.

Navigating this uncharted territory may be daunting, but I am ready to face whatever comes our way. The path ahead may be uncertain, but with Saturn by my side, I know we will triumph. Our journey together is just beginning, and I am committed to seeing it through to the end.

CHAPTER 12

"LUNAR REVELATIONS"

As Miles sets off on his errand to collect supplies for our upcoming flight home, I find myself alone in Aunt Sage's quiet abode, cradling The Book of Shadows. This, to me, is no ordinary book; it's a repository of arcane wisdom passed down through generations, and it holds an aura of mystique that seems to radiate from its very pages.

The aged leather cover, etched with the traces of countless fingertips, tells the story of its long existence. The once-supple leather now bears the weathered patina of centuries, and its rich, earthy brown hue hints at the deep mysteries concealed within.

At the center of the cover, the Eridanus constellation shines. This celestial pattern of stars resembles a winding river, symbolizing the flow of knowledge and power. It's said that those who connect with this constellation are destined for great magickal feats.

Around the constellation, ancient runes spiral outward, their intricate curves and angles invoking forgotten tongues. These glyphs seem to pulse with latent energy as if they're whispering long-forgotten spells to anyone brave enough to decipher them.

The edges of the cover bear delicate illustrations of lunar phases: waxing crescents, full moons, and waning gibbous. Each phase represents a different aspect of magick—the waxing for growth, the full for power, and the waning for release.

Turning the book over, I discover the back adorned with silver crescent moons—celestial guardians frozen in time. These moons seem to protect the gateway between realms, ensuring that the Book of Shadows remains a sanctuary for those seeking magick. The spine, wrapped in midnight velvet, cradles the pages like a protective cocoon. When touched, it yields slightly, as if it's a living conduit between the mundane and the mystical.

Upon opening the book, I encounter yellowed parchment pages, each thick and substantial. The uneven edges give the impression that they've been torn from ancient grimoires by unseen hands. The ink, a deep sepia, seems to carry the weight of countless spells cast and woven destinies.

As I turn the pages, the scent of dried herbs—sage,

lavender, and mugwort—wafts up from within. These leaves have been pressed between the pages by generations of witches, infusing the book with their protective energies.

Certain pages bear faint candle burns, remnants of rituals performed under the moonlight. The wax has seeped into the fibers, sealing intentions and binding spells.

Amidst the spells and incantations, I find hand-drawn constellation charts—maps to navigate both earthly and astral realms. Orion and Eridanus are prominent guiding lights for those who seek their wisdom.

Lifting a corner of a page, I discover hidden compartments—tiny envelopes containing dried petals, crystals, or locks of hair. These treasures hold memories, blessings, and whispered secrets, adding layers of depth to the book's mystique.

At the very end of the book lie blank pages—an invitation to inscribe one's own magick. Here, the veil between worlds is thinnest. It's a place to write desires, weave intentions, and let the Book of Shadows absorb one's essence.

Tonight, a full moon bathes the room in its glow, streaming through the stained-glass window overhead. I'm captivated by the way the book in my hands catches the moonlight, its pages casting a soft, silvery luminescence around me.

It becomes a conduit for ancestral voices, a bridge to realms beyond. In the stillness of the night, under the alignment of stars, the Book of Shadows awaits, its pages rustling with eagerness to reveal their secrets to those who seek the ancient, the mysterious, and the magickal.

Seated amidst the tranquility of Aunt Sage's sanctuary, my heartbeat quickens as I delve deeper, unearthing the hidden riddles and latent powers nestled within its pages. Each puzzle I decipher is a step closer to unraveling the enigma of my burgeoning abilities, a journey of enlightenment that is both exhilarating and daunting.

As I continue my solitary exploration, a remarkable discovery unfolds before my eyes—a breathtaking portrait of a woman. Her likeness is so strikingly similar to mine that it feels as though I'm gazing into a mirror reflecting my own soul. Beneath her captivating image lies a handwritten note, a precious message from my mother, Willow. It's a heartfelt testament to our unbreakable bond, a repository of love and wisdom that transcends time.

In her note, she speaks of the sacrifices made out of a mother's protective love. She expresses deep regret at not being there to personally guide me through life, entrusting my care to Aunt Sage. Her words are a poignant reminder of the profound love she holds for me. The final entry, penned by my mother's hand, is a tender farewell—a declaration of her unwavering love for me. "I will always love you, my darling Saturn. When you gaze upon the stars, remember that I am watching over you eternally until we reunite in the boundless universe, my little star seed." These words shimmer in silver, a radiant testimony to our eternal connection.

Overwhelmed by emotion, tears blur my vision as the reality of my mother's love and the magnitude of her sacrifice wash over me. My hands tremble as I clutch the book closer, feeling an indescribable connection to the generations of women who have wielded its magick before me. This journey of discovery, once embarked upon in isolation, now feels like a shared pilgrimage with the spirits of my ancestors guiding me, their wisdom illuminating the path ahead.

Despite my longing to share these revelations with Miles, a protective instinct holds me back, a remnant of past betrayals that have taught me caution. The secrets of The Book of Shadows and the power they promise are mine to explore alone for now. Yet, as I venture deeper into the mysteries of my heritage, the invisible thread that connects Miles and me tugs at my consciousness, a reminder of the uncharted destiny we are yet to navigate together.

Lost in the mystique of The Book of Shadows, I am a solitary voyager on a sea of arcane knowledge, each discovery a beacon in the night, guiding me towards a future where the past's shadows dance with the light of newfound understanding.

First, I find the Power named "Whispering Winds," accompanied by a riddle, a sign, and a note that says that the answer to the riddle is the secret of this power.

Riddle:

"The zephyr speaks the story of spring
As secrets softly murmur in the breeze.
Where the sun rises in the eastern sky,
What kind of power does the wind realize?"

Sign:

"A symbol resembling an intricate whirlwind."

I am dragged into the core of the natural world as I think about the Whispering Winds' enigma. The phrases seem to address me directly and allude to a potential hidden power.

I keep thinking, "The zephyr speaks the story of spring," picturing the wind as a storyteller, telling the tales of the passing seasons. To me, it seems that Spring, with its new life and rejuvenation, holds the key.

I think of the beautiful melodies of the wind as it rustles through the leaves and branches, "As secrets softly murmur in the breeze." A song with a melody of nature's secrets is heard in the air.

I focus on the last hint, "Where the sun rises in the eastern sky," The dawn of a new day, a time of awakening and promise, is signaled by the sun's rising in the east.

The last sentence, "What kind of power does the wind realize?" gets my attention. It seems to me that the wind is aware of the strength of secrets, the hidden stories about nature and existence that are carried in its winds and whispers. It possesses the ability to reveal truth and the aptitude to understand the world's mysteries.

I hear the solution as a breeze-borne whisper. The secrets of dawn, the knowledge stored in the early morning light, are the strength that the wind understands. It is the connection to nature's delicate equilibrium, a profound grasp of the environment.

After solving this riddle, I now know that I have a unique ability called "Whispering Winds." As I continue to read the inscriptions that follow, I learn this power allows me to communicate with nature, especially the wind, to learn about the world's mysteries. This power lets me understand nature's secrets as the wind shares its wisdom with me.

To use Whispering Winds effectively, I need to be calm and positive, ideally in open spaces or a forest where the wind flows freely. This enhances my ability and lets me connect deeply with the environment, learning its hidden truths. It's a precious gift from nature, and I'm committed to using it responsibly to maintain the balance of the natural world. The wind is my guide, teaching me through the whispers in the breeze.

However, I learned this gift comes with a downside. It turns me into an empath who feels the pain, sadness, and secrets carried by the wind from people's lives. This empathy is constant and forces me to deal with the emotional and physical pain that comes with the wind's stories. Using Whispering Winds means accepting this curse, linking me to the world's suffering without escape, a burden I'll have to learn to live with. As I read on, I discovered that Whispering Winds is not impervious to stealing. A potential burglar would have to use the "Ephemeral Whispers" approach. The "Zephyr's Tear," a crystal amulet made with a gemstone that captures the essence of the wind, is a specific tool used in this process.

The thief must first acquire a Zephyr's Tear, a priceless jewel that can only be discovered in holy nature areas where the winds are at their strongest. Once they have this tool, they must carry out a complex ceremony outdoors or in a setting like a forest, where the winds can blow freely and whispered secrets are revealed.

The thief uses the gemstone's affinity for the winds to invoke their power during the ritual and engages in communion with the Whispering Winds. This strategy's key component is persuading the authority to change its allegiance from the present wielder to the thief by utilizing the secrets and suffering already woven into the wind.

The Whispering Winds will separate from the present wielder and bind to the Zephyr's Tear if the thief is successful in convincing it to divulge its secrets. The original wielder will lose its link to the power and will be left without its sympathetic link to the winds.

This stolen power, which the thief can release and master as their own, is preserved in the Zephyr's Tear amulet. The thief will then be affected by the same curse, turning into an unwitting empath to the people's secrets and suffering as it is whispered by the winds. As a result, the thief will become the new bearer of Whispering Winds, leaving the prior wielder helpless and severed from the sympathetic gale.

As I dive deeper into The Book of Shadows, I find spells that let me unlock and control this magickal force on my own terms. It's like my ancestors laid out a guide for my journey towards understanding myself better. I'm amazed by these spells; they're the key to harnessing the power of the wind. With them, I can tap into my special ability fully and use it skillfully. These spells allow me to call upon the elements and reveal their secrets to light my way.

"By the zephyrs' grace, the earth's gentle sway,

I call upon the winds to guide my way.
With respect and humility, my heart is in the right place,
I harness the secrets with nature's gentle embrace.
Whispering Winds, reveal to me your song,
As I tread lightly where I belong.
Guide me through the secrets of dawn and morn,
With the wind's gentle whispers, my powers are reborn.

But let it be known, with the responsibility I wield,
For only in balance, nature's secrets revealed.
This power, a gift, I must cherish and protect,
To the earth and its whispers, my respect I'll reflect."

There's also another spell that comes with a big responsibility. It's called the bound spell, designed to keep these powers safe from falling into the wrong hands. As I grow and discover new skills, I must document them in The Book of Shadows. This step of protection and accountability ensures that only the right people can wield these powers.

"In the realm of secrets, where mystic powers reside,
I bind these words from wandering eyes outside.
With incantations whispered a guardian I shall be,
For those who hold the keys, in trust, like the earth, sky, and
sea."

I update The Book of Shadows with new information and use the binding spell to reinforce the protections around these age-old secrets. This book is more than a collection of knowledge; it's a physical representation of the connection between nature and those chosen to preserve its balance.

As I explore the spells and incantations, I feel a deep gratitude for the heritage I've inherited. I understand that my journey involves not only self-discovery but also sharing this ancient wisdom with future generations to keep the balance between the mystical and the mundane. In the quiet of my aunt's cottage, under the soft moonlight, I'm once again drawn into the magick of The Book of Shadows. With Miles not yet home, I have the opportunity to explore a new ability hidden within its pages, named "Lunar Dreams." The very name suggests a link to the moon's mysterious powers, and I'm eager to uncover its secrets and understand its mysteries.

Riddle:

"When the night is ruled by Luna's gleam,
And the realm of dreams is as it seems.
Under her gaze, the unseen's door,
What magick lies in her silver floor?"

Sign:

"A crescent moon entwined with stars."

Diving into the mysteries of Lunar Dreams, I've realized the moon plays a crucial role in unlocking this power. It's like there's a hidden path, maybe even a gateway to another realm, where the moon's magick is kept.

The clues start with an ode to the night under the moon's glow, suggesting a special time when the moon's influence is strongest. The idea is that when the moon shines, the line between dreams and reality blurs, making the extraordinary possible.

The riddle hints at the moon revealing a doorway to the unseen and magickal. It asks what magick the moon's light holds, nudging me to explore the secrets of Lunar Dreams. This power connects deeply with the moon, affecting dreams and emotions.

Through Lunar Dreams, I'll grow closer to the moon and come to understand its impact on our dreamscapes and feelings. This ability lets me influence not just my dreams but others' as well, shaping emotions and experiences while asleep.

However, with this power comes responsibility. I must use Lunar Dreams ethically, aiming for emotional healing and positive influence in others' subconscious.

Lunar Dreams comes with its own set of challenges. The moon's phases affect me more intensely, making me especially sensitive during the full moon. It's a reminder of the dual nature of this power, reflecting the moon's serene and unpredictable sides.

The Book of Shadows reveals that Lunar Dreams could be vulnerable to theft, but there are protections in place. To misuse Lunar Dreams, one would have to break through several magickal defenses, an almost impossible feat ensuring only those truly understanding its nature can wield it.

I'm fascinated by the connection between Lunar Dreams and Whispering Winds, showing The Book of Shadows holds the key to mastering these powers in harmony with the moon's cycles.

"When Luna's radiance bathes the night,
And dreams dance in her tranquil light.
To awaken this power's ethereal streams,
Inscribe its secrets within The Book of Dreams.
To control it, let empathy guide your hand,
For emotions' touch is its true command.
In moonlight's grace, unleash the spell,
And Lunar Dreams shall serve you well.
Remember, the curse within the moon's embrace,
Its powers you must yield in gentle grace.
With kindness and care, your rule must stand,
For harm, it shall not tolerate within its land."

This riddle describes a way to not only awaken the Lunar Dreams' power but also regulate and harness its magickal powers while highlighting the significance of empathy and compassion in doing so. The curse inside the moon's gaze serves as a reminder to use this power with compassion to keep it a force for good.

> *"Under the moon's tranquil, silver gleam,*
> *Inscribe the spell and fulfill the dream.*
> *In Luna's light, the binding's grace,*
> *To seal the power in its rightful place."*

I'm considering writing a binding spell for the Lunar Dreams power in The Book of Shadows, especially under the moonlight. The moon's significance in these powers is unmistakable, closely tied to its phases and the enchantment of the night.

Realizing the gravity of Lunar Dreams, I recognize its need for cautious handling and safeguarding. It's a power that demands respect and thoughtful use, not to be wielded recklessly.

As I delve further, I encounter an oddity: the Whispering Winds puzzles seem to reset, making it appear as though I hadn't solved them at all. It suggests that The Book of Shadows offers its secrets only momentarily, to be understood temporarily before they retreat into obscurity.

The book uniquely embeds its wisdom into me, as if transferring its knowledge directly into my consciousness. This mechanism seems to serve as a protective measure for those brave enough to engage deeply with its mysteries.

My contemplation is broken by Miles returning home. I hastily conceal the book; although he's aware of my powers, the realm I'm currently exploring is far more profound. It feels premature to unveil these deeper mysteries to him. His presence underscores the distinction between our shared experiences and the aspects of my journey that remain solely mine.

The knowledge from the book excites me, deepening my connection to my heritage. Yet, I'm conflicted about sharing this with Miles, pondering how it might transform our relationship.

Miles stands on the brink of this magickal world, not yet fully enveloped. I envision a future where we uncover these secrets together. I eagerly anticipate the day I can open up fully about this magickal universe to him, tackling its mysteries as a united front. Until that moment arrives, I'll continue my solitary exploration, preparing for when our paths converge into one enchanted journey.

CHAPTER 13

"A PROPOSAL IN THE SHADOWS"

As the soft light of dawn paints the Castro District of San Francisco with hues of gold and amber, I find myself ensconced in the luxury of my penthouse, close to the office in case of a long night, a vantage point that offers a panoramic view of a neighborhood vibrant with life and history. The Castro, known for its colorful streets, bustling cafes, and the spirit of inclusivity, seems to pulse with the energy of a community that thrives on diversity and unity. Yet, within the confines of my luxurious abode, I wrestle with a tumult of emotions that stand in stark contrast to the lively scene below. I head out and head to my office downtown.

I sit in my office, surrounded by the trappings of my professional world, and I can't escape the anguish that rages inside me. The coven has its intentions, a legacy

I'm supposed to continue, but Saturn's presence has cast a shadow over the road I had long imagined was mine to walk. Loyalty to the coven is something I've learned over many years since the untimely death of my parents; they were there at a time I believe I needed them the most, but Saturn's presence in my life has uncovered a completely unanticipated bond.

My life has always been one of structure and discipline, working as the CEO of a family-run antiquities business. This role, inherited from my parents—loving and kind witches who believed in the goodness of magick—has shaped my existence. They would have been saddened to know that Lysandra and I had become entangled with the Conclave of Shadows, a coven that strayed far from the values they held dear. Saturn's entry into my life has upended the delicate balance I had maintained. Her effervescent spirit, coupled with an innate kindness and a fascination with the mystical, has effortlessly dismantled the barriers around my heart. She represents everything pure and good, challenging the darker path the coven expects me to tread.

The conflict inside me is unending. Being loyal to the coven means betraying Saturn, using her unique talents for their dark intentions. Yet, choosing my bond with Saturn means I have to abandon a legacy that's part of my essence. This inner turmoil haunts me constantly, muddling my thoughts and seeding doubts.

Stepping away from the confines of my office, I reach out to Saturn, proposing an impromptu escape into the evening's embrace. The city, with its vibrant lights and dynamic pulse, beckons us with the promise of a brief respite from our encircling dilemmas. Hand in hand, we navigate the lively streets of San Francisco, finding ourselves, almost by a magnetic pull, outside an inviting Italian restaurant in the heart of Little Italy.

The ambiance inside, marked by gentle lighting and the soothing hum of jazz, offers us a haven from the storm brewing in our lives. Amid the lively banter of fellow diners and the soft chime of wine glasses, Saturn and I carve out a moment of simplicity. Sharing a meal under the melody of jazz, we allow the complexities of the outside world to blur into the background. For the time being, we indulge in this transient peace, a crucial break from the ongoing turmoil. As we're enjoying our meal, our conversation drifts, touching on the light and moving into the deep. "Hey, Love," I start, gently taking her hand to offer a bit of warmth, "this whole rollercoaster we've been on—it's a lot, isn't it? I just want you to know that no matter how wild it gets or how quiet it becomes, I'm right here with you through it all." Her response, laced with gratitude, warms me. "Miles, your support has been my anchor in this tumultuous sea. In our short time together, we've weathered storms I never imagined possible."

The humor and affection that flow between us

lighten the heaviness that has settled in my heart. For a moment, we're just two souls entwined by fate, finding joy in each other's company amidst the complexities of our intertwined destinies.

Towards the end of the evening, I decide to broach the subject of her book of shadows. "Saturn, have you found anything in the Book of Shadows you brought back with you? It's more than just a family heirloom, isn't it?"

Saturn shifts uncomfortably. "Yes, it is," she admits, her voice tinged with a mix of reverence and apprehension. "It's a repository of my family's magickal knowledge, containing secrets about my abilities. But it's also filled with puzzles and spells that I'm still trying to unravel."

Intrigued, I lean in, eager to bridge the gap her hesitation has created. "Why don't we explore it together?" I suggest, hoping my offer will light a spark of shared adventure. "It could be a way to unlock more about your incredible abilities."

She pauses, biting her lip in thought before meeting my gaze. "I appreciate that, Miles, I really do. But I need to confront some of these mysteries on my own first. It's... personal. But I promise, if I hit a wall, you'll be the first I turn to." I sense her internal struggle, the desire to share battling with the instinct to protect her vulnerabilities. Respecting her wishes, I nod, though a part of me longs to dive into those mysteries with her. Our conversation continues, touching on the mundane and the extraordinary. "You're a mystery, Saturn," I muse, sipping my wine. "What do you hope to find within yourself with these abilities?"

She ponders, her eyes shimmering in the candlelight. "I want to understand," she declares. "I need to know the extent of my powers to connect with my family's legacy." Her determination is palpable, stirring something deep within me.

"I admire your quest for knowledge. Just be careful," I caution, feeling a protective surge. "Your journey into your powers... it's laden with unknowns."

Her expression sobers. "I know, Miles. These powers are mine to master but also mine to guard."

The impulse to protect her is overwhelming. "You have a strength in you that's undeniable, Saturn. And remember, you're not alone in this. I'm here, always."

Her smile, warm and genuine, fills me with hope. "Thank you, Miles. Your support means the world to me."

Later, as I reflect on the evening and the bond we share, I realize that my love for Saturn is a beacon in the darkness, guiding me towards a path of truth and light. The decision that looms ahead is clear—my allegiance is to Saturn, to the promise of a future where love and magick intertwine.

I have made a choice that is exceedingly difficult for me to live with. I want to ask her to be my wife so we can enjoy every little moment of our lives together and create a future full of love, laughter, and adventures.

I have come to discover that Saturn is the missing piece in my life, providing the kind of connection I have never felt before. I have a nagging dread that Saturn will not entirely commit to our relationship and that she will not truly trust me. It is terrifying to consider that she will reject me, but after going over it in my head millions of times, I decide to make a significant move, and I intend to inform The Conclave of Shadow members of my plans to ask Saturn to be my wife. The following day, I board a flight bound for New York, my mind buzzing with anticipation and determination.

As the plane soars through the skies, I can't shake the lingering doubts and fears that gnaw at the edges of my consciousness. The prospect of confronting the Conclave with my audacious plan to propose to Saturn is both exhilarating and nerve-wracking. However, I know that this pivotal moment can potentially alter the course of our clandestine operations.

Upon my arrival, I am met with a mixture of surprise and intrigue from the members of the Conclave. Their initial shock quickly gives way to curiosity as I lay out the intricacies of my strategy. Then there's annoying Seraphina.

"But wait!" Seraphina interjects and yells, "Not again!" as the tension in the room rises and becomes more and more irate, "Why am I unable to read your mind?"

I reply, with a hint of cynicism and a smirk that hides my discomfort, "How many times do I have to tell you, Seraphina, you simply lack the strength to get past my strong mental defenses? It's not about you!"

The atmosphere in the chamber is charged with anticipation and a chilling resolve. Lysandra's words cut through the tension like a knife, her tone incredulous and mocking. "Wow, really, Miles? You're gonna marry her? Now I definitely know something is up! You've fallen in love with her, haven't you? I know you very well, big brother, and I know there is nothing that would make you marry anyone unless you're in love." Her accusation hangs heavy in the air, and I can feel the eyes of the other members of the Conclave boring into me, awaiting my response. Suppressing a flicker of panic, I muster a confident facade, masking the tumult of emotions swirling within me.

"Lysandra, you're delirious if you think I would betray our coven for something as trivial as love," I retort, my voice tinged with irritation. "My loyalty lies with the Conclave, and I would never jeopardize our goals for the sake of personal desires."

I shoot a pointed glance at Seraphina, silently urging her to redirect the conversation before it spirals out of control. She nods imperceptibly, seamlessly guiding the discussion back to the matter at hand. But Lysandra's words linger in the air, casting a shadow of doubt over my carefully constructed facade.

Seraphina, ever the voice of reason, interjects with a measured tone, "Let's not jump to conclusions. Miles has proven himself to be a loyal member of the Conclave time and time again. We must trust in his judgment and the integrity of his intentions."

Lucius, always the diplomat, adds his perspective, "Indeed, Seraphina is correct. Miles' actions may seem unconventional, but we must remember our ultimate goal: to harness Saturn's powers for the greater good of The Conclave of Shadows." Isolde, her expression thoughtful, chimes in, "However, we must proceed with caution. If Miles' sentiments for Saturn cloud his judgment, it could jeopardize our plans."

Meanwhile, Malachi, usually reserved, speaks up with a hint of concern in his voice, "I agree with Isolde. If Miles' personal feelings interfere with our objectives, it could prove disastrous for all of us."

Seraphina intervenes to speak up for me, asking, "What other option do we have? She has confided in him the most. If we send someone else, Saturn may move even further away. Utilize the confidence Miles has established to advance toward our objective."

Isolde cocks an eyebrow and lowers her arms, still having second thoughts. "Alright, I'll follow your lead. But Miles, if something goes wrong, you're responsible."

The exchange, filled with barbed remarks and veiled threats, underscores the delicate balance of power within the Conclave. But amidst the turmoil, my determination only grows stronger. I nod, accepting the weight of their expectations, but deep down, I know I'm ready for whatever comes next.

Back home and in the shadow of the city of San Francisco, beyond the twinkling lights and the bustling streets, Nightshade Mansion lies in a secluded enclave of a lavish, gated community, standing as a testament to the Nightshade family's legacy and affluence. It's here, amidst the manicured gardens and sweeping vistas, that I wrestle with a decision that could alter the course of my life.

My family home, Nightshade mansion, with its vast halls and hidden spaces, feels like a reflection of the turmoil inside me. I wander its corridors, feeling the heavy anticipation of proposing to Saturn pressing on my heart. This mansion, grand and steeped in history, strikes me as the ideal setting for such a significant step. Yet, as I walk through these age-old rooms, I find myself caught up in a quiet debate. "Why here, at Nightshade Mansion?" I wonder, my thoughts drifting like the mist that often shrouds the grounds at dawn. "Because it's not just any building; it symbolizes what we could be together. If Saturn says 'yes,' this place becomes more than walls and floors—it becomes a haven for our shared hopes and love."

The mansion's opulence is not merely a display of wealth but a promise of security and belonging. Each artifact, each portrait hanging in the bright corridors, whispers stories of the Nightshade lineage—a lineage I hope to extend with Saturn by my side.

However, it is not just the space setup that needs to be perfect; my choice of words is also very important. I spend hours practicing my speech while pacing back and forth, attempting to communicate all of my thoughts to Saturn in a way that she will understand.

The large and stunning sapphire ring, which is encircled with diamonds, seems like a pledge and a dedication. Knowing that Saturn will recognize the significance of such a special piece of jewelry, I pick it with care. It represents our powerful, vivacious, and unshakable relationship.

First, I will take her to a magnificent overlook of the city where we have shared a meaningful moment. It's a location rich with memories, and I want to make a new, unforgettable experience there. Then, we will head back to Nightshade mansion, where I will propose.

Nightshade Mansion, with its sprawling grounds and opulent interiors, has been transformed into a setting out of a fairytale, thanks to the diligent efforts of the staff. Maids flit through the rooms with grace, their hands deftly arranging floral displays and lighting candles, while butlers ensure that every detail is meticulously in place, from the polished silver to the soft jazz music that now fills the air with a soothing melody. In the kitchen, the cook is busy preparing a selection of delicate treats, including fresh strawberries and chilled champagne, set to complement the evening's enchanting ambiance.

The living room, where I plan to unveil my heart, is a vision of romance. Candles flicker in harmony, casting shadows that dance across the walls, telling tales of love and commitment. At the center, a table adorned with a bouquet of Black-Eyed Susans stands as a vibrant emblem of encouragement and resilience, each blooming a testament to the enduring spirit of love that I wish to convey.

As the golden hues of the setting sun bathe the city in a warm glow, Saturn and I find ourselves on the crest of our favorite hill, the city sprawled out beneath us like a tapestry of dreams and memories. The day has been perfect, filled with laughter, shared stories, and quiet moments of companionship. Yet, as we return to Nightshade Mansion, the air seems charged with anticipation, the mansion itself standing majestic and welcoming, its gates opening to a future yet unwritten. As Saturn enters the room, her eyes widen in amazement at the transformation. The magickal setting, coupled with the soft jazz enveloping us, seems to transport her to a world where only we exist.

"Miles, this is...incredible," she whispers, her voice a mixture of astonishment and delight. Taking a deep breath, I find the courage to speak my heart, "Saturn, ever since our lives intertwined, you've sparked a light in me I didn't even know was missing. The love you bring into my life has reshaped who I am, pointing me toward a future I want to embrace with every fiber of my being. You fill my days with a brightness that rivals the sun and my nights with a radiance that makes it feel like every star in the sky is shining just for us. Your energy, the kindness you carry—it lights up every moment, making each day worth living. And this mansion, with its grandeur and stories, could be the perfect backdrop for us, a place where we can weave our dreams into reality."

As I drop to one knee, the sapphire ring in my hand catches the flickering candlelight, shining as brightly as my hope. "Saturn, will you marry me? Will you be with me always, sharing every step of this adventure, making Nightshade Mansion our sanctuary, where our love and dreams can flourish?" Saturn stands frozen, her emotions a whirlwind of joy, surprise, and a flicker of uncertainty. The silence stretches between us, a testament to the gravity of the moment.

"Miles, I... this is all so much," she finally says, her voice trembling. "I love you more than words can express. But this is a big step, and I need a moment to breathe, to understand the depth of this commitment."

Feeling a mix of disappointment and understanding, I nod. My heart's heavy, but it's also holding onto hope.

"Take the time you need, Saturn. I'm here for you; no rush. Your happiness is what's most important to me."

In the days that follow, I can't ignore the distance Saturn puts between us. It's like a tangible gap, and I find myself aimlessly wandering Nightshade Mansion's halls, each room echoing with my swirling thoughts. Did I push too fast? Was the idea of us here, building a future together, just too much for her right now?

This mansion, which I've always seen as a place of hope and shared dreams, now mirrors my solitude, each corner filled with longing for some clarity. I'm learning, maybe the hard way, that patience is key and giving Saturn her space is essential. But this quiet, this waiting, is tougher than I expected, really putting our connection to the test.

Sitting in my study, surrounded by all the history that Nightshade Mansion carries, I remind myself that what Saturn and I have is worth every bit of this uncertainty, every moment of wait. I cling to the hope that she'll see just how deep my love runs and understand the true intention behind my proposal. I hope she'll decide to join me in turning this place from a symbol of my family's history into the start of our own story, our life together.

CHAPTER 14
"ECHOES OF ENCHANTMENT"

Since my return to San Francisco, the quiet moments alone have become sacred, a time to delve into the enigmatic depths of my lineage and powers. The Book of Shadows, a legacy from ancestors who whispered their secrets across the ages from the star-strewn Eridanus, awaits my attention, its pages brimming with arcane knowledge and veiled mysteries.

Today, as the golden afternoon light floods the room, creating shadows that dance like echoes of the past, I'm alone again. Sitting down, the Book of Shadows opens before me, stirring a whirlwind of emotions inside. My feelings for Miles have deepened, becoming more intricate with each glance we share, every quiet conversation. Yet, there's a weight on this growing bond—I worry that bringing someone so undeniably mortal into my magickal realm might lead to unforeseen consequences. How can I, a child of the stars with a legacy of magick, justify exposing him to such risks? This concern sends waves of anxiety through me, yet the idea of distancing myself from him is unbearable.

Right now, I have decided to shelve my concerns and focus on what's in front of me. The Book of Shadows lies open, its old pages laying out a roadmap to understanding my abilities better. I'm here to dive into my third power, one that's been subtly hinting at its existence during quiet moments and in dreams where the lines between realms get fuzzy. The air around me seems to hum with anticipation as I trace my fingers over the intricate symbols and script that adorn the page. Words in a language forgotten by time whisper secrets meant only for those born of the Eridanus lineage. The room fills with an ethereal glow, the boundaries between the mundane and the mystical blurring. In this moment, I let my mind broaden, reaching into the magick that courses through me, a gift from the celestial lineage of my ancestors. The Book of Shadows reacts, its pages rustling like leaves in a soft wind, landing on a passage pulsating with unique energy—a sign pointing me toward the dormant power I'm about to unlock.

As I delve into the mysterious challenge before me, I sense an exciting change inside, marking the awakening of my third power. This section, labeled "Feline Instincts," connects me deeply with the realm of animals, particularly cats.

This newfound ability brings me closer to the essence and acute senses of felines. The moment the puzzle's words blend with my thoughts, everything shifts. It's like the book's ancient magick recognizes something in me. "Feline Instincts" offers me the remarkable ability to access the primal senses and sharp awareness inherent to cats. The world around me bursts with details; the rustling of leaves, a gentle breeze, and the distant heartbeat of the forest become as vivid to me as if I were a cat, fully immersed in my surroundings. I feel a stronger connection to these animals, understanding their language and feeling the earth with the same sensitivity as their quiet paws.

This ancient and profound magick doesn't just give me the agility and grace of felines; it also imparts their natural understanding of nature's balance and harmony. I move with newfound ease, my senses enhanced to perceive the world in depths and nuances I've never experienced before. This is all new to me, and I'm eager to see how this dormant power unfolds and integrates into my life and magick.

Riddle:

"In the realm of felines, fierce and wise,
A hunter's heart in untamed eyes.
With spotted coat and jungle's sprawl,
What power connects to them all?"

Sign:

"A pair of enigmatic feline eyes."

Facing the riddle, I quietly think, "In the realm of felines, fierce and wise." It's an intriguing start that hints at a bond with the world of big cats—creatures known for their sharp instincts and strength. "Fierce and wise" points to a power blending both strength and intelligence. The riddle unfolds, "A hunter's heart in untamed eyes," evoking the image of a predatory cat, alive with the thrill of the hunt, embodying the wild and free spirit of these animals. It seems this ability might awaken my inner predator, enhancing my instincts.

The riddle describes a habitat "With spotted coat and jungle's sprawl," suggesting a link to big, spotted cats like leopards or cheetahs and their dense, wild environments. This hints at a power tied to creatures of the jungle, emphasizing a sense of wildness.

"What power connects them all?" ends the puzzle, challenging me to discover the common thread among these feline traits. The emblem, featuring enigmatic cat eyes, seems to call out to me, hinting at the mysteries I'm about to unveil.

Feline Instincts sharpen my senses and agility, tapping into my primal side to heighten my reflexes and physical abilities, imbuing me with cat-like stealth, decision-making, and environmental awareness.

An interesting aspect of Feline Instincts is its connection to a specific flower, the 'Feline's Grace,' drawing me closer to nature in unexpected ways. Cultivating this flower is crucial, as it's intimately linked to my ability to harness this power. The flower's health directly impacts my access to these instincts, highlighting a unique bond with nature.

The power's presence is transformative, offering enhanced senses, agility, and a deeper affinity for cat-like behaviors. Yet, there's a twist. Encounters with cats or cat imagery can involuntarily trigger these instincts, leading to cat-like actions. Keeping the 'Feline's Grace' flower close can mitigate this effect.

A ceremonial knife, linked to the 'Feline's Grace' flower and adorned with forest symbols and jaguar imagery, is key for anyone looking to acquire this power through less honest means. The ritual involves cutting a flower's petal with this knife and reciting a specific spell, with the petal holding the power's essence.

This journey into Feline Instincts is a complex challenge, pushing me to explore my primal side and connect with nature's raw elements. Trusting my instincts and senses will be crucial in fully embracing this ability, marking a journey of discovery into the depths of my own nature. "Like the Lunar Dreams and Whispering Winds abilities, this power also necessitates specific binding spells and activation spells for control," I whisper to myself, delving further into the mysterious realm of my newfound abilities.

Binding Spell:

"In shadows deep, with secrets rife,
I bind this power in the still of night.
With feline grace and instincts keen,
Its secrets are hidden, its essence unseen."

Activation Spell:

"In the world of beasts that prowl and hunt,
A gift unique in every confrontation.
The feline instincts within me reside
in a predator's prowess, with nowhere to hide.
But with this power comes a solemn vow,
A curse to bear, both then and now.
To maintain this gift, my senses refined,
I must embrace the wilderness, body, and mind.

The curse befalls those who seek to steal,
My instincts are true, the secrets that conceal.
Only when the heart aligns with feral grace,
Can they unlock the power's rightful place?

To bind this power, I must recite the verse,
In the language of the felines, it will disperse.
The instincts awakened, with nature's thread,
In my life's tapestry, they shall be spread.

So shall I wield this power, fierce and untamed,
With instincts sharp, my destiny unchained.
To fully activate and control this might,
I embrace my feline instincts, day and night."

Discovering Feline Instincts isn't just about finding a new skill; it's like being invited to see the world through a cat's eyes. It's about embracing their freedom, curiosity, and deep ties to the mystical forces of life. I begin to realize that the evening no longer marks the day's end for me but the start of a new phase in my life. Now, I walk the earth not only as myself but with the keen senses and spirit of a cat, tuned into nature's hidden whispers and secrets. Now, as I gain a grasp on feline instincts, my curiosity shifts to another power known as "Earth's Resonance." I've always been drawn to the connection between nature and its elemental forces, feeling a special kinship with this power.

Throughout the night, I focus on deciphering the riddle and its clues, aiming to piece them together to reveal their hidden strength.

I turn my attention back to the puzzle of Earth's Resonance, scrutinizing the text for insights. The riddle suggests a deep connection with the earth, its patterns, and the wonders it conceals, inviting me to explore this bond further.

Riddle:

"In the realm where roots embrace in nature's choreography,
Beneath the soil's surface lies a hidden opportunity.
For those who champion the earth's progression,
They are graced with the essence of proliferation."

As I ponder the phrase, "In the realm where roots embrace in nature's choreography," I can almost see the vast network of roots beneath us, interlocking in a complex dance, each drawing life from the earth. My thoughts then drift to, "Beneath the soil's surface lies a hidden opportunity." It suggests that the earth holds secrets of life and growth waiting to be uncovered. But what exactly is this 'hidden opportunity'? It's a question that lingers just beyond my grasp, pushing me to delve deeper into this enigma. The journey continues as I reflect on "For those who champion the earth's progression." Championing the earth means to deeply engage with and understand the natural world. I feel poised at the threshold of this adventure.

Pondering the final line, "What graces them with the essence of proliferation?" I'm intrigued by the promise of a unique bond with the earth and the ability to foster growth. The anticipation of unlocking this capability fills me with excitement.

The rule for accessing this power is simple yet profound. It requires direct contact with the earth, like standing barefoot on the ground or touching natural objects. This deep connection enhances the understanding and insights gained from the earth.

However, Earth's Resonance carries the risk of harming nature if misused. Irresponsible use can disrupt ecosystems, cause abnormal plant growth, and imbalance the environment. The consequences include losing control over this and possibly other abilities, with nature itself withdrawing its trust.

To recover from such a misstep involves sincere efforts to repair the damage and restore balance, demonstrating a renewed respect for the natural world. This power is also closely tied to a personal symbol of the user's relationship with nature, such as wooden totems or stone pendants, serving as an anchor to their abilities.

For someone to take this power, they must perform a complex ritual under a full moon, creating a new bond with nature while breaking the old. However, this can only happen if the original wielder has severely violated the power's ethos. Maintaining a harmonious relationship with nature protects the power, making it nearly impossible to be taken by force. This dive into my heritage is mesmerizing, revealing the vast scope of what I can become. It's more than just learning about my abilities; it's a journey of self-discovery, confirming my role in the world's vast mosaic. Closing the Book of Shadows, I marvel at these revelations and feel a thrill of excitement; a thread of concern weaves through my joy, especially when I think of Miles. How do I follow this path and embrace my destiny without endangering him, someone whose soul has grown so intertwined with mine? This dilemma lingers as I turn the page, the fading light outside mirroring the shadows of doubt in my heart.

Exploring my fourth ability has not only led me to the realization of otherworldly fascinating realms but also highlights the complexity of living at the intersection of the ordinary and the magickal. Balancing my legacy with my deep feelings for Miles places me between two worlds, each with its own strong pull.

CHAPTER 15
"ECHOES OF LEGACY"

I continue to explore the mysterious pages of The Book of Shadows and stumble upon another riddle: "Ancestral Guidance." The puzzle entices me, promising ancient wisdom.

Riddle:

> *"In the pages of time, old and wise,*
> *The spirits of kin, a noble prize.*
> *To tap the wisdom of those long gone,*
> *Where must your connection be drawn?"*

Sign:

"A symbol representing a chain of ancestors."

Reading aloud, "In the pages of time, old and wise," the room echoes back. It's about the ancient knowledge passed down through generations. Next, "The spirits of kin, a noble prize" hints at the value of family heritage and the invaluable lessons from our ancestors.

The puzzle goes on, "To tap the wisdom of those long gone," pushing me to seek out my ancestors' knowledge. It's a call to connect with the wisdom of those who've come before. "Where must the lines of your connection be drawn?" leaves me pondering. It's a deep, soulful question, suggesting that the real connection with my ancestors lies beyond the physical, in the spiritual ties that bind us across time.

I start piecing together the mystery, realizing it's not about literal genealogy but a spiritual bond transcending time and death. Closing my eyes, I sense my ancestors' presence, their voices guiding me to their wisdom.

The symbol of intertwined threads, representing ancestral lines, becomes clear. It's about an unbroken link to my forebears, offering their guidance and wisdom. Ancestral Guidance isn't about manipulating the elements but connecting with my past to access a collective ancestral wisdom.

This power lets me tap into my ancestors' memories and wisdom, offering insights and guidance through life's challenges. It's about forging a deep connection with my family's history and learning from their experiences.

The rule is intriguing yet strict: I can only access wisdom from ancestors within the last century, ensuring the advice is relevant and discouraging overreliance on the distant past. This limitation makes me thoughtful about the ancestors I reach out to, adding a layer of responsibility.

Ancestral Guidance is a profound way to connect with my family's legacy, a privilege I handle with care, honoring the path they've set for me. It deepens my understanding of my place in the world.

Yet, this power also merges my emotions with those of my ancestors, sometimes overwhelming my own feelings with theirs. It's a vivid reminder of their lives and experiences.

However, stealing Ancestral Guidance isn't straightforward. The "Ritual of Reflection" requires crafting an object to symbolize the ancestral connection and engaging the power's current holder in a mental duel. It's a risky endeavor, as the object might also capture the thief's emotions, exposing them to my ancestors' emotional imprints.

Securing this wisdom involves an Activation Spell, rooted deeply in my ancestral ties and performed in a sacred space, symbolizing my connection to my lineage. This ritual, steeped in respect and focus, is my gateway to the ancestors' guidance, a journey I approach with both excitement and solemnity.

Activation Spell:

"In the hallowed realm where past and present entwine,
I seek the wisdom of my bloodline, divine.
With the flicker of a candle's gentle light,
I call upon my ancestors, spirits bright.

Their voices, echoes of time's embrace,
Shall guide me forward in life's complex maze.
Yet with control, this bond shall stay,
To heed their wisdom and find my way.
With reverence profound, a sacred space I make,
The symbol of our lineage, a journey to undertake.
As I light the candle, our spirits draw near,
I speak these words, removing doubt and fear.
In the pages of time, old and wise,
The spirits of kin, hear my cries.
To tap your wisdom, so profound,
With reverence, I seek and surround.
With each utterance, the ancestral connection awakens
A bridge between past and present, as my spirit quickens.
The warmth of the candle, their whispers in the air,

I maintain control with intent, as our destinies pair.

After finishing the incantation, I refocus on The Book of Shadows and discover a concealed note nestled between its pages. This power can be stolen, and this note unveils a crucial detail about the process. To activate the reverse binding spell, one must use a special item: the Mirror of Mirastella, a rare artifact known for its reflective properties that transcend mere physical appearances, reflecting the true essence of both the holder and the world around them.

This mirror is said to be hidden in the ruins of an ancient temple dedicated to a forgotten deity of wisdom and magick, located deep within the heart of an untouched forest. The journey to retrieve the Mirror of Mirastella is perilous, filled with trials that test the seeker's strength, wisdom, and purity of intent. Only by proving themselves worthy can the person attempting to claim a new power hope to find and use the Mirror of Mirastella to cast the binding spell in reverse, severing the connection between the original owner and the stolen power.

Binding Spell:

"To balance their insights with the present demand,
I invoke this bond with a steady hand.

In the threads of time, past's embrace,
With kin's wisdom, finds my space.
Evoke the bond, firm but gentle,
To guide my path, ancestral channel."

Uncovering new layers of my abilities has shown me their boundaries and underscored the importance of protecting The Book of Shadows from falling into the wrong hands.

As the night wraps the sky, adorning it with stars, I find myself sitting in my loft, enveloped by a sense of magick and eager anticipation.

It's Saturday night, and outside, there's a hush, a pause in the world's rhythm, while I grapple with Miles' absence, feeling the stretch of three silent weeks between us like a gap yearning to be closed.

To distract myself from the emptiness his absence has left, I focus on the yet-to-be-discovered secrets of my powers.

I've recently been reading up on my sixth power, "Elemental Manipulation," and it's drawing me in with the promise of unlocking ancient secrets and dormant energies. It's as though the elements themselves are whispering to me, inviting me to explore the mysteries they've held for centuries.

Riddle:

"In the heart of creation's prime, Where elements merge through space and time. To master this force, a puzzle you'll unchain; What binds the elemental realm to your domain?"

Sign:

A complex emblem materialized before my mind's eye, a multifaceted array of elemental symbols entwined in a circular dance, each connected by a web of interlocking gears. This emblem spoke of unity and control, a representation of the elemental forces that governed the natural world, waiting for me to discover the key to their dominion.

As I dive into the mystery that the riddle lays out before me, its words resonate deep within me. "In the heart of creation's prime," it starts, painting a picture of the beginning where all elements come together, a place full of power and possibilities.

"Where elements merge through space and time," I find myself whispering, feeling the energy around me respond. It's a call to the natural balance and harmony of the elements, reminding me of their continuous dance across the universe.

"To master this force, a puzzle you'll unchain" presents a challenge, an adventure to unlock the vast power at the intersection of the elements. It's like an open invitation to gain control over the very forces that mold our world. "What binds the elemental realm to your domain?" This question hangs in the air, asking for more than just smarts but a deep bond with the elemental spirits. It seeks the key that will link the elemental world to my influence.

A symbol made of intertwined gears and elemental signs lights the way, helping me understand the complex relationship between me and the elemental forces. It's a roadmap to learning how to shape these energies to my will.

As the solution to the riddle becomes clear, I sense a connection to the elements around me, communicated in whispers of the wind, the flicker of fire, the touch of water, and the stability of the earth. I've turned into a channel for their strength, ready to harness the primal energy of creation itself.

Handling this power is a serious matter. Controlling the elements comes with guidelines and boundaries. I can command only one element at a time, requiring concentration and skill. Changing from one element to another involves a ritual, a moment where I'm open and must carefully align with a new elemental force.

Discovering Elemental Manipulation has been an eye-opener, revealing a connection not just to nature but to the universe's rhythm.

It's a privilege that demands respect and a deep bond with the elemental world. Now, as I stand ready to perform the activation spell, anticipation pulses through me. Each word of the spell connects me more deeply with the elemental energies, ready to weave them according to my intention.

Activation Spell:

"In the heart of creation's prime, Where elements merge through space and time. To master this force, a puzzle you'll unchain, What binds the elemental realm to your domain?

When fire's passion and water's flow unite, And air's swift grace with earth's strength alight, Recite the words and call the elements near, With this incantation, let the path be clear.

Invoke the blaze to dance with fervent desire, Bid waters to calm and quench, never tire. The breezy zephyrs and solid ground's embrace, Combine as one, their essence you shall trace."

This riddle's answer reveals the binding key,

To the elemental powers, to set them free.
But know dear bearer, this path is a solemn one,
For only the worthy shall see what's done.

As each element's fury and harmony blend,

With the wisdom of time, their powers extend.
The ancient magick shall your heart and soul empower,
Only then, claim dominion over the elemental tower."

After I finish the spell, the room feels charged, buzzing with a kind of energy that you can't see but definitely feel. The Book of Shadows is open in front of me, its pages like doors to other worlds, each word guiding me closer to mastering these mysteries.

Then, the intercom cuts through the quiet, pulling me back to reality. It's a jolt, reminding me there's a world outside my magickal studies. Miles is here, breaking the long silence between us. It's like my everyday life and my magickal one are colliding, promising to start weaving a new story made of both ordinary moments and magickal ones. Here I am, standing at the crossroads of elemental magick and personal connections, ready to dive into whatever mysteries and adventures lie ahead.

CHAPTER 16

"WHISPERS OF THE HEART"

The buzzing of the intercom continues to cut through the silence of my loft, feeling more like an alarm than a simple alert. Miles is on the other side of that door, unexpectedly throwing a wrench into my evening. It's been weeks since we've spoken, with me choosing silence as a shield to protect both my heart from further damage and Miles from the chaos of my world. Despite my efforts to keep him at a safe distance, believing it was for the best, his presence now stirs up a mix of emotions and second guesses. My attempts to keep my feelings locked away are suddenly under siege as Miles, ever persistent, challenges the barriers I've so meticulously erected around my heart.

I'm dead set on staying silent, leaving Miles out in the cold (figuratively speaking) to keep my heart from shattering. Deep down, though, I'm dying to open the door, to feel his arms around me, to hear his promises whispered just for me. But the terror of opening up and getting burned—again—is a massive roadblock, and the idea of putting Miles in harm's way is a much stronger emotion I can't deal with right now.

"Baby, it's me," comes Miles' voice, dripping with a mix of hope and despair. "I know you're in there. Just let me in; let's figure this out."

His words manage to squeeze tears out of me. There I am, glued to the spot, hand on the door, speechless. My emotions are raging, trying to breach the dam of my heart, but I can't let them.

"Why are you shutting me out?" he continues, his voice trembling like mine. "If the proposal scared you, that's okay. You don't have to say yes. I just want to be with you. We can just be ourselves without all the formalities? Saturn, please, let's talk," he pleads. I remain stiff as a statue, trapped by my own turmoil. The doubts, the walls I've built to avoid getting hurt, are now feeling more like a prison.

Miles, fueled by a mix of determination and affection, isn't giving up. "I'm not the cheating ass from your past, not the friend who let you down," he insists. "My love for you is the real deal, and I will never hurt you. I promise. I'm not Daniel. Baby, just open the door. I can't handle this—not seeing you or talking to you for weeks. My love for you is too strong to simply walk away, and I understand trust is hard to give, but you've managed to break down my barriers, showing me the true meaning of love."

Tears stream down my cheeks, yet words fail me, swallowed by the sheer weight of everything. How can I protect him? Miles views himself as my protector, unaware of how much I need to protect him from plunging into a world of magick that even I am still navigating. Moreover, the thought of marriage terrifies me; it's barely been a year since I emerged from a marriage that left me shattered and betrayed by a man who cheated and broke my heart. How do I risk that pain again, and how do I risk Miles in a world he thinks he understands but is far more dangerous than he can imagine?

As the sounds from the hallway finally die down, I pull back from the door, my emotions still in turmoil. With the outside noise gone, I move away, feeling a tremble run through me from all the emotional chaos. Tears slip down my face as I sink into the couch, caught in a storm of feelings torn between fear and love. I deeply care for Miles and can see a future with him, but the pain of Aunt Sage's loss, the journey of discovering who I am, and the fear of marriage disappointment weigh heavily on me.

Dealing with Aunt Sage's passing and the quest for my true identity makes it hard to think about starting something new with Miles, let alone marriage. Since moving here, Miles has become my go-to person, the only one I truly open up to for advice or to share different opinions. But now, with all this uncertainty, I feel more alone than ever, lacking someone to confide in with my deepest concerns.

In solitude, I mull over Aunt Sage's cryptic guidance, which suddenly begins to resonate with clarity. Her mysterious advice and the enigmatic aura of her crystal shop and cottage, where I discovered our family's Book of Shadows, now seem like pieces of a puzzle falling into place. "Life is fraught with shadows, Saturn, but it's within those shadows we discover our strength," she had once told me. Realizing my lineage and the powers I possess is like piecing together a map Aunt Sage has left for me, her cryptic messages a guide for the challenges ahead.

Exhausted to my core, I drift into a restless sleep, my dreams a montage of past, present, and an uncertain future. The next morning, I awake frazzled, Miles' heartfelt plea still echoing in my mind, urging me to hurry as I fear his return.

Rushing to work, I'm greeted by the vibrant buzz of the urban newspaper office. The air is electric with the hustle of deadlines, the rapid-fire tapping of keyboards, and snippets of heated discussions floating in the air – a stark contrast to the quiet turmoil of my morning. It's here, amid the flurry of journalistic fervor, that Laila Jonasson approaches my desk, her presence a calm in the storm. Her Scandinavian beauty, with striking black hair and deep blue eyes, stands out amidst the office's chaos. According to conversations shared in the past, she was raised in Los Angeles and moved to San Francisco two years ago; Laila's easygoing nature and sharp wit made her an instant friend. "Saturn, you look like you're off in another galaxy," Laila remarks, her tone light but laced with concern. Her intuition, a testament to the close bond we've formed, offers a momentary escape from my inner turmoil.

I manage a small smile, grateful for her presence. "Just wrestling with some ghosts from the past. But I'm managing," I admit, finding solace in her understanding gaze.

Laila leans closer, lowering her voice to a whisper amidst the background noise of ringing phones and bustling colleagues. "Listen, if you need to vent or just escape for a bit, I'm here. We can grab a coffee or just take a walk. Whatever you need," she offers, her sincerity shining through.

"Thanks, Laila. That means a lot to me," I respond, feeling a glimmer of hope in her supportive words.

Our conversation meanders through work gossip to deeper reflections on life's unpredictable paths, her humor and insight making the day's burdens a little lighter. Laila's ability to navigate our conversation from light-hearted jokes to meaningful advice showcases the depth of our friendship, a rare find in the frenetic pace of city life.

As the day fades, my mind drifts back to Miles and the looming choices about where we're headed. Laila's unwavering support shines through my darkest times, reminding me I'm not journeying through the complexities of love and vulnerability alone.

Arriving back to my loft, the sight of Miles curled up in front of the door, oblivious to the world, sharply reminds me of the shared pain lingering between us. Torn between my deep feelings for him and the haunting fear of past mistakes, I find myself frozen, wrestling with indecision.

Choosing to quietly tiptoe past him, hoping to avoid a conversation I'm not ready to have, I feel a twist in my heart. But he notices, and with slurred words slices through the quiet of the night; laying bare the depth of our bond and the turmoil within.

CHAPTER 17

"SHADOWS UNVEILED"

I had stayed outside Saturn's flat all night, begging her to let me in so we could have a conversation. She had not wavered, though, and I soon found my way back to my own house. I was walking alone for a long time, and my head was racing and spinning out of control with a mashup of different feelings.

My house is a massive estate outside of San Francisco, tucked away in a quiet, gated community that is home to the wealthiest and elite in the city. It stands here as a stronghold of exclusivity and elegance within the serene surroundings of verdant woodlands. This remote location provides relief from the city's hustle and bustle, as well as solitude and security.

Constructed in the mid-1920s by my grandparents, this opulent mansion is a tribute to riches and power. What makes it even more impressive is that, despite its age, it has maintained an imposing air and a flawless façade, as if it had been built just yesterday. The architecture with modern components creates an intimidating sight. The real wonder is within, like a time capsule from another era. Antique furniture, vintage paintings, and antique objects are used to decorate each room, creating a fascinating historical tapestry within the walls. There is something intimidating about this mansion, a structure that has stood the test of time and still manages to have a commanding presence.

Upon entering my house, I notice a familiar figure sitting in the living room. That would be my sister Lysandra, and judging from the way our last interaction went, I know there will only be more underlying tension, so I want to avoid her from getting into another argument. There she sits, with a glass of wine in the dimly lit room, the ethereal light swirling around her from the crystal chandelier above. I pause for a while, my desire to avoid a confrontation clashing with my awareness of her proximity. She speaks, the first blow of a storm in her voice, with a sharp edge. "Did you not see me, brother, or are you just being rude?"

Here I am, under the heavy gaze of Lysandra, drowning in the complexities that the moment brings. It's rare for Lysandra to seek me out, so her timing isn't coincidental. The room seems to pulse with all the things we haven't said to each other, thick with a tension begging to be broken.

She confronts me, irritation and concern lacing her voice, "Where have you been, Miles?" Her tone carries a hint of annoyance. My life's already a mess, and the last thing I need is another fight.

Exhausted by my own turmoil, I sigh. I'm frustrated with myself for just walking past her without a word. Heading upstairs to my room, I can feel her stare boring into me, her words echoing in the silent hallway.

As I try to breeze past her, she blocks my path, her voice laced with frustration and suspicion. "So, what's this about marrying Saturn, Miles? You and I both know you're not one to mix business with... romance. What's going on?"

I hesitate, knowing she's not going to let this go, and finally stop to face her, feeling the seriousness of her inquiry. "Look, Lysandra, it's complicated," I start, trying to find a way to skirt around the truth without lying outright. Her arms are crossed now, and her stance is telling me she's not buying the official line. "Complicated? Since when do you risk everything for a mission? This isn't you, Miles."

I attempt a diversion, hoping to steer the conversation away. "And what would you have me do, sister? Ignore the Conclave's commands?" My tone is light, but there's an underlying tension I can't mask.

She pierces me with a look that says she knows me too well. "This isn't about orders. I saw the way the look in your eyes changed when you were talking about the whole plan. It was different, Miles, and you're lucky I'm the only one who caught it. Are you actually in love with Saturn?"

Her direct hit catches me off guard, and I struggle to maintain my composure. "Lysandra, love is a luxury I can't afford. You know the stakes."

But Lysandra's not letting up. "No, Miles. I know you. You wouldn't endanger everything for a cover story. There's something more here, and I want the truth."

The room feels smaller, the air between us charged with years of sibling understanding and the current weight of my secrets. "It's not as black and white as you think. The situation with Saturn... it's evolved."

"Evolved?" She repeats, disbelief and concern mingling in her voice. "You're playing a dangerous game, brother. And for what? Love?"

I look away, the conflict within me growing. "I'm handling it, Lysandra. It's under control."

Her frustration bubbles over. "Under control? Miles, if the Conclave catches wind of your true feelings, it's not just you who's at risk. It's Saturn, too, and me! They will come after me as well."

Feeling the weight of Lysandra's words, a surge of vulnerability overtakes me. The truth, long buried under layers of duty and deception, finds its way to the surface. With a heavy heart, I admit, "Lizzy, you are right; I love her. I love Saturn, and I've loved her since the first time I laid eyes on her." The confession feels like a release, a burden lifted as I share this deeply held secret. "Please keep this to yourself. If you've ever felt any kind of loyalty to your big brother, now would be the time. I will explain everything, but please, I'm begging you, don't say anything."

At this moment, stripped of pretenses and the complex facades we've built around ourselves, I'm just a brother seeking understanding from his sister, holding onto the hope that the bond we share is strong enough to carry this secret.

Lysandra pauses, her expression softening at the mention of the childhood nickname. "Wow, bro, you haven't called me that name since we were little kids. I'll keep your secret for now."

After spilling my guts to Lysandra, feeling that mix of relief and dread, I escape to my room. It's like stepping into another world compared to the rest of the mansion's showy vibe. This room, with its down-to-earth feel, is my hideout. The dark floors and those thick curtains blocking out the world just get me. And my desk—more like a treasure chest of the weird and wonderful, covered in books that speak of other realms and my own sketches that seem to crawl off the page. It's my own corner of the universe where I can drop the act, kick back, and try to make sense of the rollercoaster my life's become.

My room's dim and quiet vibe is exactly what I need

to chill out right now. The darkness around me feels like a cozy blanket, helping me see things more clearly and really get my thoughts in order. Those long shadows stretching out because of the dim light just add to the whole mysterious mood, making it the perfect spot for some serious life reflection.

I'm sprawled out on my bed, mulling over everything. I kind of knew Lysandra would catch on sooner or later, but man, I didn't expect her to put two and two together so fast. Proposing to Saturn wasn't just a whim; it was all about deep, complicated feelings that I can't just brush off. And yeah, the path I've picked is pretty risky.

In this quiet, dark corner of mine, Saturn's all I can think about. She's like this shining light in the middle of my messy life.

The idea of not seeing her again or hearing her laugh is freaking me out. My nerves are shot, and just thinking about her leaving town and disappearing from my life, especially when she's been giving me the cold shoulder, is too much.

As the night gets darker, I find myself reaching for a bottle of Balvenie. That 40-year-old Scotch is like a temporary escape hatch from the bucketload of sadness and anger I'm drowning in. I'm feeling totally alone, pissed off at myself, and kind of anxious.

Next morning, I drag myself to work, but I'm still stuck in this dark mood. Saturn's silence feels like she's completely erased me from her life, and our thing, which was just starting to bloom, feels like it's been cut off at the roots, leaving me hollow.

Later, sitting in my office, I hit the bottle again, and that's when this wild, desperate idea hit me. What if I just come clean to Saturn and tell her I'm not just some regular guy but a witch with my own set of powers? Maybe that would get her to see things differently and clear up everything that's keeping us apart. I'm trying to figure out how to break it to her, but yeah, the booze isn't exactly helping me think straight.

I realize Saturn's probably heading home from work by now. Sobering up a bit and full of resolve, I tell my driver to head to her place. I make my way to her door and just sit there, waiting for her to come back.

I barely keep my eyes open, but then I hear the sounds of keys and the door unlocking. Seeing her there, it's like a punch to the gut. She tries to sneak past me, pretending I'm not even here, which just twists the knife even more.

Feeling this mix of panic, anger, and sheer desperation, I can't hold back anymore. I stand up and let it all out, "Wow! You're just going to act like I'm invisible, my love?" That came out all raw and real, just laying out everything that's been tearing me up inside.

Saturn stops dead, clearly taken aback by me being there and all the emotions I'm throwing her way. You can see the surprise, the worry, and something like curiosity on her face. It's clear she wasn't expecting this - me, here, all messed up and emotional.

I keep going, trying to dial back the anger and show her I'm really worried. "Saturn, I've been here waiting for you," I say, feeling all this turmoil boiling up inside me despite the buzz from the drinks.

For a moment, it's like time stands still. You can almost feel the tension and all those things we've never said to each other just filling up the space between us. I'm just hoping for some sign she still cares, anything to show there's still a connection between us.

I see it, the worry and maybe a hint of pain in her voice when she says it's not the time to talk, suggesting we wait until I'm sober. But I can't; I need to sort this out now. "No, Saturn," I insist, my words more urgent, "I need to know where we stand. Ignoring me like this is just tearing me apart."

That seems to get through to her. She steps closer, offering her hand, ready to help. "Let's go inside, Miles. We'll talk," she suggests.

I nod, letting her lead me into her flat. Walking in, I'm filled with all these thoughts - is this the moment everything changes? She guides me to the couch, and as I sit, the room feels charged with all this unsaid stuff between us. She heads to the kitchen, leaving me to my thoughts for a moment. When she comes back with water, our hands touch briefly, and I'm just trying to make sense of everything.

Here we are, sitting together, wrapped in silence. It's like the whole universe conspired to get us to this point, forcing us to really see each other and all the complicated stuff that's been going on with us.

"Are you okay, Miles?" Saturn's voice cuts through the silence, gentle and filled with a love that seems to push past her doubts. Her question hits me hard; she's clearly wary, but it's like she's trying to bridge the gap that's stretched out between us. The silence is heavy, sure, but it feels like we're finally getting somewhere.

I try to swallow the lump in my throat, aiming for some semblance of calm. "I'm fine, Saturn," I manage, but my voice is heavy with everything I'm not saying. We've got a lot to unpack, but for now, I just want us to find our way back to some kind of normal.

Just as she's about to say something else, I realize I can't hold back any longer. "There's something you need to know," I blurt out, desperate for her to understand.

"Miles," she starts, but I can't let this moment slip away. "Please, Saturn, let me get this out first."

Her initial shock softens into a resigned sigh. Even though she seems ready to argue, my urgency wins out. "Okay," she concedes, "go ahead."

I take a deep breath, the weight of my confession pressing down on me. "There's something I haven't told you. Something I've had for the past ten years since I was twenty. It's been a part of me, something I got from my parents and learned to manage over time."

Saturn looks puzzled, her voice shaky. "Miles, what are you talking about? What's been with you for ten years?"

I know this is going to shock her, but it's time. "I have powers, abilities. Like you do. And I've kept them a secret because I didn't want it to change how you see me."

Her confusion is evident. "Powers? What the hell? Please, just give it to me straight."

"Okay, hear me out," I say, hoping to ease her into it. She nods a bit reluctantly. "Alright, I'm listening."

So, I lay it all out there. "I've got these powers, Saturn. I can change shape, disappear into shadows, or become anything I want. I can also connect with the dead and use their knowledge or powers. I can even make things decay or manipulate energy. And yeah, I've got a bit of a knack for messing with time loops, changing small things from the past."

Saturn looks at me, searching for the truth. "So, you've had these supernatural abilities for like ten years, and you never told me, even knowing I have my own powers. And you proposed without coming clean about this huge secret?"

Her voice is full of hurt and disbelief, and I realize just how much I've risked by keeping this from her.

Her words hang heavy between us, and I can see the

hurt and betrayal in her eyes, mirroring my own internal turmoil. "Miles, why didn't you tell me sooner? You should've shared this with me when we first met, or at least when I discovered my own powers. It's really messed up that you kept this hidden just to use it now to win me over for marriage." The air is thick with tension as Saturn tries to wrap her head around my bombshell. She's a mix of hurt, confusion, and anger. I've kept such a big part of me a secret from her, and now, when she's finally let her guard down and trusted me, she has to face this shocking truth. Her gaze cuts right through me, filled with a sense of betrayal.

"I know this is a lot," I whisper, my voice barely above a breath. "I always planned to tell you, honestly. I didn't mean to keep it a secret this long, but with everything going on with you, it never seemed like the right time. I'm so sorry, Baby. I should've been upfront with you."

Saturn's silent for a moment, and the complex mix of emotions on her face says it all. She's trying to find some sliver of truth in my eyes, wondering if we can somehow navigate through this emotional minefield we're in now.

"How can I trust anything now?" Saturn's voice breaks, her disappointment clear. "You hid something so big from me, and it just breaks my heart, Miles."

Feeling her pain, I'm shaking. "I get why you're mad at me, Baby. I should've been honest from the get-go, but I was scared. I didn't want to overwhelm you further, and I couldn't bear the thought of losing you."

As she tears up, her anger and hurt echo in her voice. "Scared of losing me? By not telling me, you've just made me doubt you even more. How am I supposed to trust you now?"

Seeing Saturn cry tears me apart. "I'm truly sorry, my love. I realize now how wrong I was. I thought I was protecting you by not sharing everything right away. I believed telling you would just be too much, but I see I was wrong." Saturn's response hits me hard, her voice laced with bitterness. "I'm relieved I didn't say yes to your proposal. It would've been another deception by someone who claimed to love me. If I had agreed, who knows if you'd ever have shared your truth with me? Why, Miles? I opened up to you, trusted you, and you've just shattered that trust."

Her words are a gut punch, and I suddenly find myself fighting back tears. I've never felt so exposed, so broken. Saturn's words slice through me, leaving me feeling like everything's crashing down around me, and there's nothing I can do to stop it.

Hearing her words cut deep, I find myself saying in a voice full of regret and desperation, "No, love, please don't say that. I messed up, big time. But I'm begging you, believe me, I want to fix this. Just give me a chance to make things right."

Tears start rolling down my cheeks as I see Saturn crying, too, and it feels like my whole world is hanging by a thread, hoping for a chance to fix the mess I've made.

I can't stand seeing her so upset. The air is thick with everything we haven't said, all the tension and hurt between us, so I stand up and pull her into a hug. Holding her close, I'm silently telling her I'm sorry. I'm hoping against hope we can weather this storm together and start to rebuild the trust that's been damaged.

As Saturn keeps crying, I just hold her, whispering, "I should've told you everything right from the start, but I didn't know how. On the day I asked you to marry me, I wanted to come clean about my secret. But you looked so taken aback that I chickened out. And the distance between us since then has been killing me. I had to tell you now, no matter what because I couldn't stand the gap growing any wider. I needed to be upfront about everything. I give you my word; I will never keep anything from you again."

After a while, Saturn seems to collect herself. She sits back on the couch, giving me this look that's a mix of curiosity and concern.

I stay close to her, my heart aching for her. I gently kiss her forehead, whispering, "My powers, like yours, have been in my family for generations. I didn't choose them; they were handed down to me, just as yours were to you. It's taken me years to get a handle on them, to really accept that they're part of me."

Saturn listens intently now that her tears have stopped. The revelation of how much I've kept from her, though, just piles on more stress. She's torn between feeling hurt, confused, and angry. She had put her trust in me, and now she's forced to reckon with the fact that I've kept such a big part of my life hidden from her.

CHAPTER 18
"UNVEILING TRUTHS AND EMBRACING LOVE"

After a brief pause, I got off the couch and walked over to my bedroom to grab my family's Book Of Shadows. When I returned with it in my hands, I noticed Miles' bewildered expression as he glanced at me.

"Baby, why did you bring out your Book Of Shadows?" he asked.

Keeping a determined expression on my face, I said, "Now it's my turn." With a bewildered expression on his face, Miles questioned, "Your turn? For what?"

His gaze was fixed on mine as I opened The Book Of Shadows. I gestured to the pages that were covered in symbols and riddles. "Miles, are these visible to you? How do you feel when you look at them?"

"Yes, I can see it," he said, nodding. "However, they

look very hard to understand with all of the symbols and riddles."

I grinned, "Yeah, I was able to solve a few of them. A couple at my aunt's place when you left, and the rest following your proposal to me."

As I shared my skills with Miles, I could see his eyes light up with curiosity. The anticipation in his gaze was evident as he leaned closer. "Saturn, what powers do you have?" he asked. Which ones are comparable to mine?"

Taking a deep breath, I made the decision to reveal my abilities. Miles was inquisitive, and his sincere curiosity motivated me to reveal them.

"Um, let's start with 'Whispering Winds,' a power that enables me to speak with the wind and other elements of nature. The mysteries of the earth are communicated through the wind. It enables me to comprehend and interact with the natural world's mysteries through the medium of wind. It makes it possible for me to record the wisdom that the wind conveys, akin to the whispers of messages."

I went on, "The second is called 'Lunar Dreams.' This ability allows me to manipulate the lunar cyclical rhythms, influencing not just my dreams but also the dreams of others. With this capacity, I may comfort or disturb anybody I choose to contact in their dream worlds, thereby influencing the subconscious."

Miles listened to me describe each of my skills with increasing fascination.

"Then there's 'Feline Instincts,' which gives me greater awareness and agility," I went on. "By releasing my inner predator, I can hone my physical capabilities, reflexes, and senses. I can move silently, make accurate decisions, and sense my surroundings because of its wildcat-like powers."

My ability to converse with plants is based on my sharing of the fourth power, called 'Earth's Resonance.' I can hear the murmurs of the flora, comprehend their wants, and mold their forms and growth. I can use this ability to heal by utilizing the vitality of the land or to direct nature's strength when needed by developing a strong connection with the roots of nature."

As I described the fifth power, "Ancestral Guidance," my voice became more solemn. "Using their memories and experiences, I can draw on the wisdom, insights, and abilities of my ancestors. It seems as though I can speak with the ghosts of my ancestors and ask for their help when I'm having trouble or need direction."

I then displayed my sixth power, 'Elemental Manipulation.' "I can reach a special energy that permeates the cosmos thanks to it. I can control elements like fate, time, space, fire, water, and air with it."

Astonished, Miles blurted out, "Shit! Yours are so different from mine."

"Yes, but they have their own rules and curses as well," I said, nodding and a little dejectedly.

"Curses and rules?" Miles wondered, fascinated. "What do those look like?" Breathing deeply, I went on, "It's a long story, Miles."

Still, he persisted and enquired, saying, "Well, I'm here. I've got all the time in the world, so please go on."

"These powers each have their own binding and activation spells, curses, rules, and even special tools in hidden locations with high protection to prevent them from being stolen," I explained. "My understanding is that I inherited some of these abilities, but I also have my own that are unknown to me, and I'll have to figure them out, register them in The Book Of Shadows, and bind them with the appropriate spells."

Confused, Miles enquired, "Bind with spells? What does that mean?"

"Yes, each power has a binding and activation spell," I clarified. "The spells are required to utilize these powers successfully and responsibly. Additionally, they aid in maintaining control over them because exercising these powers carelessly may result in unanticipated outcomes."

With genuine curiosity, Miles asked, "What about the unknown ones? For them, do you have any spells, curses, or guidelines?

"No, I have to find everything on my own for the unknown powers," I shook my head. "No prefabricated rules, curses, or spells exist. I'll have to start from scratch in order to acquire and comprehend these skills."

Another urgent inquiry from Miles was, "What about the tools you mentioned earlier?"

I clarified, saying that every power has a special instrument that is well-protected and concealed in an unidentified place. "These tools are intended to prevent anyone from stealing the powers by reversing the binding spell. I will, therefore, need to find or manufacture the tools necessary for my mysterious powers. It's a difficult procedure."

These insights seemed to captivate Miles. "That's so interesting," he remarked. "All I had to use my powers for were laws, activation spells, and curses. I've never heard of binding and tools before."

"Not only that, but each power also has its own unique rules," I said with a sardonic smile. "Each of them has unique complexity."

"How many rules do you have to follow and remember, baby? Isn't this getting too overwhelming for you?" Miles asked in frustration.

I acknowledged with a sigh, "I know it can be overwhelming. One law is that you must use every ability you have, will or not, or else it may become uncontrollable and endanger innocent people."

"The Book Of Shadows has some mysterious powers, too," I said after pausing. "It is aware of who really owns it. It will only divulge details about the abilities it detects in its owner. Moreover, it is capable of sensing the owner's latent power."

Miles became more and more fascinated as I talked about my Book Of Shadows. He appeared to be truly enthralled with the mystery surrounding this antiquated relic. I could tell he was excited to delve further into our common history.

Miles leaned in closer, curiosity shining in his eyes. "Saturn, this is fascinating. It's like something out of a Syfy movie or book. The book can detect latent powers. That's freaking amazing!"

His head was obviously full of questions when he eventually managed to ask, "Why didn't you tell me about all of this earlier? You never brought it up when I had asked."

"It was difficult, and I was overwhelmed," was my mixed-emotion response. "I didn't want to involve you, an ordinary mortal man, in this. Well, at least I thought you were just an ordinary mortal at the time, and I had some misgivings about you. I needed to establish boundaries because of my past, and I had trouble trusting people."

As my words float through the air, lingering between us, his gaze locks on mine, filled with an intensity that makes the world around us fade away. The dim light of the room casts shadows across his face, highlighting the sincerity in his eyes. He pauses, collecting his thoughts before he begins, his voice soft but firm, "My love, I'm sorry for not being open with you sooner. I'm not just some ordinary guy, and there's something essential I need you to remember."

Caught off guard by his sudden change of direction, my curiosity piques, and I lean in, asking with a blend of curiosity and caution, "What's that?" My eyes search his, trying to decipher the emotions behind his next words.

Miles takes a deep breath as if bracing himself for what he's about to confess. "I'll never betray you like Daniel and Dianna did," he asserts with a conviction that reverberates through the quiet room. "I'm not going to leave you behind. So, please, don't shut me out. I value you for exactly who you are. You don't need to prove yourself to anyone, not even to me. I'll guard you with all I have; trust me, baby."

His words strike a chord deep within me, stirring emotions I've kept at bay. Tears well up, spilling over and tracing warm paths down my cheeks. "Baby, did I say something wrong?" Miles asks, his worry casting a shadow over his previously determined demeanor.

He leans closer, his voice dropping to a whisper, "I guess I shouldn't have said anything." He looks away for a moment. "I won't mention it again."

Perplexed, I ask, "Why won't you bring it up again?" My gaze finds his again, searching for an answer. He stumbles over his words, "Because... it made you cry."

I'm quick to correct him, my voice stronger than I feel, "I wasn't crying because of what you said." I wipe the tears from my cheeks, determined to make him understand. "I cried because nobody has ever asked me not to change or put-up walls before. Miles, those were tears of joy."

The revelation seems to take him by surprise, and the tension in his shoulders eases as a genuine smile breaks across his face. Enclosed in a hug that feels like a haven, I find a sense of safety and belonging I hadn't dared to hope for.

Enclosed in the warmth of his embrace, the words linger between us, filled with hope and a promise of something deeper. "So, you'll say it again, right? " I persist my voice a blend of need and assurance, craving the repetition of his vow as if to etch it into the very air we breathe.

Without hesitation, Miles pulls me closer, his hug enveloping me in a fortress of comfort and security. "Yes, definitely," he affirms, his voice steady and sure. In that moment, the room around us, with its dim lights and shadows, transforms into a cocoon of our shared future, a testament to the depth of our bond and the sincerity of his pledge. As we're wrapped up in this heartfelt moment, I throw a curveball into the mix, asking, "So, when are we tying the knot?"

The question seems to blindside Miles completely. It's as if, amid all our heartfelt exchanges tonight, the thought of actually getting married had slipped his mind entirely. For a second, he's speechless, lost for words in the surprise of the moment.

Not letting him off the hook that easily, I press on with a bit more edge to my voice, "I said, when are we getting married, Miles Nightshade?" There I am, challenging him, pushing for an answer, watching as he stands there, piecing together his thoughts amidst the emotional whirlwind we've found ourselves in.

Finally, catching his bearings, he looks at me, disbelief and hope mingling in his eyes, "Are you... are you accepting my proposal? You want to marry Me?"

I can't help but let a playful warmth flood my gaze as I respond, "No, I'm just inquiring on behalf of a friend," my words dripping with sarcasm, a playful smirk dancing on my lips.

Catching on to my teasing, Miles scoops me up effortlessly, his actions transforming words into motion as he spins me around. Laughter fills the space between us, a testament to the joy and lightness we've managed to salvage from the night's emotional rollercoaster.

"Saturn, I love you so much! I've never felt this way about anyone or anything in my life," Miles exclaims, his eyes gleaming with emotion, reflecting the dim light of the room that wraps around us like a cocoon.

As he gently lays me down, a chuckle escapes me, breaking the intensity of the moment. "You didn't just wing that proposal without any thought of what comes next, did you?" I tease, my voice laced with humor, watching as his expression shifts from one of earnest declaration to mild panic. His surprise is palpable, a delightful confusion that dances across his features. "I gave you a whole month after popping the question, Miles, and you still haven't come up with a plan," I continue, poking fun at the seriousness of our earlier conversations. "Does this mean you hadn't really thought about 'us' in the grand scheme of things?"

He stumbles over his words, a mix of affection and surprise. "No, no, sweetheart, that's not it at all. You've been on my mind every second. I just... didn't have any concrete plans yet."

Hearing his earnest response, I can't keep my laughter at bay any longer. "Take it easy, love. I'm only pulling your leg." I see the tension wash from his face, replaced by a dawning relief, our exchange injecting a playful ease back into the air.

I give him a reassuring smile, the warmth in my heart spilling into my words, "Now we've got all the time in the world to plan together." Our laughter fills the room, a light-hearted end to a moment charged with the depth of our connection.

He smiled at me and said, "I have missed you." He leaned in for a kiss. I felt my heart melt as his lips touched mine.

I had missed him too. We kissed passionately, and I

wrapped my arms around his neck, pulling him closer to me. He ran his hands through my hair and down to the back of my neck. His hands were strong and yet gentle.

I loved how he touched me. After we broke our kiss, he pulled away from me and looked into my eyes. "I love you so much," he whispered. "I love you too," I replied. He smiled again and then kissed me on the lips.

After weeks of separation, the distance between Miles and me has felt like an ever-expanding void. Yet, standing here in the gentle glow of the evening light, I sense the magnetic pull between us, drawing us inexorably closer. The air vibrates with the energy of reunion, filled with the promise of healing and reconnection.

Miles steps toward me, his eyes searching mine, uncovering the whirlwind of emotions swirling within —longing, love, and a flicker of uncertainty. He reaches out, brushing a stray strand of hair from my face, igniting a warmth that seems to fill the room.

"Miles," I breathe out, barely a whisper, as he draws nearer. "I've missed you more than I could ever express."

With a soft sigh, I close the distance between us, my hands finding his. Our fingers intertwine, weaving a silent vow of forgiveness and new beginnings.

As Miles pulls me closer, our lips meet in a kiss that starts tender and cautious but deepens with every heartbeat. It's a kiss brimming with apologies, the ache of absence, and the sweetness of return. We're rediscovering each other, reaffirming a bond that, despite the distance, remained unbroken.

Held in Miles's embrace, the world outside fades away. Doubts and fears dissolve, leaving only the rhythm of our hearts in sync. Miles lifts me, carrying me to the couch, where we continue to explore the depth of our connection, each kiss, each caress, reaffirming our love.

We whisper declarations of love, laughter blending with tears of happiness as we exchange stories of our time apart, cherishing every shared second. In the hush that follows, we pledge to face whatever comes together, our bond stronger and more unified than before. Wrapped in Miles's arms as dawn's light begins to filter through the curtains, I realize that, with him by my side, we can overcome any challenge the future might hold.

I never thought I would ever love someone like this. I was wrong. I was so wrong. I didn't care what anyone else thought. I cared only for him. I loved him with all my heart.

CHAPTER 19

"ENCHANTED EVENINGS"

As the sun sets over the picturesque Napa Valley, Miles and I find ourselves enveloped in a cocoon of blissful solitude. This evening was meant to be ours alone, a precious moment away from the hustle and bustle of wedding planning and the excitement of our impending nuptials. With a gentle breeze caressing our faces and the scent of blossoming vineyards in the air, we savor the tranquility of the moment, relishing in the intimacy of our connection.

Our decision to leave our guests to explore the beauty of Napa Valley on their own was a deliberate one. We wanted this time to be just for us, a chance to bask in the magick of our love without any distractions. As we stand hand in hand, watching the sky transform into a canvas of vibrant colors, I'm grateful for the opportunity to share this moment with the person who means everything to me.

As we make our way back to our suite at the Carneros Resort, the anticipation of the evening ahead fills me with excitement. The thought of being alone with Miles, away from prying eyes and the demands of the outside world, ignites a spark of desire within me. Tonight is about more than just celebrating our love; it's about cherishing each other in the most intimate of ways.

We step into the elevator, a sense of anticipation hanging in the air, mingling with the warmth of our shared affection. With a soft smile, Miles wraps his arm around my waist, pulling me close as the doors close behind us. In this moment, surrounded by the gentle hum of the elevator and the intoxicating scent of Miles' cologne, I feel more alive than ever before. As we step into our suite at the Carneros Resort, the soft glow of candlelight dances around us, casting shadows that seem to shimmer with anticipation. Miles' thoughtful gesture of having oysters, fresh strawberries, and champagne waiting for us fills me with warmth and excitement. The air is fragrant with the scent of roses, their petals scattered on the floor, leading us towards the luxurious bathtub for two.

A delighted gasp escapes my lips as I take in the romantic scene before us. "Miles, this is amazing," I breathe, turning to him with a smile that mirrors the joy in my heart.

He grins, his eyes sparkling with affection. "I wanted tonight to be perfect for you, my Love. Just like you deserve," he says, his voice soft with love.

Taking his hand in mine, I lead him toward the bathroom, the anticipation building with each step. The sight of the bathtub, surrounded by flickering candles and delicate rose petals, is breathtaking. It's as if Miles has transported us to our own private paradise, where time stands still and love knows no bounds.

"Wow, Miles, you've outdone yourself," I say, unable to contain my excitement as I run my fingers through the water, feeling its warmth against my skin.

He smiles, his gaze never leaving mine. "Tonight is a celebration of our love, Baby, and what better way to start than with a relaxing soak in this beautiful tub?" he replies, his voice filled with tenderness.

As we ease into the warm embrace of the water, the world outside fades away, leaving only the two of us lost in the moment. The soft glow of the candles casts a gentle light on our faces, illuminating the love that shines in our eyes. With each passing moment, the tension melts away, replaced by a sense of peace and contentment. We talk and laugh, sharing stories and dreams as we revel in the intimacy of the moment.

But soon, hunger gnaws at our stomachs, reminding us of the delicious spread waiting for us in the other room. With a reluctant sigh, we unwillingly step out of the bathtub, wrapping ourselves in plush robes before making our way to the dining area.

The sight of the oysters, fresh strawberries, and champagne beckons us, promising a feast fit for royalty. We indulge in the decadent treats, savoring each bite and sip as we bask in the glow of our love.

And as the night wears on, our passion ignites once more, culminating in a beautiful union of body and soul. In each other's arms, we find solace and ecstasy, our love reaching new heights with each tender touch and whispered vow.

As we lay tangled in each other's embrace, the world outside fades into oblivion, leaving only the two of us wrapped in the warmth of our love. And as we drift off to sleep, I know that this is just the beginning of a lifetime of love and happiness together.

CHAPTER 20
"THE CELESTIAL UNION"

As the sun dips low on the horizon, casting a warm glow over the Carneros Resort in Napa Valley, the air hums with anticipation. The sprawling grounds of the resort, adorned with lush gardens and rolling vineyards, provide the perfect backdrop for our wedding ceremony.

In the heart of the resort, beneath a canopy of swaying trees, sits the Arbor – a picturesque setting for our vows. The trellis, adorned with delicate flowers and trailing vines, frames the scene like a painting, while the soft murmur of a nearby fountain adds to the serene ambiance.

Stepping into the bridal suite, I feel a rush of excitement and nerves as I lay eyes on the gown that will soon become a part of my most cherished memories. Laila, my dearest friend, and confidante, and I gasp as we gaze upon the dress customized to fit my petite frame. The gown, "Celestial Seraphina," chosen for its celestial beauty, holds a special significance for me, symbolizing the stars and moons that have guided my path to this moment.

Admiring the dress, my heart skips a beat at the sight of the Celestial Seraphina gown awaiting me. Designed by the renowned House of Lumière Étoilée, this gown transcends earthly confines, singing a celestial symphony that weaves dreams into silk and lace. It's the perfect ensemble for my wedding day, a day that promises to be as enchanting as the stars themselves.

The Celestial Seraphina gown unfolds before me like a cosmic ballet, with bolts of silk organza unfurling like comet trails. The bodice, sculpted with whispers of moonlight, cradles my heart, its delicate neckline mirroring the lunar phases—the waxing and waning of love. As I run my fingers over the fabric, I can feel the celestial magick woven into every stitch.

"That wedding dress! It's freaking stunning; breathtaking, Saturn," Laila whispers, her eyes filled with awe as she admires the intricate details.

"I know! Right? It's like something out of a dream," I reply, my voice filled with wonder.

The skirt cascades like a meteor shower, layers of tulle and chiffon catching stardust as they fall. Each tier bears embroidered constellations—the Eridanus, Pleiades, Orion—etched in silver thread, a testament to the cosmic wonders above and my lineage. Trailing behind, the train resembles a comet's tail, leaving a luminous trail for those who follow.

"Imagine walking down the aisle in this," Laila muses, her eyes sparkling with excitement.

"I can't wait," I say, a smile spreading across my face at the thought of wearing such a stunning gown on my wedding day.

Adorned with celestial jewels, the dress shimmers with an otherworldly beauty. Crystal dewdrops sparkle on the bodice, capturing starlight and holding it captive. Moonstone buttons trace the spine, invoking lunar secrets whispered through millennia, while the sleeves bear constellations of pearls—Eridanus, Orion's Belt, and Lyra—each one a tribute to the stars that guide us.

The veil, with its ethereal beauty, stands out as the centerpiece of my attire, visible only to me and soon to Miles. Crafted from the whispers of the universe itself —comet's breath and supernova sigh—it rests upon my face like a secret shared with the cosmos. Through its delicate fabric, I see the universe unfold: the Andromeda with its spiral arms, the Triangulum with its nebulas, and the Magellanic Clouds, each a silent guardian watching over the night. As I move, the veil floats behind me, tracing my steps with a trail of stardust, a celestial path visible only to those who share this magickal heritage. To others, it may appear as nothing more than a beautiful accessory, but to me, it's a bridge to the stars, a reminder of the magick that courses through my veins.

Climbing onto the riser, I can't help but feel like a celestial being in this magnificent gown. The mirrors reflect the universe itself, and for a moment, I feel like I'm twirling among the stars.

"Laila, can you believe this?" I say, breaking the seriousness with a chuckle. "I never thought I'd feel like a space princess on my wedding day!"

Laila laughs, her eyes sparkling with playful energy. "Well, you do make a pretty stunning space princess, Saturn. But let's save the galaxy-saving adventures for after the wedding, okay?"

I nod, joining in her laughter. "Deal! But can we at least have a little champagne and girl talk before we conquer the universe?"

"Absolutely," Laila replies, already reaching for the champagne bottle. "After all, what's a wedding day without a little celebration and laughter?"

As we clink our glasses together, the seriousness of the day fades away, replaced by the warmth of friendship and the anticipation of what lies ahead.

Setting down our glasses, I stand before the mirror, and Laila presents me with a crown fit for a celestial queen. This was a surprise from Miles and he did not want me to see it until it was time to wear it. I'm totally shocked because those are real diamonds on it. I scream excitedly to Laila, "Those are real fricken diamonds, dude! Oh, my Goddess, I can't believe Miles got this for me. The dazzling sun halo crown, delicately crafted from the purest white gold, seems to glow with an otherworldly radiance, each curve and contour reflecting the brilliance of the world's finest diamonds.

I reach out to touch it, feeling the weight of its exquisite craftsmanship in my hands. At its core sits an authentic diamond, ethically sourced and flawlessly cut, its radiant sparkle captivating all who behold it. The diamond's brilliance seems to dance with the light, casting a spellbinding glow that illuminates the entire room.

The crown's design is inspired by the celestial elegance of a sun halo, with rays of white gold extending outward in a breathtaking display of artistry. Each ray is meticulously adorned with meticulously set diamonds, creating a shimmering halo that seems to dance with light.

As Laila places the crown atop my head, I feel a sense of regal elegance wash over me. The centerpiece of the crown, a magnificent diamond carefully selected for its exceptional quality and unparalleled beauty, seems to ignite a spark within me, filling me with a sense of confidence and grace. The weight of the crown feels both regal and comforting as Laila, and I admire its splendor in the mirror. Its delicate curves and shimmering diamonds seem to capture the essence of our love, a love that transcends time and space.

Laila walks over to the dresser, her steps light and graceful, and retrieves a beautiful card in my favorite color. With a knowing smile, she hands it to me, her eyes twinkling. "Last but not least, this is from Miles," she says, her voice filled with warmth and affection.

Curious, I open the card, feeling a rush of anticipation coursing through me. As I read Miles' words, my heart swells with love and gratitude:

"My Dearest Saturn,

As I stand here on the brink of our wedding day, my heart is filled with an overwhelming sense of joy and gratitude. To think that I am about to marry my best friend, my soulmate, my queen from the stars—it's a dream come true.

When I saw this crown, adorned with the finest diamonds, and crafted from the purest white gold, I knew it was meant for you. Every diamond, every curve, every detail speaks of my love for you and my desire to give you the world.

I wanted this crown to be as extraordinary as you are, my love. To shine as brightly as your spirit, and to remind you every day of the love that we share. You are my light in the darkness, my guiding star, and I am eternally grateful to have you by my side.

With all my love,
Miles"

After reading Miles' heartfelt letter, a tear escapes my eye, and I can't help but chuckle through my emotions. "Wow, Miles really knows how to make a girl feel special," I say, wiping away the tear with a laugh.

Laila joins in on the laughter, her eyes sparkling with mischief. "I'm starting to feel jealous here," she jokes, a playful grin tugging at the corners of her lips. "I might need to find myself a Miles of my own."

Her comment lightens the mood, and we share a moment of laughter and camaraderie, basking in the joy of the upcoming wedding. With Miles' words and Laila's humor, I feel more loved and supported than ever before.

With the crown resting upon my head, I feel ready to embark on this journey into matrimony, confident in the love and support that surrounds me. As we make our way to the ceremony, the crown becomes a beacon of hope and joy, guiding me toward a future filled with happiness and fulfillment.

The suite is alive with activity as we put the finishing touches on our attire, and clean up the makeup we've cried away, the air buzzing with our laughter and excitement. Laila's words of encourage-ment and support fill me with confidence, her presence a comforting anchor in the whirlwind of emotions.

As we make our way to the Arbor, the air is filled with the soft strains of music, adding to the magickal atmosphere. Guests mingle and chat, their voices blending into a joyful symphony as they await the start of the ceremony. In the radiant glow of the golden sunlight, the Arbor stands tall and majestic, its wooden beams embracing the warmth of the day. It serves as a sacred sanctuary, a testament to the strength and beauty of our love. As we stand beneath its canopy, surrounded by our friends and loved ones, the Arbor becomes the focal point of our ceremony.

The High Priestess, a vision of grace and wisdom, presides over the ceremony with a quiet authority that commands attention. Her fiery red curls cascade down her back, a striking contrast to her elegant attire, and her presence exudes a sense of reverence and solemnity.

With each word she speaks, the High Priestess weaves a spellbinding tale of love and commitment, drawing us deeper into the sacred union we are about to embark upon. Her voice, rich with emotion and wisdom, resonates through the air, filling the space with a sense of magick and enchantment.

As witches, we have chosen to incorporate elements of our spiritual practice into the ceremony. The handfasting ritual, steeped in tradition and symbolism, serves as a poignant expression of our commitment to each other. With cords woven from strands of silk and satin, the High Priestess binds our hands together, symbolizing the joining of our hearts and souls in love and unity. As the cords are wrapped around our clasped hands, we feel the energy of our bond intertwining, creating a powerful connection that transcends the physical realm. With each knot tied, we affirm our vows and pledge ourselves to each other for eternity. Following the handfasting ceremony, we move to the next part of our ritual – the jumping of the broom. This ancient tradition, rooted in African and Celtic cultures, symbolizes the crossing of the threshold into a new life together.

With laughter and joy in our hearts, we take each other's hand and leap over the broom together, our spirits soaring as we embark on this new chapter of our journey. As we land on the other side, we are filled with a sense of exhilaration and anticipation for the adventures that lie ahead.

The handfasting ceremony and jumping of the broom serve as powerful symbols of our love and commitment, marking the beginning of our life together as partners and equals. And as we stand hand in hand beneath the Arbor, surrounded by the warmth and love of our friends and family, we know that our union is blessed by the magick of the universe.

The reception that follows is a celebration of love in all its glory. Guests mingle and dance, their laughter merging with the soft melody of the music. Each toast, each embrace, is a testament to the bond we share, a reminder of the joy that love can bring.

As the celebration unfolds, Miles takes the opportunity to introduce me to his sister, Lysandra. With a warm smile, he leads her over to where I'm standing, and I can't help but feel a mix of excitement and nerves at meeting someone so important to him.

"Lysandra, I'd like you to meet Saturn," Miles says, his pride evident in his voice. "And this is Laila, Saturn's closest friend."

I extend my hand graciously, trying to ease any tension that may exist. "It's a pleasure to meet you, Lysandra," I say, hoping to convey sincerity in my words. Laila chimes in with her trademark warmth. "Yes, we've heard so much about you. It's lovely to finally meet you face to face."

Despite our efforts to make her feel welcome, I can sense a hint of hesitation in Lysandra's demeanor. Her smile seems forced, her eyes guarded as she sizes me up.

As the conversation progresses, Lysandra becomes increasingly tense, her unease palpable. Eventually, she pulls Miles aside, leaving Laila and me exchanging puzzled glances.

As Lysandra storms off during her conversation

with Miles, a wave of confusion washes over me. Miles follows her, leaving Laila and me standing there, bewildered by the sudden tension.

I exchange a look with Laila, a silent question in my eyes. Before I can voice my concerns, she takes my hand gently, her expression somber yet resolute.

"Hey, love, there's something I need to talk to you about," she says, her voice tinged with seriousness.

Her words only deepen my sense of unease, but I nod, silently urging her to continue. Whatever it is, I know we'll face it together.

CHAPTER 21
"VEILED WATCHER REVEALED"

In the midst of all the wedding chaos, with Lysandra and Miles having their own drama show, I feel the weight of my secret role as Saturn's guardian pressing down on me like a ton of bricks. Seriously, the tension in the air could cut through steel.

But hey, no more beating around the bush. The party's almost over, and it's time to spill the beans. I've been Saturn's silent guardian angel for too long, lurking in the shadows and keeping her safe from all the craziness out there.

Now, with danger knocking on our door, I can't hide in the shadows anymore. From the moment Saturn walked into In the Cut, I've had my eyes on her, silently watching over her like a stealthy ninja.

As our bond grew stronger and Saturn began navigating the wild ride of her new life, I've been there every step of the way, pulling strings behind the scenes to keep her safe. But now, with trouble brewing, it's time to come clean.

With the spirits of my ancestors and the wisdom of my parents backing me up, I'm ready to step out of the shadows and reveal the truth to Saturn. It's time to show her who I really am and why I've been lurking in the shadows all this time.

So, as the reception goes on and the champagne flows, I pull Saturn aside for a heart-to-heart chat. It's time to spill the tea, spill the secrets, and let her know that she's got a guardian angel in her corner.

"Saturn," I begin, my voice hushed as we wander through the garden, "there's something I need to tell you."

Saturn's eyes meet mine, brimming with curiosity and uncertainty. "What is it, Laila? Is everything okay?"

"There are truths that have been hidden from you, secrets that have been kept for your own protection," I confess, my heart heavy with the weight of the revelations to come.

"What do you mean?" Saturn presses, her voice tinged with urgency and a hint of anger, as though she's about to be betrayed by yet another friend.

With a steadying breath, I begin to unravel the tangled threads of her past, weaving a tale of ancient prophecies and hidden alliances. I speak of Eridanus, of her parents, of a legacy passed down through generations. And as I speak, I watch as recognition dawns in Saturn's eyes, piecing together the fragments of memory that have long eluded her.

"I've been with you since the beginning, Saturn," I confess, my voice barely above a whisper. "But I've had to keep my true identity hidden to protect you from those who would seek to harm you."

Saturn stands before me, her expression a mixture of disbelief and wonder, as the truth of her origins begins to sink in.

"And now," I continue my tone grave, "the time has come for me to reveal myself to you fully. To stand by your side and help you face any challenges that lie ahead." Emotions swirl within me, a tumultuous storm of fear and determination, as I watch Saturn come to terms with the magnitude of what I'm telling her. But amidst the uncertainty, I see a glimmer in her eye, and tears start welling up. "Oh, my goddess, Laila, I thought you were going to tell me something bad like that you've betrayed me somehow. I can't believe this. So, you are a star seed too, with powers?" Saturn quietly asks, excitement shining in her eyes.

"Yes. I was chosen, prepared, and trained in Eridanus to protect you," I respond, feeling a sense of relief wash over me as the truth is finally revealed.

As Saturn absorbs the truth, her emotions flicker

like a candle in the wind, uncertainty mingling with curiosity and a hint of disbelief coloring her features.

"Wait, so you've been with me all this time, and you have powers too?" Saturn's voice quivers with a mix of awe and apprehension. I nod, a wry smile tugging at the corners of my lips. "Yes, Saturn. I've been shadowing you, protecting you from the shadows that lurk in the corners of our world."

Saturn's eyes widen, her mind racing to grasp the magnitude of what I've just revealed. "But why keep it a secret? Why not tell me sooner?"

"It wasn't safe," I explain, my voice tinged with regret. "There are forces at play, Saturn, forces that would see you harmed. I had to bide my time, wait for the right moment to reveal myself." Saturn's brow furrows, her gaze shifting to the night sky above us. "And what about now? Why tell me all this now?" "Because the time has come for you to embrace your destiny," I reply, my tone solemn. "There is a threat coming, a threat unlike any other, and you'll need allies by your side if you and Miles are going to get through it."

Saturn nods, determination flickering in her eyes. "I understand," she murmurs, her voice filled with resolve. "Thank you, Laila, for everything."

With a sense of relief washing over me, I take Saturn's hand in mine, a silent vow passing between us.

Together, we'll face whatever challenges lie ahead, our bond stronger now that the truth has been revealed.

We return to the festivities; a nagging sense of unease gnaws at the edges of my consciousness. The Conclave of Shadows looms on the horizon, their sinister presence casting a shadow over our future. I'm acutely aware of the threat they pose, but I'm bound by ancient laws and forbidden from revealing the full extent of the danger to Saturn. Everything must unfold in its own time.

As the evening winds down and guests start to bid their farewells, I can't help but feel relieved by Saturn's reaction. She's taking everything in stride, showing the kind of resilience and grace that I've always admired in her.

Helping Saturn and Miles gather their belongings. I offer a reassuring smile as we say goodnight to the last of the guests. It's been a whirlwind of emotions, but seeing Saturn and Miles together, ready to face whatever comes their way, fills me with hope for the challenges ahead.

As we part ways and head to our respective rooms, I can't shake the feeling that our journey is going to be a crazy one. But with Saturn and Miles by my side, I know we'll face whatever lies ahead together, stronger than ever before.

CHAPTER 22

"SHADOWS OF CONFLICT"

As Saturn lies peacefully beside me, illuminated by the gentle moonlight, an unexplainable restlessness stirs within me. It's like the universe itself is nudging me, urging me to step outside the comforting confines of our room at the Carneros Resort.

So, I slip out into the night, greeted by the cool breeze and the whispering of leaves. It's just me, the stars, and a whirlwind of thoughts swirling in my mind.

That tension from last night with Lysandra still lingers, weighing me down. And Saturn's inquisitive glances only add to the weight. She keeps shooting me looking like, "What's going on with you and your sister?" I wish I had all the answers, but the truth is, I'm as clueless as she is.

I try to ease Saturn's worries, telling her everything's

fine, but deep down, I know I'm only adding to her concerns by keeping things vague. The air feels heavy with uncertainty, and it's messing with my head.

Out in the night, a strange feeling takes hold, like someone's watching me. And before I know it, a figure cloaked in black appears before me. He looks like he just stepped out of some dark fantasy novel—mask and all.

As I stand face to face with the shadowy figure, an electrifying tension fills the air, crackling with potential energy. I can feel the weight of his malevolent presence pressing down on me, but I refuse to yield. With every fiber of my being, I am determined to protect Saturn and vanquish this darkness once and for all. "You shouldn't have come here," the shadow hisses, his voice dripping with malice. "You cannot stop what is already in motion."

"I won't let you harm her," I retort, my voice steady despite the adrenaline coursing through my veins. "She's under my protection, and I'll do whatever it takes to keep her safe."

The shadow chuckles darkly, tendrils of darkness swirling around him like an ominous cloak. "Your efforts are futile, little witch. She belongs to us now, and there's nothing you can do to change that."

With a surge of determination, I draw upon the depths of my power, channeling the energy of the earth and the elements themselves. A wave of force emanates from my outstretched hand, crashing against the shadow with the strength of a tidal wave.

But he is resilient, his form dissipating into mist before reforming once more. "Is that the best you can do?" he taunts, his voice mocking. "You're no match for the darkness that awaits her."

Gritting my teeth, I summon a vortex of wind, whipping around us with hurricane force. The air crackles with energy as I struggle to contain the shadow's onslaught, each blast of power pushing me to my limits.

"Give it up, Miles," the shadow sneers, his voice echoing in the darkness. "You can't protect her forever. Sooner or later, she will die, and we will have her powers." I refuse to back down, drawing upon every ounce of strength and determination within me. With a fierce cry, I unleash a torrent of fire, engulfing the shadow in flames. For a moment, it seems as though I've gained the upper hand, but the darkness only grows stronger, feeding off my desperation. As the battle rages on, the ground trembles beneath us, echoing the intensity of our struggle. The very fabric of reality seems to warp and shift as though unable to contain the sheer magnitude of our clash.

But I refuse to be defeated. With a final surge of power, I summon a blinding light, piercing through the darkness and banishing the shadow once and for all. As his form dissolves into nothingness, a sense of relief washes over me, mingled with exhaustion and triumph.

Gasping for breath, I collapse to my knees, the adrenaline slowly ebbing away. But even as I catch my breath, I know that this battle is far from over. The shadows may have been vanquished for now, but the darkness still lurks on the horizon, waiting for its chance to strike again. And when it does, I'll be ready to face it head-on for the sake of Saturn and all that I hold dear.

Back in our room, Saturn's still fast asleep, unaware of the night's events. I decide to keep it to myself, a mix of bravery and concern swirling inside me. The encounter reveals secrets and hints at challenges to come. But with Saturn by my side, I know we will get through it.

CHAPTER 23

"ECHOES OF POWER"

Last month, Miles and I embarked on this beautiful new journey together, stepping into a happiness that feels both exhilarating and profound. The honeymoon in the Maldives was like a dream, with days spent basking in the sun and nights under a tapestry of stars, every moment steeped in love and the kind of peace that feels rare and precious. Yet, amidst this sea of joy Miles brings into my life, there's a shadow of longing for my Aunt Sage. She wasn't merely family; she was my compass, my teacher, guiding me through life's complexities with wisdom and patience. Her absence has left a void in my heart, a space filled with memories and whispers of what used to be, making me ache for her presence in a way that seems to deepen with time.

Miles, with his incredible sense of perception,

notices the gap left by Aunt Sage. He does everything within his power to support me, providing comfort in ways I hadn't even realized I needed. But the understanding and connection I shared with Aunt Sage are irreplaceable. I miss her advice and her comforting presence every single day.

This feeling doesn't lessen my love for Miles. It's a different kind of longing for a piece of my heart that belonged to Aunt Sage. Being with Miles feels like home, yet there's always this reminder of the unique bond I've lost.

Then, our quiet life morphs into something out of a fantasy novel. It starts with objects floating around our room as if gravity has taken a hiatus. At first, it's surprising, even thrilling, but the wonder quickly turns to concern. Our home, once a haven of peace, now thrums with the chaos of my uncontrolled powers. Miles, always the observer, stands by me, attempting to unravel the chaos. "Saturn, what's happening? Why are things floating?" he asks, his concern evident in his gaze.

I sigh, overwhelmed by the mystery. "I don't know, Miles. It started out of nowhere, and now it feels like these powers have a mind of their own." Miles reassures me, "We'll figure this out together. Maybe it's just something temporary."

But as the night falls, my powers seem to amplify, stirring the wind outside with a mere gesture. "Saturn, that's incredible, but we need to understand this," Miles voices, his worry palpable.

The thought that my powers are beyond my control scares me, not for myself, but for the chance of accidentally harming someone. My efforts to master these abilities lead to frustration and a sense of inadequacy.

Miles and I talk about everything, sharing our fears and determination. Throughout, our love is the anchor, grounding us and giving us the strength to face the unknown together.

One day, while at the grocery store, my powers caught me off guard again. Just thinking about grabbing a juice can makes it float right into my hand. It feels like discovering a hidden talent but also a reminder of the responsibility it entails.

Miles listens intently as I recount the experience. "That's amazing, Baby, but what if it gets out of hand?" he inquires, his concern obvious.

"I have a plan," I assert, filled with a newfound sense of determination. I focus on my abilities, seeking answers and guidance.

As I explore my powers deeper, I start to see them in colors and shapes. Whispering Winds manifest as spirals in green and turquoise, carrying secrets of the natural world. Lunar Dreams are silver and indigo, calm and tranquil. Feline Instincts appear in earthy ochre, reminiscent of a cat's silent grace. Each power reveals itself through unique sensations, colors, and energies. It's like uncovering a new part of myself, a realm of potential I had never known existed.

But with this revelation comes fear. I'm unsure of what lies ahead on this path of self-discovery. Nevertheless, I'm determined to learn, grow, and harness these powers that have become a part of me.

Sharing this with Miles, I try to describe what I've experienced. "It's like the wind is whispering secrets to me," I attempt to explain the sensations and colors.

Miles, ever supportive, asks, "What do these powers say to you?"

I remember the gentle voice of the wind, "Whispering Winds speaks of nature's mysteries, revealing itself in patterns of green and turquoise."

Our conversation swings between wonder and concern, but through it all, Miles and I stand united, prepared to face whatever lies ahead.

Standing in the glade, surrounded by the grandeur of an ancient tree, feels like stepping into a world where magick isn't just real—it's alive. The whispers of the night, blending seamlessly with the soft hum of my newfound abilities, create a symphony that only Miles and I are privy to. Lunar Dreams, one of these mysterious abilities, seems to cast a shimmer around me, revealing dreamlike visions against the backdrop of the star-filled sky.

"I'm seeing dreams... fragments of people's thoughts," I find myself whispering to Miles, almost in disbelief. It's as if I've tapped into a stream of consciousness, catching fleeting glimpses of others' fears, hopes, and moments they cherish in their dreams.

Miles, with his unwavering curiosity, leans closer, his eyes reflecting the moon's glow. "What does it all mean?" he asks, his voice a mix of wonder and concern.

I ponder for a moment, feeling the weight and the warmth of his gaze. "I think... I think it's teaching me and guiding me on how to wander through not just my dreams but others as well. Lunar Dreams is showing me how to navigate the subconscious realm," I try to explain, my hands moving as if to grasp the elusive threads of understanding that danced just beyond my reach.

As we stand under the watchful presence of the great tree, another voice makes itself known—Earth's Resonance. It isn't a voice you could hear with your ears but one you feel deep in your bones. It speaks in the language of rustling leaves and the steady pulse of the earth under our feet. I reach out with my arm, palm facing downward, feeling the energy flow through me, connecting me to the very essence of nature.

"This place... it's in harmony," I murmur, a sense of wonder washing over me. "I'm beginning to understand the life force that binds everything. It's teaching me about balance, about being one with nature." Miles, always the observer, takes in the serene scene around us. "You seem to connect with everything here," he remarks, clearly amazed at how I seem to engage in a silent conversation with the elements around us.

Then come the whispers of Ancestral Guidance, a power I hadn't fully grasped until now. It's like hearing the voices of those who came before me, offering wisdom through the breeze, showing me shadows of the past that I didn't even know existed within me.

"I'm receiving guidance," I confess, the awe evident in my voice. "It's as if my ancestors are reaching out, trying to reveal parts of me I haven't discovered yet."

As we allow the tranquility of the glade to envelop us, a new sensation begins to emerge. My Feline Instincts, which had lain dormant, start to awaken, sending out a tender, almost imperceptible energy. Near the base of the tree, a blossom of feline grace unfurls its petals, casting a soft light around it—a sign, perhaps, of the awakening of this particular power.

Miles points to the glowing flower, a hint of surprise in his voice. "Is this one of your abilities?" he asks, intrigued by the unexpected bloom.

With a nod, I confirm, my expression a blend of curiosity and excitement. "Yes, it's tied to my Feline Instincts. It seems to be a sign, a clue to understanding these powers."

Each revelation, each whisper of power that chooses to reveal itself, feels like a piece of a puzzle clicking into place. The feline grace blossom is more than just a flower; it's a beacon of enlightenment, pointing the way to the deeper mysteries of my abilities that lay waiting to be unlocked.

"It's here," I say softly, a mix of surprise and determination in my voice. "I think I'm getting closer to unlocking the secrets of these powers."

The glade, with its ancient tree and whispered secrets, seems to promise that here, amidst the natural world's gentle embrace, I will find the keys to understanding the depths of my abilities. Guided by the subtle energies and the messages of the past, I feel a surge of resolve to explore this path further, to unlock the potential that whispers my name under the cover of the night.

CHAPTER 24

"THE POWER OF TELEKINESIS"

As I delve deeper into the depths of my inherent powers, each holds a sliver of understanding, a whisper leading me closer to the mystery's heart. The "Whispering Winds" led me to a hidden grove in the woods, where the echoes of ancient rituals permeate the air. The breeze wraps around me, bringing back memories of lost customs. In these visions, I witness celestial dances and mystics tapping into elemental forces using lunar energies.

"Elemental Manipulation" lures me into a cave adorned with pulsating glyphs that appear to emit cosmic energy. The symbols evoke emotions and create a harmonious blend of earth, water, fire, and air. The cavern reverberates with mysterious celestial alignments—an intricate language intertwined with the elemental rhythm.

"Ancestral Guidance" displays fleeting images of aged faces, their eyes burdened by the passage of time. My ancestors' cryptic instructions caution me about the latent power awakening within me. The fragmented insights start to come together, showing a stronger focus on accountability and self-control. The authorities demand respect, not carelessness. It's a sacred responsibility.

Later back at Nightshade mansion, I sit beside the crackling fireplace in quiet contemplation; the ancient Book of Shadows resting gently on my lap. Dancing flames cast shifting shadows upon its weathered pages, setting the stage for the enigmatic puzzle that consumes my thoughts and steers my actions. With careful reverence, I turn the fragile pages, each one a repository of my lineage's timeless wisdom. An empty canvas is just waiting for me, eager to soak up the secrets the wind whispers, the elemental harmonies, and those ancestral murmurs, all circling around the magick of telekinesis. As I dive into the mystical tome before me, the riddle of telekinesis calls out to me, enticing me with its mystery.

"Whisper of Telekinesis," it reads, and I can't help but be drawn in.

"I am the whisper in the wind's gentle sway, Unseen, unfelt, yet mighty in its way. No touch, no words, no uttered decree, Through my command, all bends to me."

This puzzle, right here in my hands, is consuming me. Each line, cryptic yet clear, pushes me closer to unlocking my power. "I am the whisper in the wind's gentle sway," I repeat to myself, the essence of telekinesis captured perfectly in words. It's like it's talking about the power to command without being seen, a silent yet forceful presence.

"No touch, no words, no uttered decree," I muse, thinking about how this isn't about physical gestures or spoken words. In the world of telekinesis, it's all about what you can do with your mind. "Through my command, all bends to me," it concludes, promising control and dominion through sheer will.

Diving deeper, I feel a surge of excitement as the secrets of telekinesis unravel before me. This isn't just about moving stuff with my mind; it's about respecting the unseen forces at play. "The essence of telekinesis lies in trust, where manipulating thoughts and intentions is forbidden. Use wisdom to guide your actions and aim for the good," I add my own thoughts to the ancient spell, making a personal vow to handle this power with care and to always consider its impact.

I make a note for the future, a personal touch to ensure empathy and ethical use. This isn't just about rules; it's a commitment to use telekinesis wisely and compassionately. I emphasize, "No manipulating thoughts, no unfair control," as I write, pledging to navigate the mental realm with respect and empathy.

"Let wisdom guide your intentions," I declare, penning down my promise to use this power for healing and understanding, not harm. "Use it to mend, not to rend," I finish, feeling the solemnity of my words. I'm making a vow here, to use telekinesis to bring people together, not tear them apart.

The spell I compose is a careful balance of warning and guidance. "Misuse this power, and you'll disturb the delicate balance," I warn, knowing the risks of telekinesis gone wrong. I lay out the steps for using this power responsibly, emphasizing the importance of a pure heart and clear intentions.

Diving deeper into my exploration of telekinesis, I realize the importance of a specific crystal in unlocking this power. This isn't just any crystal; it's a rare, iridescent stone known as an Astral Quartz, known for its connection to the ethereal realms and its ability to amplify psychic energies. I remember the day I found it, nestled within the heart of a secret cavern beneath the ancient roots of the Nightshade estate, its luminescence catching my eye in the dim light.

As I carefully extracted the Astral Quartz from its resting place, I could feel its raw energy pulsating through my fingers, a silent yet profound resonance with my own magickal essence. This crystal, with its unique connection to the astral planes, would become the key to unlocking telekinesis for those who come after me.

To transform the Astral Quartz into a magickal item capable of awakening telekinesis, I needed to infuse it with my own energies and intentions. On a night when the stars aligned with ancient celestial patterns, I held the crystal aloft under the moon's silvery glow, chanting an incantation that wove together the essence of wind, will, and wisdom. The ritual was not just about empowering the crystal but also about creating a bond between it and the lineage of future wielders.

As the incantation reached its crescendo, the Astral Quartz began to shimmer with an inner light, its surface reflecting the cosmos above. I could feel the crystal's energy harmonizing with my own, a sign that it had been successfully imbued with the potential to unlock telekinesis. To complete the process, I carefully placed the enchanted crystal within a specially crafted box made from the wood of the Nightshade estate's oldest tree, inscribed with symbols of protection and growth.

This crystal, now a magickal item, would serve as a guide for future generations seeking to unlock the power of telekinesis. By holding the Astral Quartz and connecting with its energy, they would be able to tap into the same forces that now coursed through me. I made sure to document the ritual and the properties of the Astral Quartz in The Book of Shadows, ensuring that the knowledge would not be lost to time.

With the crystal safely stored and the knowledge

preserved, I knew that I had taken a crucial step in safeguarding the future of telekinesis. It was a legacy that went beyond my own time, a gift to those who would walk the path of magick after me. The Astral Quartz, once a mere stone hidden in the earth, was now a beacon of potential, a key to unlocking powers undreamed of by those who would inherit the mantle of magick from me.

"To fully awaken this power, you'll need a special crystal," I write, detailing the ritual of connecting with the moon's energy. It's a moment of communion with the cosmos, a step closer to wielding this incredible ability.

But with great power comes great caution. "Speak not for power or greed," I remind myself and future readers, aware of the darkness that misuse can bring. The spell to safeguard telekinesis is my final touch, a binding promise to keep this power safe and to use it wisely.

Closing the book, I feel the weight of responsibility settling on my shoulders. I've pledged to uphold the integrity of telekinesis, to use it not just as a tool but as a gift that demands respect and wisdom. It's a commitment that stretches beyond the pages of The Book of Shadows, a promise to future generations and to myself.

CHAPTER 25

"JOURNEY OF UNITY"

It's been six months since diving into this shared journey with Saturn, and every discovery about her powers amazes me. Yet, beneath the surface of our growing connection, there's a turmoil churning within me—a secret that shadows every moment of awe and wonder.

Our training sessions, serene on the surface, hide the storm of my internal conflict. We share looks that say so much, yet I'm holding back a truth that could change everything. As Saturn reveals more of herself, I find myself at a crossroads, deeply entrenched in her story while hiding a crucial part of mine.

Watching Saturn practice her powers in the forest behind Nightshade Mansion, I'm struck by her beauty and grace. She's truly amazing, her essence a beacon of light in the darkness that surrounds us. As she focuses on her Whispering Winds power, her hair dances in the breeze she conjures, a testament to her control and harmony with nature.

Her growth and our deepening bond have become the heartbeat of my days. But as she learns to master her chaos, I'm caught in my own tempest, wrestling with the shadows of the Conclave of Shadows and their plans. The trust Saturn places in me, especially in our quietest hours, feels like both a gift and a burden, heavy with the secrets I've vowed to keep from her.

Together, we've faced challenges that have only brought us closer, but the weight of my undisclosed secrets presses down on me. It's not just about supporting her anymore; it's about the silence that lies between us—a silence filled with things unsaid and actions not taken. The emotional intimacy we've built, sharing fears and dreams, now feels tainted by the deceit I carry. This journey of discovery, meant to be about trust and understanding, is clouded by my struggle to keep the dark intentions of the Conclave hidden from her.

Amidst the silence that speaks volumes between us, my mind races with possibilities. How can I protect Saturn from the truth without breaking the promise of honesty I made to her? The fear of losing her if she learns the full extent of my deceit gnaws at me, yet the realization that I must do something to dissolve this looming threat becomes increasingly urgent.

Could swaying Lysandra away from the Conclave be the answer? Winning her support might be a way to shield Saturn from the truth and dismantle the threat looming over us. But the question remains: Should I confide in Saturn, risking our relationship but honoring our vow of honesty? The thought of her ever discovering my betrayal on her own is unbearable.

As our bond deepens, so does the complexity of my dilemma. How do I navigate this web of secrets without losing the one person who's become my world? The decision looms large, a shadow over the connection that's become my haven. As I ponder our future, the challenge of maintaining our trust while shielding her from the darkness of my world is a tightrope walk I never anticipated.

CHAPTER 26
"SHADOWS OF DOUBT"

This morning, I woke up to the sun peeking through the curtains, casting a warm golden glow all around the room. It's been six months since Miles and I tied the knot, and each day feels like we're living out some incredibly magickal tale. Our love just keeps growing stronger, adding layers of depth and warmth to our lives.

Navigating this intertwined path of love and otherworldly powers with Miles by my side is transforming into something magickal. We're not just learning to use our powers; we're learning to use them together, creating a formidable force where once there were two separate witches. It's like we're two halves of a whole, our abilities complementing and enhancing each other, making us stronger than we ever were apart.

At first, the journey seemed daunting, a tangled web of superhuman abilities that felt almost too vast to comprehend. But as we face each challenge side by side, our connection deepens, solidifying us not just as partners in life but as allies in magick. The mysteries of our powers, once a source of trepidation, become less fearsome with Miles at my side. Our combined strength feels like an invincible shield against the uncertainties that lay in our path.

The beauty of our exploration lies in its harmony. Miles, ever my rock, offers his strength and wisdom generously, making the unraveling of each new ability feel like a shared triumph. He's more than just my husband; he's my fellow magician, my confidant in this mystic journey. Together, we're peeling back layers of ancient knowledge, discovering not just the secrets of our powers but the depths of our bond. This shared quest has a surreal grace to it, a dance of discovery that's uniquely ours. Miles's insights shed light on aspects of my abilities I hadn't even considered, his perspective opening new avenues for us to explore. As we navigate this enchanting world together, our powers intertwine, weaving a potent tapestry of magick, that's far more powerful than anything we could achieve alone.

The experience of mastering these powers as a duo is exhilarating, a testament to the strength of our unity.

Every moment of discovery, every breakthrough, feels like a step closer to understanding the full extent of what we can achieve together. It's a journey of mutual growth, of becoming not just powerful witches but a single, unstoppable force. Together, we're charting a course through the mystical, our love and powers combined, leading us into the unknown with a sense of invincibility and wonder.

In the midst of the enchantment that fills our lives, there's always a shadow, a distant memory of Aunt Sage. Every day, I find myself missing her presence, yearning for the wisdom and warmth she brought into my life. Sometimes, it feels like her absence hovers around me like a ghost, reminding me of what I've lost. But as time passes, I come to terms with this loss, knowing she's here in spirit and we'll be reunited upon my return to the stars. The constant sadness fades and is replaced by the moments Miles and I share now and the bond that grows stronger with each passing day. I'm falling deeper in love with my wildly handsome husband as we continue to grow together. The way he looks at me, the understanding in his gaze, brings me a sense of comfort. It's a silent reassurance that no matter what challenges we face, we can conquer them together. Our love becomes our anchor, guiding us through the uncertainties of life and keeping us steady as we navigate this incredible journey.

Months blend into one another in the ethereal fabric of our shared existence, yet a persistent question lingers in my mind like an unspoken truth. It revolves around Miles' sister, Lysandra, whom I encountered only briefly at our wedding. Despite our limited interaction, my claircognizant senses prick with an intuitive knowing that her absence carries a dark undertone.

As the soft hues of twilight cascade through the room one evening, I feel compelled to broach the subject with Miles. With an innate understanding that transcends verbal explanation, I sense there's a troubling reason behind Lysandra's conspicuous absence from our lives.

I ask Miles about his sister with a light heart, yet a sense of worry clouds my thoughts. "Miles, I've been thinking about Lysandra," I start nervously, wanting to tread softly on what seems like a sensitive issue.

A shadow passes across his face as he looks up. "What about her, baby?" He sounds cautious as if he expects me to ask him questions.

"It's simply that... We got married, and I haven't seen her since. She hasn't been around for months," I voice my concern while attempting to sound reassuring.

Miles hesitates, speaking in small, deliberate steps. "She is busy running our family business and spends most of her time in New York at our corporate headquarters. It keeps her away for a long time," he states, but I sense something more lurking beneath his words.

"She was like a whirlwind at our wedding, barely taking time to even speak to me. Does she not like me? Was she not happy we got married?" I have a lot of questions on my mind, and doubt starts to eat away at me.

Miles' expression softens a trace of distance in his eyes. "She was actually very eager to finally meet you. When I told her about you, she was overjoyed. I'm not sure why she was so distant at the wedding; maybe she just had a lot of things on her mind. I can invite her over for lunch or dinner this weekend if you'd like. I know she'll be in town." The chat leaves me contemplative, with a renewed desire to bridge the gap and learn more about his sister and their family dynamics.

Although I would love to have Miles' sister over, my heart races with surging nervousness and uncertainty, and I am not ready, nor do I have the energy to host a lunch or dinner. "Let's hold off on the invite, Babe. This weekend is too soon; I'm too exhausted to have guests. Maybe next time she's in town, we can plan to have her over?" I say. Miles replies, "Of course, my love; I will make a note of it and find out when she will be back in town."

Lately, I've been dealing with these totally bizarre sensations—like nothing I've ever experienced before. It's like my body's playing this weird trick on me, and I can't quite figure out what's going on. I mean, I've been feeling nauseous all the time, and it's not just a passing thing. It's this constant, nagging feeling that just won't go away.

Today, I reached a point where I can't brush it off any longer. Summoning my courage, I head to the store to grab a pregnancy test. But as I stand in the aisle, surrounded by options, uncertainty hits me like a tidal wave. What if I'm pregnant? What if my entire life is about to change in ways I can't even fathom?

The signs are all there, impossible to ignore. It's been over a month and a half since my last period. After a small dinner, I slip into the bathroom with the test kit clenched tightly in my hands, nerves fluttering in my stomach. I'm not ready for this, not prepared for the idea of becoming a mom.

I try to follow the instructions on the test, but my hands are shaking so much I can barely hold onto the stick. The wait for the positive or negative sign feels like an eternity. My heart pounds in my chest, and I'm consumed by anticipation, wondering what lies ahead —if motherhood is truly on the horizon.

As I wait, doubt gnaws at me, each minute dragging by painfully slow. When the result finally seemed to appear, it resulted in catching me off guard. The plus sign stares back at me from the test stick, shaking my world to its core. Just two weeks ago, I took a test, and it was negative, but now it's positive. I'm going to have a baby. We're going to have a baby. It's a monumental moment, a realization that our lives are on the brink of a profound transformation.

The weight of the results presses down on me, stirring up a whirlwind of emotions in my mind. Despite the turbulence caused by our powers and the challenges they bring, the idea of having a child has never been discussed. Questions swirl in my head—how will Miles react? How will we navigate this uncharted territory?

Amidst the overwhelming flood of emotions, there's a spark of joy, a glimmer of excitement for the new reality unfolding before me. It's a fresh chapter, promising adventures unlike any we've faced before in lives woven with enigmatic energies and unpredictable abilities.

Heart pounding, I rush from the bathroom to our dining room, bursting with the incredible news that's about to reshape our world. But Miles isn't there. Thinking he might be buried in his work, I make my way to his office, where the muffled sounds of a tense conversation drift through the open door as I approach.

At first, judging by the tone of his voice, I assumed it was work-related—a big problem at the office perhaps, or some mistake that had rattled Miles, disrupting his usual calm demeanor. Disappointed with the timing, I opted to delay sharing my news for the time being.

I start to back away when his comments stop me in my tracks. He's talking to someone about "taking me to someone else after our marriage, assisting in taking powers and telling them not to be so fucking impatient as he is working on that." The words sting like a slap in the face, lingering in the atmosphere, swirling around like a tornado.

"I cannot be going through this bullshit again!" I think as his words echo in my head, transporting me back in time to when I overheard Daniel deceiving me with Dianna.

Questions ricochet through my mind, each one like a hammer striking my heart. Am I a target? What would make him want to take my powers? Why is he keeping secrets from me, and who the fuck is he talking to? His remarks rip through my entire being, causing a rush of anxiety, irritation, and a deep sadness that I am unable to overcome.

I experience a kaleidoscope of emotions I've never felt before. It's like trying to find a firm foothold while navigating a choppy sea of uncertainty and bewilderment. I trudge back to our room, my mind tangled in a maze of uncertainty, seeking answers in a haze of feelings I can't describe. Approaching him now feels impossible. Doubt tears at me, causing me to question the foundation of our union, our love. The lingering effects of past betrayals overwhelm me, clouding my judgment.

It seems silly to have such doubts about my husband, the love of my life. Yet, the crippling anxiety of being deceived again weighs heavily on me. I decide to keep this to myself for now. I must seek the truth and answers, but I also want to do it without outside pressure. It's a painful realization that contradicts my feelings of trust and love for Miles. But I can't risk sharing my vulnerable reality until I'm certain of his intentions.

Now, my primary concern shifts to the safety and well-being of my unborn child. The excitement I once felt about revealing the positive pregnancy test to Miles is now overshadowed by fear. What if he orchestrated everything to gain control of my powers? In that case, he certainly won't be pleased about the news of the baby. He might even try to manipulate me into aborting the baby, concocting excuses about the potential dangers of raising a child with magickal abilities. It's a frightening thought, considering the already complicated nature of our lives intertwined with magick. Tonight's events have left me feeling like I don't truly know Miles anymore. I've made the difficult decision to leave him until I uncover the truth and ascertain whether he genuinely loves me and would accept our unborn child.

I bide my time, waiting for Miles to drift off into sleep before I start to strategize my covert exit from Nightshade Mansion. I've got to be slick about slipping past our security team. After our blissful honeymoon in the Maldives, Miles, for reasons that are still a bit fuzzy to me, told them to keep a close eye on me. He doesn't want me stepping out solo or leaving without him saying it's okay. Maybe he's worried I won't come back, or worse, that someone out there might be after me—or more specifically, after my powers. But now, lying here in the dark, I'm starting to feel like the person I should be wary of isn't lurking outside; it's the man sleeping next to me.

CHAPTER 27

"WHISPERS OF DECEIT"

The tranquility of the evening is shattered by the shrill ring of the phone, and my heart sinks when I see Lysandra's name flashing on the screen. While I eagerly anticipated Saturn's pregnancy announcement ever since I saw her bring home a pregnancy test earlier this afternoon, I restrained myself from pressing her for information. Instead, I opt to wait patiently, understanding that she will share the news when she feels ready, without any added pressure from me.

As I answer the phone, her voice cuts through the line, devoid of any concern for my well-being or the fact that we haven't spoken in months. Without a preamble, she launches into the conversation, her eagerness thinly veiling her underlying agenda involving Saturn. Despite my efforts to maintain composure and engage in rational discourse, she meets my attempts with annoyance and a tinge of frustration. She demands immediate answers regarding my plans and the strategies I had meticulously crafted during my unwavering loyalty to the coven, showing little regard for the time and effort invested in them.

Her impatience not only annoys me, but it infuriates me, and I'm so frustrated that I can't help but ask why she's behaving like such a petulant child.

Lysandra's tendency to be overly impatient often leads her to act like a complete bitch! Struggling to rein in my escalating emotions, I find myself more determined to break my ties with the Conclave of Shadows. She remains relentless, her impatience palpable even through the phone line. I struggle to contain my anger as I strive to quell the mounting frustration within me, and her urgent tone only adds to my unease. "Yes, I know I said I'd bring her to you, and I'm working on it. Why the fuck are you being so impatient, sister?" At last, I lost it, just a mild hint of frustration creeping into my voice.

I'm boiling with rage. How can they be so damn impatient? I mean, they're striving for ultimate supremacy and power, aren't they? If anything requires patience, it's this! Idiots! When things come to a head, I lose it on my sister over the phone. After screaming my frustrations at Lysandra, I hurl the phone onto the table, a physical manifestation of my anger. In the eerie calm that follows, a sense of someone else's presence lingers in the air. My mind races. Could it be Saturn? Nonetheless, I open the door of my office, half-expecting to find her, only to be met with a deserted, undisturbed hallway.

Shutting the door behind me, my mind races as I seek refuge in my office. I'm haunted by the idea that Saturn might have overheard my unintended confession. Yet, as I collect myself, I resolve to maintain a calm façade. I don't want to unsettle or scare Saturn with the inner demons that plague me at this moment.

Amid the quiet of my office, I'm caught up in a whirlwind of thoughts, trying to find some calm. That call from Lysandra just won't leave me in peace; its unsettling message loops in my head, cranking up my worries for Saturn's safety. Every ring of the phone now feels like a jolt, echoing Lysandra's urgent voice and her barely hidden concern, which only fuels my frustration even more.

I can't shake off the image of Saturn, her innocence tangled in the web spun by a coven blinded by their desires and, frankly, a bit too caught up in their own drama. Lysandra's actions, while they sting, have pushed me to a crossroads. On one side, there's the call of my loyalty and the destiny I'd chosen before finding Saturn, a destiny that's increasingly hard to align with. On the other, there's Saturn—my unexpected, earth-shattering love that has rooted itself deep in my heart, reshaping my world in ways I hadn't dared dream.

Walking through the mansion's luxurious halls feels different now, like I'm caged in. Our heavy security setup suddenly seems paper-thin against the looming threat of a determined coven. Every step I take is heavy with the burden of figuring out a way to shield what matters most to me.

I'm wrestling with the urge to spill everything to Saturn and the dread of dragging her into this mess. Staying silent feels like I'm betraying the very foundation of trust we've built.

As daylight gives way to the evening, my mind never rests, always alert to the dangers inching closer. Lysandra's dogged determination to keep pushing reminds me just how thin the ice we're skating on is, threatening the delicate peace I've found with Saturn.

Here's the plan: I need to flip the script with Lysandra. It's time to shift from being on the defensive to making her an ally. If anyone knows the ins and outs of the Conclave and how to safeguard against them, it's her. Plus, as my sister, there's a bond there that I'm hoping still counts for something. I'm banking on the fact that, deep down, she doesn't want to see me—or Saturn, for that matter—in harm's way. The challenge is convincing her to switch sides, to see that her loyalty to the Conclave is misplaced and that her true allegiance should be with us. It won't be easy, given our past, but if

I can just get her to listen, to really hear me out, I believe I can bring her over to my side. It's a long shot, but Saturn's safety—and our future—depends on it.

As I ponder this, a plan begins to take shape. I need to approach Lysandra, not with accusations or anger but with an appeal to the sister and brother bond we share. I have to remind her of the stakes and make her see that what we're up against is bigger than any of us. And maybe, just maybe, I can sway her to become our protector, our secret weapon against the looming threat of the Conclave.

It's a delicate dance, one that requires all the finesse and diplomacy I can muster. But for Saturn's sake, for the love that's become the center of my universe, I'm willing to try anything. Because in the end, keeping Saturn safe isn't just my duty; it's my everything. And if bringing Lysandra into our fold is what it takes, then I'm all in.

The descent into New York is a mix of anticipation and a gnawing sense of unease. As night cloaks the city, its lights a dizzying array of neon blinks and halos, I find myself back in my penthouse, the skyline a mere backdrop to the turmoil brewing within. I pace, restless, the city's vibrant pulse in stark contrast to the tight knot of apprehension in my gut. Lysandra's arrival is imminent, and with it, a confrontation years in the making.

The door opens, and there she stands. "Why the

sudden call, Miles?" Lysandra asks, her voice tinged with caution, her gaze probing.

"We need to talk about Saturn... and the Conclave," I reply, struggling to mask the urgency in my tone.

Her stance hardens. "What about them?" The guarded edge in her voice is unmistakable.

I exhale, bracing myself for the plea I never imagined making. "It's time to rethink our loyalty to the Conclave. Their darkness and evil intent, Lysandra, is dangerous not just to Saturn but to all of us. Once they succeed at killing Saturn and taking her powers, they will have control over all the covens, and because of the darkness that lives inside of them, they will have the potential to destroy every magickal being and the humans living on this planet."

She scoffs, disbelief and skepticism mingling in her expression. "You're asking me to turn against the Conclave?"

"It's not about betrayal; it's about protection," I insist, my words careful, pleading. "Saturn's caught in a web she didn't weave. She's innocent, and it's up to us to shield her from a fate she doesn't deserve. Just like us, she's inherited her lineage, but that shouldn't mean she should die and have all of her powers taken away by an evil coven hell-bent on using them for their own evil agenda."

Her gaze falters, a tumult of emotions flickering across her face. "And why should I help you?" Her words are laced with a bitterness born of years of estrangement.

"Because I believe the sister I grew up with, the one whose kindness knew no bounds, is still in there," I counter, my voice softening. "Remember us, Lizzy, before the world told us who we should be? Before Mom and Dad died. We have a chance to do right by Saturn. With her, I've seen what our powers can truly achieve when guided by love, not ambition."

A moment stretches between us, heavy with unsaid words and buried memories. Then, slowly, a flicker of the sister I knew peeks through the armor she's built around herself.

"Alright, Miles. I'll stand with you," she relents, her resolve mingling with a hint of the warmth I remember. "But what's the plan? How do we protect her without igniting a battle?"

A sense of relief washes over me, mingled with determination. "Oh, there's no way to do this without a battle, but we play the game. We make them believe we're still their loyal soldiers, all the while building a sanctuary around Saturn and gathering alliances. It's a dance of shadows, Lizzy, but together, I believe we can lead it."

Lysandra nods, a truce forming in the space between us. "Okay, big brother. For Saturn and for us, I'll join your cause. Just tell me what to do."

As the city continues its restless hum below, I'm

struck by a newfound hope. Together, Lysandra and I will weave a new narrative, one where love and kinship might just outshine the darkness that up until now, has engulfed us. The path ahead is fraught with peril, but for the first time, I dare to believe that we might just find our way through the shadows.

And as we head out, bound for the Conclave's meeting, I realize this is more than just a mission to save Saturn. It's a chance to redeem ourselves, to break free from the chains of power and control. Tonight, Lysandra and I embark on a path of deception, but with the noblest of intentions. For the first time in a long time, I feel like we're fighting for something truly worthwhile.

Stepping into the heart of the Conclave's lair feels like entering a storm, each member a tempest of power and suspicion. Seraphina cloaks the room in her web of illusions while Malachi's sharp eyes cut through the air, attempting to unveil secrets and lies. Lucius, with his command over the elements, mirrors the tension within us, his powers reflecting the storm brewing in our midst. Isolde's shadows, meanwhile, dance ominously around us, hinting at the darkness we're all steeped in.

Here I am, standing with Lysandra, our facade of conflicting loyalties a thin veil over our true intentions. The atmosphere is electric, charged with the skepticism of the Conclave towards my fidelity. Lysandra meets my gaze, her voice laced with a pretense of worry that's almost convincing. "So, Miles, are you still with us? Truly with the family, with the Conclave?" Her words, meant for the ears of our peers, sting with the irony of our situation.

It's a delicate dance we're doing, her question a carefully placed chess piece in our game of deception. Internally, I'm a whirlwind of emotions, battling between the act I must maintain and the rebellion simmering in my heart. Facing the Conclave, we wear masks of unity, yet beneath the surface, our resolve to protect Saturn from their clutches burns fiercely.

As Lysandra cleverly crafts her doubts, my mind races with counterarguments. "I've been nothing but dedicated, pouring every ounce of myself into our cause," I assert, my voice a mix of defiance and silent plea for them to buy into our act. The air tightens with suspicion and barely veiled threats, the Conclave's desperation palpable as they probe for any sign of treachery.

Our silent pact, a shared commitment to thwart the Conclave's plans, stands firm amidst the chaos. Yet, as I vocalize my feigned allegiance, the weight of our secret alliance presses heavily on me. The thought of Saturn, my beacon in this enveloping darkness, reinforces my determination to navigate this treacherous path with Lysandra by my side.

Breaking free from the Conclave's grasp looms as a

daunting yet necessary rebellion. Our unspoken agreement, fortified by the love I hold for Saturn, guides my every move, driving me to seek a future where love triumphs over ambition and darkness. With every step I take, the path ahead becomes clearer, our shared resolve a beacon guiding us through the impending storm. As the meeting unfolds, I stand ready, bolstered by Lysandra's silent allegiance and the love that fuels my defiance. Together, we navigate the treacherous waters of loyalty and deception, a bond of brother and sister against the world, ready to challenge the darkness for a glimpse of light. In the dimly lit space of the Conclave's headquarters, the air is thick with impatience and suspicion. It's been six months since Saturn became my wife, and the Conclave's tolerance for delays wears thin. Their penetrating stares and the cold, hard edge to their questions make the atmosphere nearly suffocating.

"Why the delay, Miles?" Seraphina demands, her tone sharp as the edge of a blade. "We expected progress by now."

I'm on the defensive, scrambling for an explanation that will satisfy their hunger for results without revealing the truth. "Patience is crucial," I insist, my voice steady despite the internal chaos. "Every step must be calculated. We can't risk arousing Saturn's suspicions."

Malachi leans forward, skepticism written all over

his face. "Six months, Miles. Even the most cautious plans should have borne fruit by now. What exactly is the holdup?"

I feel like a cornered animal, trapped by their expectations and my own web of lies. "The dynamics are more complex than anticipated. Gaining Saturn's complete trust isn't something that can be rushed without raising alarms," I explain, hoping to buy more time.

Lucius, ever the strategist, isn't convinced. "You've had ample time to 'gain trust,' Miles. What we need are results, not excuses. The Conclave's patience isn't infinite."

Their frustration is palpable, a tangible force pressing down on me. I'm walking a tightrope, trying to balance the Conclave's demands with my desperate need to protect Saturn. "Trust me," I plead, "I'm as committed to our goals as ever. But rushing this could destroy everything we've worked towards." The room falls into a tense silence, their dissatisfaction clear. I know I'm running out of time, and with every moment that passes, the danger to Saturn – and to the fragile peace I've found with her – grows. The Conclave's impatience is a ticking time bomb, and I'm the only one who can defuse it. But how, without risking everything I hold dear?

Their doubt hangs thick in the air, a suffocating fog, and I understand the necessity of treading carefully, prioritizing Saturn's safety above all else. "I have a comprehensive plan," I assure them, my heart burdened by the weight of deception. "But we must proceed with caution; Saturn's powers must fully manifest for our success."

I present the Conclave of Shadows with a meticulous strategy, satisfying their hunger for power with calculated precision, leveraging their desire for control.

"Everyone, please exercise patience," I assert with calculated confidence. "Saturn's powers cannot simply be unlocked; they must align with cosmic forces."

Crafting a tale of cosmic convergence, I weave intricate details of heavenly bodies, and occult alignments shrouded in mystery. "Her abilities are intertwined with cosmic cycles, mysteries, and bound by mystical resonance, vibrations, frequencies." We must harness these alignments and frequencies in a ceremonial ritual to unlock them."

The Conclave is enthralled by the complexity of my plan, enticed by the idea of manipulating the cosmos and gaining supernatural prowess. "Only when the stars align perfectly," I explain, "will Saturn's powers fully manifest, ready for us to harness and wield."

By diverting their focus from Saturn to the celestial realm, I ensure they remain oblivious to my true intentions. This elaborate ruse grants me the time needed to strategize Saturn's relocation to a secure hideaway, safeguarding her from the clutches of the Conclave's malevolence.

Each carefully crafted word weaves a tapestry of mystique, veiling my true intentions beneath a facade of celestial manipulation—a calculated deception to safeguard Saturn from the Conclave's predatory grasp.

As the meeting with the Conclave of Shadows draws to a tense close, Lysandra and I make our exit, our footsteps echoing against the cold marble floors. The air outside is crisp, a sharp contrast to the stifling atmosphere we've just left behind. We don't speak until we're safely ensconced in the sleek, shadowed interior of my penthouse, the city lights of New York sprawling out below us like a glittering, chaotic tapestry.

I pour us each a glass of whiskey, the liquid amber catching the light as I hand one to Lysandra. She takes a sip, then turns to me, a grin spreading across her face. "Good job, bro! That was quick thinking and a perfect response and plan to keep them busy!" she exclaims, her voice carrying a mixture of relief and admiration.

I can't help but return her smile, feeling a weight lift from my shoulders, if only temporarily. "Thanks, Lizzy," I say, using the childhood nickname that slips out in moments like these. "It wasn't easy, but as long as it keeps Saturn safe, I'll spin them any story they want to hear."

We clink our glasses together, the sound sharp in the quiet of the room. Lysandra's praise is a balm to the worry that's been a constant companion these past months. Her support, once uncertain, now feels like a solid foundation I can rely on.

As we settle into the plush couch, the city's nightlife providing a backdrop to our conversation, we start to plan our next steps. "We need to be even more careful now," Lysandra advises, her tone serious. "The Conclave's patience might be wearing thin, but your plan bought us some time."

I nod, fully aware of the tightrope we're walking. "We'll use that time wisely. We have to," I assert, determination steeling my voice. The thought of Saturn, unaware of the danger that shadows her every step, strengthens my resolve.

Lysandra leans back, her gaze thoughtful as she surveys the skyline. "We'll protect her, Miles. No matter what it takes," she promises, and I feel a renewed sense of purpose.

As Lysandra makes her way to leave, a thought crosses my mind—a bridge I've been meaning to build between her and Saturn. "By the way, Saturn really wants to get to know you better. Could you come to the mansion for lunch or dinner soon?" I venture, hoping to foster a connection that could strengthen our united front.

Lysandra pauses, her expression softening. "Sure, Bro. That sounds nice. Just let me know when," she responds, a hint of warmth in her voice.

The possibility of bringing Lysandra closer to Saturn fills me with cautious optimism. It's not just about forming alliances; it's about building a family, one that stands together against the shadows threatening to engulf us. As Lysandra agrees, the seeds of a new beginning are sown, promising a united future where love and loyalty are our strongest shields against the darkness.

CHAPTER 28

"THE MIRROR'S REFLECTION"

Last night, as I lay awake in the silence of the Nightshade Mansion, a realization hit me hard: I have to leave. The mansion, once a symbol of love and security, now feels like a gilded cage. My heart races, thoughts swirling like a tempest about the future of our unborn child and the true intentions of Miles.

With every tick of the clock, my resolve hardens. I can't shake off the anxiety that Miles might be entangled in plans that could harm our baby. The fear that our child, destined to inherit remarkable abilities, could be in danger under the same roof that was supposed to protect us is unbearable.

Tonight, the mansion seems eerily quiet, almost as if it is holding its breath, waiting for what I am about to do next. Miles has left for New York, giving me the perfect opportunity to leave. His absence is the perfect cover for my escape. I need clarity, away from the shadows of doubt that have crept into our home.

I hastily send a text to Laila, my fingers trembling as I type:

"Hey, Laila, I need a few days off. Won't be in the office. Can't talk about it right now, but I promise to explain everything later. Please don't worry and don't come looking for me. Love you."

Recalling the news Laila revealed to me at the wedding reception, I don't want her to know what's happened, and I need to keep her in the dark about this until I get things figured out. I wonder to myself if this was the looming threat she mentioned; plus, if Miles decided to search for me at the office, she wouldn't have any answers that could lead him or anyone else to me. The decision to leave isn't easy, but it is necessary. I decided to call an Uber for a pickup a little ways from the mansion so I wouldn't be seen or caught on any of the cameras in our secure neighborhood. I leave the mansion and head out to meet the Uber.

Telekinesis becomes my unseen hand, moving objects and clearing my path with just a thought. The mansion responds to my silent commands, doors unlocking and closing behind me as I pass, a silent accomplice to my escape.

As I step into the freedom of the night, every ability I possess harmonizes into a symphony of escape. The wind caresses my face with the promise of freedom, the earth guides my steps, and the moonlit sky bears witness to my liberation. My heart is a tumult of emotions — fear, excitement, determination — each beat a step further from my past and toward an uncertain future.

As I move, "Lunar Dreams" weaves a veil of illusions around the guards. It's like casting a spell that envelops their minds, making them see what I want them to see — nothing. Their dreams become my allies, shielding my escape in the depths of their subconscious, making me invisible to their waking eyes.

The "Feline Instincts" within me stir, lending me the grace and stealth of a night prowler. Each step I take is calculated and silent, almost as if I am gliding across the ground. The Feline Grace Flower's essence courses through me, sharpening my senses, and allowing me to move like a shadow through the darkness, unnoticed and free.

"Earth's Resonance" calls to me, the vegetation whispering secrets of escape. The leaves rustle softly under my touch, parting to reveal hidden pathways that only I can see. It's as if the earth itself is guiding me, its fertile embrace offering shelter and camouflage as I make my way through the lush grounds of the estate. ,

The voices of my ancestors, "Ancestral Guidance," echo in my heart, offering wisdom and courage. Their presence is a comforting reminder that I am not alone and that generations of strength and knowledge are with me, guiding my steps through the labyrinth of my escape.

With "Elemental Manipulation," I call upon the forces of nature to aid me. The elements respond to their power at my fingertips, allowing me to bend reality to my will. I whisper to the wind, and it answers, hiding my presence; I beckon to the shadows, and they deepen, cloaking me from view.

After walking a few blocks, I reach the corner where the Uber driver awaits. I'm heading to Eridanus Mansion, my family's home, and now a safe haven for me and my baby. The drive is a short one since the Mansion is nestled in the forest that stretches out behind Nightshade mansion, it's only an eight-block drive away around the forest. I had the driver drop me off at the edge of the forest so I could walk the rest of the way to the mansion.

I move with a purpose, blending the ancient wisdom of my ancestors with the raw power of the elements, crafting a path of escape that is as mystical as it is strategic. The world around me seems to pause, acknowledging the gravity of the moment, as if nature itself holds its breath, rooting for my success. I can't help but feel a surge of empowerment. For the first time in what feels like forever, I am not just Saturn, the one ensnared in a web of deceit and power struggles. I am Saturn, the seeker of truth, the wielder of ancient magick, embarking on a journey to discover my destiny, guided by the whispering winds, the dreaming moon, and the nurturing earth. This is my moment of rebirth, a leap into the unknown, armed with the magick that courses through my veins and the wisdom of those who came before me.

I move cautiously through the forest, my senses heightened to every rustle, every flicker of movement. Moonlight filters through the dense canopy above, illuminating my path along the forest trail. Its gentle glow serves as a guiding light amidst the surrounding darkness, leading my way with a soft, reassuring presence.

As I venture deeper into the dense forest that surrounds the Eridanus Mansion, my heart is a cacophony of beats, each one echoing my whirlpool of thoughts. The mansion, in its neglected splendor, seems to whisper tales of bygone eras, beckoning me into its arms like an old friend promising refuge from the storm of confusion that rages within me.

I feel a vice-like grasp of uncertainty that intermingles with my will to keep moving forward. Even though the mansion is dilapidated and abandoned, there is something mysteriously alluring about it—a possible oasis in a world suddenly full of uncertainties and shadows.

My heart thunders like a drum, its rhythm echoing the turmoil within me. I'm caught in a whirlwind of apprehension and fear, a tempest of conflicting emotions threatening to consume me entirely. Can this inherited mansion offer refuge, or will its labyrinthine corridors only serve to further obscure my path?

As I trek through the forest towards the mansion, memories flood my mind from almost a year ago. I remember the anticipation of walking through those majestic French doors, imagining the cherished experiences of my ancestors. It feels like I'm watching an old film reel playing out before me.

But suddenly, the memories fade into the mist of uncertainty. The desire for safety clashes with the fear of being alone in this unfamiliar place. Yet, despite my apprehension, the mansion's allure pulls me closer with an undeniable force.

A flurry of questions about Miles, my abilities, and the mysterious forces that now appeared to be invading my life swirl around me with every step closer. I am desperate for answers, for clarity, anything to calm the storm inside of me.

As I walk through the dark woodland behind the Eridanus Mansion, an awful discomfort comes over me like a ghostly mist. The shadows flicker, tricking my senses into thinking there could be an unidentified presence. I write it off at first as a figment of my overactive imagination, a frazzled mind, a fantasy of my own making in this lonely space.

However, as I cautiously move forward, the figure in front of me comes to life and approaches with purpose.

I am overcome with panic, erasing all illusion and uncertainty.

My heart pounds out of my chest as I realize—someone is actually walking up to me; somebody is really there. I'd only seen shadows before, here and there leading up to this moment, and no matter how ultimately powerful I am supposed to be, the shock that it is an actual person approaching me terrifies me.

My mind races, trying to figure out who it could be. It doesn't seem right that Miles would arrive so quickly. The gravity of the situation cuts through my fear and makes me turn, and run for cover instead of giving in to the unidentified threat.

As I turn, an incredible sight meets me—a figure soaring from the air with otherworldly elegance, landing before me in a spectacular display of supernatural prowess. I am filled with fear and confusion when I suddenly realize that I have been followed and that my ability to leave has been obstructed.

In that bizarre moment, an extraordinary and astonishing female appears in front of me. Her stylish clothes reflect her otherworldly beauty, commanding attention. Her icy-blue eyes, framed by raven-black hair, possess a mystifying charm.

An internal wave of emotions swirls in my belly; dread, curiosity, and a strong urge to survive. I cling to my protective instincts and abilities and the developing life inside of me with all of my being. I brace myself, prepared to face the unidentified being and protect the two of us with all I have inside of me from this unanticipated danger that suddenly stands in my way.

When my tear-stained eyes meet hers in that unsettling moment in the nocturnal shadows, a world of confusion and inner struggle engulfs me. I am stunned to pick up on the energy of this beautiful woman. In this eerie forest, I come to the realization that this person has a strong bond with Miles.

In a confused and shaky voice, I utter, "Who the hell are you?" The shock on my face is evident, a spark of optimism blended with suspicion. But in her reply, she reveals something that completely upends my frail understanding of my new reality: "What do you mean? You don't know me? Hasn't Miles mentioned me?"

"Who are you?" I repeat with a hint of frustration and confusion in my voice.

She answers, "No worries, I'll tell you who I am, little witch. I'm Seraphina, and I have known Miles for more than a decade." The name Seraphina hovers there, her words weaving a complex web of deceit and betrayal. Tears form, a torrent of feelings overtaking my senses.

I figure Miles had deceived me, just like Daniel had, but when Seraphina sees the tears, she says, "Look at you, crying already, and I haven't even told you the best part yet. Typical for someone so young and pure!" Again, I ask, "What do you mean?"

"I asked Miles so many times to bring you to me, to us, but he didn't, he just kept making excuses and ignoring us, I couldn't wait any longer, so I came myself. What are you doing here in this forest?" After midnight? Alone? Without Miles? Did you leave him?" She continues on in a humorous manner. "I must tell you; I am very surprised to learn the true depths of yours and Miles' relationship, Mrs. Nightshade."

"What if I have left him?" I ask. "You can't leave him," she adds, her attitude shifting to one of rage and frustration. "We haven't gotten what we came for from you."

As I try to make sense of all the bullshit coming out of her mouth, my confusion grows. I ask about Miles' true intentions, "You are the one Miles was talking to about a week ago, right?" He was chastising you and asking, no demanding that you exercise patience, right? "Oh snap, so this is the reason you're here all alone? You're having doubts about Miles, that he doesn't really love you, right?" Seraphina asks as if she senses my internal anguish. She goes on, "Let me tell you a little secret, little witch: Miles was planning to propose to you and get married in order to gain your trust and eventually all your powers. But now that you've decided to run away and hide, it's ruining everything, WITCH! He doesn't love you.

We knew about your powers even before they awoke inside of you." Her look shifts to one of frustration with a tinge of fury as if she is trying too hard to control her patience.

Seraphina's story unravels, presenting a harsh picture of the coven's plans, of schemes hatched to trap me, to harness the powers that lie dormant within.

I am overcome with a wave of shock and heartbreak, realizing that everything, including Miles' proposal and our marriage, had been an entirely evil plan to get me to awaken all of my abilities that I had been completely oblivious to.

My thoughts race, repeating what she had said, and the broken pieces of trust feel like they would swallow me whole. With the shards of love and the truth of yet another deceit tearing at my heart, the air becomes heavy.

As she continues, her revelations break me, and I find it difficult to comprehend the immense wave of emotions that wash over me as Seraphina's admissions crush me. I stand in that dark woodland, a broken soul amid the eerie whispers of the night, filled with betrayal, hurt, and a deep sense of loss.

Seraphina's abilities surge, dark energy enveloping her as she seems to prepare to unleash what seems like a ritual. Panic and desperation churn within me as I struggle to process the devastating revelations she has just laid bare.

"I can't let her succeed. I won't let her strip me of

everything I hold dear," I vow silently to myself, determination igniting a fierce flame within my core.

My stomach drops when I realize what she is doing. The Ritual of Reflection commences; its sinister purpose unfolding before my eyes. My heart clenches with fear as Seraphina wields her powers, her intentions clear and menacing. With every incantation, every movement, she draws closer to severing my connection to my ancestors, to stealing the wisdom and strength they bestow upon me.

"Fight back, Saturn! You can't let her win," I urge myself, the urgency of the moment driving me to action. With trembling hands and a racing mind, I summon every ounce of my own power to resist her dark magick.

The ritual demands a mirror-like object engraved with the names of chosen ancestors, a conduit through which the ancestral spirits will be forced to acknowledge their presence. It is a battle of wills, a struggle for control over the very essence of my being.

"Hold on, Saturn. Don't let her break you," I whisper to myself, the echoes of my ancestors' voices urging me to stand firm against the encroaching darkness.

As Seraphina continues to channel her malevolent energies, I feel a profound sense of loss wash over me. The bond that has always anchored me, the connection to my ancestors that has guided my every step, is slipping through my fingers like grains of sand. "No! I won't let her take this from me," I cry out inwardly, my defiance ringing loud and clear amidst the chaos of the ritual. With every fiber of my being, I fight against the tide of despair threatening to engulf me, clinging desperately to the fragments of my shattered identity.

But despite my best efforts, I can feel myself weakening, my resolve faltering in the face of Seraphina's relentless assault. The realization hits me like a physical blow, the crushing weight of defeat bearing down upon me with suffocating force.

"I can't do this alone. I need help," I admit to myself, the admission a bitter pill to swallow. With one final, desperate plea to the spirits of my ancestors, I reach out into the void, grasping for the lifeline that will save me from the abyss.

CHAPTER 29

"ECHOES OF ABSENCE"

As I return to San Francisco, a whirlwind of emotions swirls within me. The anticipation of seeing Saturn fills me with excitement and longing. Her embrace has always been my sanctuary, offering solace and comfort in times of uncertainty.

Approaching our house, excitement courses through me. I miss Saturn's warmth, a guiding light amidst my conflicting loyalties. My heart hastens as I remember the pregnancy test and wonder to myself, "Was it positive or negative?"

Walking into our home, my heart's racing with the thought of seeing Saturn, but instead, I'm met with a deafening quiet. Our bedroom, normally a cocoon of our shared lives, feels hollow without her. It's like the air's been sucked out, leaving a chill of loneliness that wraps around me.

I roam through the house, from the living room where we've shared countless nights talking and laughing, to the kitchen that's seen us cooking together, but she's nowhere. Each room echoes back my own footsteps, a stark reminder she's not here. The anticipation I had walking in turned into a knot of worry in my stomach.

"Saturn?" My voice echoes off the walls, sounding more desperate with each call. But there's no response, just the silence that's growing heavier by the second. The realization hits me hard—she's gone, and I'm here, left in the wake of her absence.

With a sense of desperation clawing at my chest, I pull out my phone, dialing her number only to be greeted by the impersonal tone of her voicemail. "Baby, it's me. Please, call me back as soon as you get this. I love you." I plead into the silence, my voice betraying my growing panic.

Next, I send a barrage of texts, each one more urgent than the last, but the lack of response only serves to amplify my worry. The digital silence from her end feels like a chasm widening between us, and I'm powerless to bridge it.

As the night deepens, so does the sense of isolation that envelopes me. Each unanswered call and text is a reminder of how quickly warmth can turn to cold, how suddenly presence can shift to absence. The house, once a sanctuary of our shared life, now feels like a maze of unanswered questions and unspoken fears, leaving me adrift in a sea of uncertainty.

I make a beeline for the security team, heart pounding in my chest. "Guys, have you seen Saturn? She's not in our room, not anywhere I've checked," I blurt out, trying to mask the rising panic in my voice.

There's an awkward shuffle among them, eyes not quite meeting mine. "Sir, we... we haven't seen Mrs. Nightshade since early evening," one of the guards finally speaks up, his voice laced with unease.

"What do you mean you haven't seen her? Isn't monitoring her whereabouts part of your job?" My frustration bubbles over, fear tinging every word.

Another guard steps forward, "We've been on high alert, Mr. Nightshade, but she didn't inform us of any plans to leave the mansion tonight. We assumed she was in for the night."

The room spins a little as their words sink in. "So, you're telling me, she could be anywhere right now? Alone, without any of you knowing?" I press, desperation creeping into my tone.

"Yes, sir, but we can start a search right away, check the cameras, the perimeter..." the first guard suggests, already moving towards the security panel.

I nod, barely registering his words as my mind races with worry. "Do it. Find her. She can't have gone far, right?" The silence that answers me is deafening, the quiet of the mansion now a screaming absence of her presence.

Moment by moment, my uncertainty deepens, morphing into a tangible fear. Did Saturn step out driven by fear, or was there a pressing need she couldn't ignore? Silence is my only companion as I sift through my thoughts, desperately searching for a clue. It's a gut feeling that steers me towards Eridanus Mansion, an instinct I can't shake off.

Fueled by a mix of hope and dread, I make my way to the Eridanus Mansion. Each step feels heavier than the last, the distance between Saturn and me growing with every breath. But as the mansion's imposing silhouette cuts through the tree line, a faint spark of hope flickers to life inside me.

The mansion's grand appearance, with its pristine white walls and soothing teal accents, strangely feels like a beacon of hope. I ascend the familiar steps, drawn in by the warm glow emanating from behind the windows, half-expecting, half-hoping to find Saturn here. The foyer's opulence strikes me anew as I step inside—its elegant wallpaper, the sparkling chandelier above, and the grand staircase all stand as silent witnesses to the life within. Yet, for all its beauty, the mansion feels hollow, echoing my own sense of loss. As I navigate the silent halls of Eridanus Mansion, the thought strikes me out of nowhere, "When did she find the time to clean this place up? It looks amazing." Even amidst my growing worry, I can't help but be taken aback by the meticulous care evident in every corner of the mansion. The polished surfaces, the dust-free environment, the perfectly arranged decor—all of it speaks to an attention to detail that's both impressive and bewildering given the circumstances.

This observation, while minor in the grand scheme of things, momentarily distracts me from the gnawing concern for Saturn's whereabouts. It's a testament to her enduring spirit, a reminder of her presence even in her absence. The thought lingers as I prepare to leave, a mix of admiration and curiosity about when and why she took the time to transform the mansion into such a welcoming space.

Pushing through the weight of the silence in Eridanus Mansion, a thought suddenly sparks within me, "She's not here; maybe she went to her loft." With a surge of renewed hope, I quickened my pace, heading towards the familiar comfort of what used to be her home. My steps echo through the empty mansion, each one amplifying the anxious rhythm of my heart.

Arriving at Saturn's loft, I punch in the door code, head up to her floor, and pause at the threshold, my breath catching in anticipation. Opening the door with my key reveals a space that, while impeccably tidy and inviting, lacks the one thing I'm desperately seeking—Saturn. The loft stands silent and abandoned. My heart sinks, the faint hope that had guided me here evaporating into the stillness of the room.

The disappointment is palpable, a heavy cloak around my shoulders as I stand in the doorway, absorbing the emptiness. "She's not here," I whisper to myself, the words barely audible over the pounding in my chest. The realization that she's not in her loft, nor anywhere else, deepens the mystery and my concern for her whereabouts.

Leaving Saturn's loft, each step I take feels heavier than the last, echoing in the staircase. The notion that she felt compelled to leave, to possibly seek solace without me, twists inside me like a knife.

Dragging myself back to Nightshade Mansion, my mind races with plans and possibilities. "Massachusetts... Aunt Sage's house. She always felt safe there," I think to myself, the pieces of a plan beginning to form. The thought of Saturn, alone and possibly in need, propels me forward. "I have to find her."

The moment I zip up my bag, the reality hits me hard. "Booking a flight... That's going to take forever with public airlines; especially at SFO," I mutter, frustration building at the thought of wasting precious time on layovers and schedules. That's when an idea sparks, a glimmer of hope in the frantic pace of my planning. "Jack," I realize, the name of an old friend who's a pilot surfacing from the depths of my contacts. "He could fly me directly to Massachusetts."

I waste no time, my fingers moving swiftly over my phone to dial Jack's number. The phone rings, each tone echoing my escalating hope and desperation. "Hey, Jack, it's Miles... I need a huge favor, man," I begin, my voice a blend of urgency and hesitation. I can almost hear his eyebrows raise in surprise at my sudden call. After explaining the situation, barely pausing to catch my breath, I make my offer. "I'll pay you, Jack. Whatever you think's fair. I just... I need to get to Massachusetts as soon as possible." My plea hangs in the air, a testament to the seriousness of my request.

Jack's response, a mix of concern and camaraderie, doesn't keep me waiting long. "Alright, Miles. I'll do it. No problem." he says, his tone firm, leaving no room for doubt. Relief washes over me in an almost palpable wave. "Thank you, Jack. You have no idea how much this means to me."

The arrangement is set with efficiency that only years of friendship and a shared sense of urgency can produce. The price we settle on is more than fair, but under these circumstances, no expense could be too great. As my driver heads to the private airstrip where Jack's plane is waiting, each step feels lighter, propelled by the newfound hope that direct, swift action brings.

"I'm on my way, Saturn," I think to myself as the engine roars to life, the plane taxiing down the runway. "Just hang on a little longer." The flight to Massachusetts is a blur of anxiety and determination, the landscape below a mere backdrop to the tumult of emotions within. But with Jack at the helm, I'm closer than ever to finding Saturn, to bridging the distance that's felt like a chasm since I discovered her absence.

Landing in Massachusetts, memories flood my mind as I approach Aunt Sage's house, a place where Saturn and I had spent countless hours unraveling the mysteries of her past. "Oh my love, where can you be?" I whisper to myself, my voice barely a breath against the chilly air. This house, once a beacon of discovery and love, now stands silent, its emptiness mirroring the void in my heart. I move from room to room, each step a reminder of the moments we shared here, each space imbued with the laughter and whispers of our explorations. But now, the laughter has faded, and the whispers are gone, replaced by a deafening silence that seems to mock my desperation.

Finding her childhood home devoid of her presence, panic sets in. "She's not here," I realize, the hope that had propelled me here disintegrating with every passing second. It's then that I reach for my phone, dialing Lysandra's number with hands that tremble slightly, not from the cold but from fear.

"Lysandra, it's Miles... Saturn's missing," I say, the words feeling foreign on my tongue. "Do you know if the Conclave...?" My voice trails off, unable to finish the thought.

Her response comes quick and firm, "No, Miles, not

at all. I swear." There's a pause, and then, "I'll help you look for her. I'll start at the paper and keep an eye out around the city."

A wave of relief washes over me, not just at the reassurance that the Conclave isn't involved, but also at the offer of help. "Thank you," I manage to say, my gratitude genuine. "I... I appreciate it, Lysandra."

As I end the call, the silence of Aunt Sage's house envelops me once more, but now it's a little less oppressive, tempered by the knowledge that I'm not alone in my search. "I'll find you, Saturn," I vow, the promise to my love fueling my determination to keep searching, no matter what it takes. The dawn breaks, and I'm bone-tired, feeling every second of the night's search weigh down on me. The quiet around Aunt Sage's place is eerie like it's hiding something in the early morning mist. Before I leave, I decide to check the back, in the forest, just in case. And then I see it—a shadowy figure lurking at the edge of the trees, stirring a sense of familiarity in me, the kind I wish I didn't recognize. Daniel Darkwood vibes, no mistake about it. But as soon as I spot him, he's gone—vanished into thin air. "What the hell is Daniel doing here?" I mutter to myself, a mix of confusion and irritation bubbling up. My senses are sharp; it's one of the things I rely on, but this... this just adds another layer of mystery I don't have the time to unravel right now.

With no sign of Saturn and this unexpected twist,

my heart sinks even further. I've got to focus, can't let this throw me off. I pull out my phone, my fingers moving quickly over the screen to shoot a text to Jack. "Heading back to the airport," I type, urgency clear in every tap. This isn't over, not by a long shot. I've got to keep moving, keep searching. Whatever it takes, I'm going to find Saturn.

Heavy-hearted and filled with unanswered questions, I head back to San Francisco. If Saturn sought refuge anywhere in this turmoil, it would likely be there, a city that held significance in our journey together.

Driven by the need to close the gap that yawned suddenly between us, I leave the mystery of her past behind, focusing on the now. Landing back in San Francisco, the urgency to cover the miles needed to bring Saturn back to the safety of our shared world intensifies with every step toward the car.

The drive swallows miles, with the road unfurling before me and the engine's roar marking the urgency of my quest. Thoughts of Saturn, missing and alone, haunt me, urging me on.

San Francisco looms ahead, a beacon of hope amid the uncertainty. Driven by the desperate need to find Saturn, unravel the mystery that had torn us apart, and bring her back into our shared life, I press on. With each passing mile, my resolve to find her again only grows stronger.

CHAPTER 30

"EMBERS OF RESILIENCE"

The moment I realize one of my powers is gone, it's like the world stops spinning. I'm gutted, feeling this gaping hole where a part of me, something ancient and vital, used to be. That connection to my ancestors, to their wisdom and guidance, it's just... disappeared. Vanished. It's not just a loss; it feels like a part of my soul has been torn out.

I'm reeling, caught in a storm of emotions. Vulnerability crashes into me, leaving me feeling naked and raw in a suddenly hostile world. The certainty I once took for granted is gone, replaced by this aching void of uncertainty. How am I supposed to face this magickal, chaotic life without the ancestral compass that's been guiding me?

Grief and disbelief wage war inside me, alongside a burning anger. It's more than just losing power; it's like losing a piece of my identity, a connection to where I come from. The depth of this loss is staggering, shaking me to my very foundation.

But then, there's this flicker of something else amidst the tempest—determination. It's fragile, barely there, but it's enough to keep me from being swallowed by despair. I might have lost a crucial part of my magick, but I'm not beaten. Not yet.

That resolve grows stronger as I approach Eridanus Mansion, the absence of my ancestors' voices a hollow echo in my heart. But there's a new kind of courage brewing, born out of necessity and the fierce desire to protect what's still mine to fight for. The journey ahead looks daunting, each step heavy with the weight of the unknown. Yet, as I stand before the mansion, a symbol of all I've lost and all I'm fighting to keep, I'm steeling myself for whatever lies ahead. For me, for my baby, I'm ready to face whatever comes, guided by a newfound strength that whispers of hope and defiance.

Losing my connection to my ancestors has lit a different fire within me—one that burns with determination and a resolve to forge a new path, guided not by the wisdom of the past but by the strength of my own spirit. Amidst the chaos and fear, I find a sense of clarity and purpose, drawing on the unseen forces that still dance within me, ready to face the future with or without the guidance I once relied on.

After I lost my access to the ancestors, a whirlwind

of thoughts swept over me. The fact that my powers had failed me when I needed them the most had me wondering what the hell had gone wrong. I was totally confused. My abilities had come to serve as a beacon and an intricate aspect of who I was. This was a reminder of how vulnerable I am, even minus just one power.

I try to push aside the memory of failure, but it lingers persistently in the recesses of my mind. Why did my abilities falter at that critical moment, right when I faced off against that blue-eyed bitch? Was it mere coincidence, a test to gauge the extent of my powers? Or could there be a darker agenda at play? Fear of the unknown mingles with frustration, triggering a sudden migraine that throbs relentlessly, a physical manifestation of the tangled emotions swirling within me. I grapple with a whirlwind of conflicting emotions—skepticism, resentment, and an insatiable urge to uncover the truth behind this baffling situation. How on earth did she manage to strip me of my power of Ancestral Guidance without performing the intricate Ritual of Reflection, a complex and meticulous ceremony outlined solely in my Book of Shadows? And more importantly, how did she gain access to my sacred book in the first place? The unanswered questions gnaw at my mind, fueling a growing sense of frustration and suspicion.

The already tumultuous situation becomes even

more perplexing as I grapple with the mystery of how she managed to acquire the information held within my Book of Shadows—and the unsettling suspicion that Miles may have played a role in it. After all, they've had a close relationship for over a decade.

As I press on toward the Eridanus mansion, the weight of unanswered questions bears down on me. The desire to reclaim what's rightfully mine clashes with the uncertainty of what lies ahead, leaving me in a state of mental and spiritual disarray.

Approaching the mansion, I'm struck by a strange blend of familiarity and unease. In the early morning light, its grandeur is imposing yet inviting, like stepping into a world frozen in time. As I cross the threshold, memories of my initial exploration upon arriving in San Francisco flood back, echoing the timeless aura both inside and out.

As soon as I step inside, I kick into high gear, determined to whip this place into shape. Being a clean freak, I head straight for the master bedroom. With this being a long-term stay, it's essential to freshen up the sheets, comforters, and any other linens I can find. It's like Auntie Sage knew I'd end up here one day, as all the essentials are already laid out. "Thank you, Auntie," I murmur, sending a grateful wink to the air.

I dive into the cleaning process with gusto, folding, creasing, spraying, wiping, vacuuming, and sweeping my way through the mansion. It's meticulous work, but

I know it's necessary. "Have I mentioned how much of a clean freak I am?" I chuckle to myself as I work, determined not to let up, knowing time is of the essence.

The kitchen and bathroom pose their own challenges, each corner revealing signs of neglect over the years. It's like they're begging for a complete overhaul. I find solace in cleaning, using it as a form of meditation to temporarily escape my nagging discomfort. The day stretches on, and by the time I finish, exhaustion weighs heavily on me.

Hungry and depleted, I realize I've forgotten to stock up on food for the days ahead. The mansion's cupboards are bare, a stark reminder of its untouched state since my mother's passing.

Standing in the newly gleaming kitchen, I feel a sense of accomplishment wash over me. Cleaning may not be my favorite task, especially when it comes to the kitchen and bathroom, but seeing the transformation is gratifying. The room now exudes a timeless beauty.

I turn to admire the polished cupboards, marveling at how different they look after a day of scrubbing them down to their original wood. As I mentally take inventory of each shelf, my thoughts shift to the next task at hand: stocking up on supplies, especially food. Going out to get supplies is going to be a real challenge. I'm so isolated here at the mansion, and I prefer walking to avoid any risk of being spotted driving like clockwork, hunger grips me. "Why didn't I bring food?"

I lament aloud, uncertain if Instacart will deliver. Yet, as a pregnant woman settling into a remote forest mansion sans provisions, I must find sustenance. Quickly accessing the Instacart app, I confirm they do deliver. "Yes!" I rejoice inwardly, placing a hefty order for groceries and essentials. Opting for a week's supply, uncertainty looms over the duration of my stay. "Done," I affirm, anticipating a bath while I await delivery.

My final task is to protect myself and veil the mansion from Miles or anyone else who might come looking for me and the baby. I weave a layer of magick around the mansion, concealing any evidence of my recent activities and dissipating any lingering energy that could give away my presence. It's the only way I can feel safe, creating a decoy to deflect any unwanted attention from this hidden oasis in the wilderness.

Suddenly, a familiar voice breaks through the silence, tinged with desperation. It's Miles, pleading for me to come out, to return and explain why I left. Despite his chivalry and the aura of the love we shared, I'm not ready to face him yet. I slide into the shadows, concealing myself behind the mansion's opulent facade, observing him as he searches, noting the solemnity of his request.

As Miles walks away, his face marked with worry, I'm caught in a turmoil of emotions. Part of me yearns to lower the magickal barrier and rush into his embrace, yet Seraphina's insinuations haunt me—the idea that his concern might not truly be for me, but rather for the powers he's after, the abilities he's hunting. When the Instacart driver arrives, I reluctantly lower the barrier spell, relieved to see the delivery of more cleaning supplies, toiletries, water, and food. It's a small comfort in the midst of uncertainty. A sense of seclusion envelops me as I return to my tasks inside the mansion, organizing supplies and preparing a meal. It's my form of meditation, a way to center myself amidst the chaos. I yearn to venture out into the garden to soak in the beauty of nature surrounding the Eridanus Mansion, but I hesitate, unsure if I can conceal myself from prying eyes for long enough.

Rummaging through my Book of Shadows, I uncover a concealment spell—a cloak of invisibility to shield me from unwanted attention. With a few whispered incantations, I shroud myself from sight, retreating further into the mansion's depths.

The mansion holds mysteries waiting to be unraveled, secrets that may hold the answers to my recent struggles with my powers. There's a surge in my abilities, followed by an unexplained halt—a puzzle I'm determined to solve.

The library, with its towering shelves of dusty tomes, beckons to me—a sanctuary of knowledge waiting to be unearthed. As I delve into the books, searching for clues to unlock the mystery of my powers' erratic behavior, I can't shake the feeling of frustration.

I should have been able to defend against the theft of my powers, and I need to understand why I failed.

Entering the library, an overwhelming urge to dust off the neglected volumes consumes me, but exhaustion weighs heavily on my limbs. Despite my eagerness to embark on this new project, I recognize the need for rest. I mean, I literally walked here! With a reluctant sigh, I force myself to abandon the cleaning impulse, knowing that giving in would only leave me more fatigued come morning. I make a mental note to return to the library after breakfast, determined to uncover its secrets then.

CHAPTER 31

"ECHOES OF REGRET"

'm sitting in my softly lit bedroom, the soothing strains of high-frequency music from Saturn's Spotify playlist filling the air. "These frequencies will calm you and make you feel like a million bucks!" she used to say as she set it to repeat while we slept. But tonight, my mind is consumed by dread, my fingers absently tracing the rim of my beloved whiskey glass. Thoughts of Saturn whirl through my head, threatening to overwhelm me.

In the midst of panic and desperation, a thought strikes me like lightning. "Boom! I can find her! With my powers, I can enter a temporal loop and see exactly what happened!" I exclaim aloud to myself. Taking a deep breath, I focus my energy and call upon my abilities to manipulate temporal loops. It's not about altering history; it's about glimpsing moments in time, searching for any sign of what led to Saturn's departure from our home.

As I delve into the recent past, time begins to shift and twist around me, unfolding like a motion picture. Scenes flicker before my eyes as I scour the hours leading up to her disappearance, desperate for answers. My powers allow me to witness events as they unfolded, searching for any clue, any hint of where Saturn might be and what led her to leave.

I immediately spot the positive pregnancy test, and my heart skips a beat. "We're going to have a baby," I whisper aloud, the words tinged with excitement and disbelief. But as the reality sinks in, I'm engulfed in a whirlwind of emotions. The joy of impending fatherhood mingles with confusion and guilt, a heavy weight settling in the pit of my stomach. As I sift through the fragments of conversations from the night before, searching for clues, a pang of sorrow grips me. It becomes clear; that she overheard my conversation with Lysandra. Each word spoken and unspoken weighs heavily on my conscience, fueling a sense of remorse.

With determination, I hone in on a faint link, a subtle connection to Saturn's spirit. Following this elusive trail, I move with purpose, driven by an unrelenting desire to set things right. Every memory of her, every moment, serves as a guide in my quest to find her.

With a determined expression, I set down my drink. My resolve to find Saturn and protect her, and our unborn child, is unwavering.

Guilt gnaws at me as I replay the events leading up to Saturn's departure. The look of mistrust and uncertainty on her face during my conversation with my sister, Lysandra, weighs heavily on me. I realize with a sinking feeling that I may have inadvertently ruined what should have been a joyous moment—the announcement of a positive pregnancy test.

As I piece together the timeline, using my temporal loop ability, it dawns on me that Saturn chose to leave on her own. She headed for the Eridanus mansion—a decision that sparked both relief and a new wave of worry, especially given her condition. My heart races as I comb through the security footage once more, only to find it void of any signs of her, confirming my suspicions that she's used a spell to conceal her presence.

I'm gripped by an urgency that propels me forward, thoughts racing as I prepare to leave. The idea that she sought refuge in her family home; the one spot she'd consider safe enough to hide, is both comforting and alarming. As I set out for the Eridanus mansion once again, the short drive is torturous, each second filled with scenarios of what I'm about to find—or not find.

I can't shake the feeling that I missed something crucial during my first visit. Maybe it was the desperation to find her, or the panic clouding my judgment, but I overlooked the possibility of her using magick to stay hidden. The mansion, with its sprawling grounds and countless memories, suddenly feels like the last piece of a puzzle I've been trying to solve in a haze of fear and confusion.

The moment I pull up to the mansion, a heavy dread settles over me, like a thick fog I can't see through. This place, steeped in her past and now possibly a refuge in her anger feels like a fortress keeping me at bay. The idea that Saturn felt compelled to leave, to cloak herself in magick so thoroughly, sends a chill down my spine. She must have been beyond furious, and the reason for that fury—my lack of honesty—twists my stomach into knots.

I had promised her transparency, an open-book approach to our life together. But that conversation with Lysandra, the one she overheard, broke that promise in the worst way. Now, standing before the mansion, I'm grappling with the enormity of what I've done. The thought that I might have lost not just my wife but my unborn child too because I couldn't uphold my word is crushing.

I rush from the car to the French Doors, each step laden with a heavy blend of fear and determination. My heart races as I'm consumed by the need to find Saturn, to apologize, to heal the rift my silence has created. The mansion looms, silent and daunting, a tangible obstacle to the reconciliation I desperately seek.

Shadows and whispers seem to hide her from me, ironically shielding her from the one who swore to protect her. This realization sharpens my resolve to bridge the gap my mistakes have widened. Yet, as I approach the doors, the once majestic mansion now seems less grand, casting doubt on my hunch about her whereabouts. "Could she really not be here?" I question myself, hope dimming.

Calling out her name yields no response, deepening my despair. I search the gloomy rooms to no avail, her absence echoing through the empty spaces.

I step into the sprawling quiet of this neglected mansion, and instantly, a peculiar sensation wraps around me, like an embrace from the unseen. It's Saturn's unmistakable vibe, her essence—a melody softly playing in the background, filling the air with warmth and a hint of jasmine, her signature scent. This place, with its peeling wallpaper and dust-laden corners, hardly feels like our home. We've only breezed through its halls a time or two, dreaming out loud of what could be, but it remains more a project than a sanctuary. The echoes of our aspirations hang in the air, so tangible yet just out of reach.

As I wander through the shadowed rooms, it's as if the mansion begins to stir, recognizing my presence. Walls that once hid themselves behind decay now start to shimmer with life, revealing the grandeur of a time when Saturn and I first dreamed up our future here. It's an uncanny transformation; signaling her presence; the entire house seems to awaken, shedding its dreariness to offer me a glimpse of the house that greeted me that first day I stepped into this place searching for Saturn.

The stark contrast jolts me, pulling me deeper into the mystery of her absence. "Saturn, baby, are you here?" I murmur into the silence, half-expecting her to emerge from the shadows with that mischievous sparkle in her eyes.

Suddenly, a noise—a thud, distant yet distinct—cuts through the stillness. My heart races, hope surging with every step as I follow the sound. The palpable shift in the mansion's aura seems to be acting as a beacon guiding me closer to Saturn, or so I wish.

"Saturn, if that's you, please come out and talk to me," I call out, my voice echoing off the walls, mingling with the lingering traces of laughter and whispered secrets. The heavy silence that follows is charged with the weight of unsaid words and unexplored possibilities.

At this moment, the mansion isn't just a structure of bricks and mortar; it's a testament to our uncharted journey together. The revival of its beauty mirrors the resilience of our connection, challenging the shadows, and daring me to believe in the impossible.

"Come out, please come out, my love," I beg, my words a blend of hope and desperation. The thought that Saturn could be here, hiding in plain sight, is both exhilarating and maddening. This game of hide and seek with fate, with our future, ignites a fire within me. I'm ready to tear down these revived walls if it means finding her, unraveling the mystery of her silence. The mansion, now a beacon of past warmth and present mystery, holds its breath, waiting for the next move in our story—a story of love, of searching, and of the undying hope that somewhere in its revived corridors, Saturn waits for me.

"Saturn!" I cry out, my voice reverberating through the empty halls of the mansion. "Are you here, my love? Please, come out. I haven't seen you in a week, and I'm worried sick. I need to see you, to hold you in my arms."

But my pleas are met with silence, save for the faint hum of magick that seems to envelop the house. I am positive now that Saturn has cast a spell, concealing herself from me, and it explains why I couldn't find her earlier.

In a desperate attempt to reach her, I implore her to break the spell. "We need to talk, Saturn. I know you're using magick to conceal yourself. Please, come out. How can we resolve anything if you won't even speak to me? Please, my love, I beg of you."

Suddenly, a voice fills the air, ethereal and tinged with emotion. It's Saturn, speaking to me from beyond the physical realm. Her words cut through me like a knife. "Why did you do it?" she asks, her voice heavy with hurt and confusion. I'm taken aback, unsure of what she's referring to. What have I done that she's unaware of, aside from the conversation with my sister, Lysandra? The question hangs in the air, a painful reminder of the rift between us. "Why did you share my spells from my Book of Shadows?" she demands.

CHAPTER 32

"UNRAVELING SHADOWS"

In the grand halls of Eridanus Mansion, shadows, dance, and whispers from the past linger. I hear Miles' voice, sincere and echoing in the silence, stirring a tempest within me—a longing to rush into his arms for refuge from the storm of betrayal that has ravaged my heart, yet fear keeps me anchored in place.

The enchantment I cast around myself was a shield, born out of necessity, not malice. Betrayal fractured my heart, making solitude my haven where I could nurse my wounds and gather the scattered pieces of myself. However, Miles' desperate pleas threaten this sanctuary. His voice, full of emotion and reaching out to me, promises understanding, forgiveness, and a love that can weather any storm.

I'm torn, battling between yielding to his pleas or maintaining the barriers I've so carefully erected. His presence beckons, promising healing and warmth, yet fear shackles me, leaving me hesitant to step forward and confront the truths that lay bare between us.

As his calls continue, the spell that cloaked me in invisibility begins to fade. The mansion, previously shrouded in darkness, bursts into life:

- Dust motes dance in beams of light, like tiny fairies celebrating their freedom.
- Chandeliers, once dim, now sparkle, casting prisms of light across the room.
- Furniture emerges from the shadows, their surfaces gleaming as if welcoming me back.

Stepping into the hallway, my footsteps echo, a reminder of the solitude that has been my constant companion. Yet, as I move forward, the mansion seems to whisper words of encouragement, its walls bearing witness to the tumult of emotions within me.

There he stands—Miles, in the doorway, his face a mix of worry and hope. A flood of emotions washes over me—relief at seeing him, fear of the unknown, and an undeniable pull towards the love we shared. I've kept him at a distance, protecting him from the darkness that consumes me. But now, I see no point in hiding any longer.

Our hands tremble as we reach for each other, locking eyes in a silent conversation. The mansion, our silent guardian, seems to hold its breath, anticipating the reunion of our souls intertwined by fate.

His touch, gentle yet filled with unspoken promises, sparks a glimmer of hope amidst the desolation. "Saturn," he whispers, his voice heavy with unshed tears, "I've been searching for you everywhere."

Yielding to his embrace, I allow myself a moment of vulnerability, letting tears stream down my face. His arms wrap around me, offering sanctuary, a refuge from the storm that has been raging within me.

Yet, as I step back, a shadow of doubt creeps in, fueled by the revelations Seraphina shared. The joy of our reunion is tainted by lingering questions, by the specter of deceit that looms over us.

"Miles, who is Seraphina?" I ask, my voice mixing curiosity and dread. His reaction, surprised and hesitant, deepens my unease.

"Saturn," he starts, struggle clear in his voice, "There's so much I need to tell you."

His words hang between us, an untraversed bridge, signifying the journey we still have to undertake together. The air thickens with unspoken truths, holding the promise of revelations that might mend or further widen the rift between us.

Standing in the dimly lit room of the Eridanus mansion, emotions battle within my heart. Seraphina's revelations cast a dark shadow over everything I thought I knew about Miles and our life together. "Why didn't you tell me about her, Miles?" I ask, my voice breaking under the weight of betrayal and confusion. "I thought we agreed on honesty before we got married. No secrets, nothing hidden."

Miles averts his gaze, looking at his hands, symbols of his guilt. "I was scared of how you'd react," he admits quietly, his voice almost lost in the room's vastness. "I couldn't bear the thought of losing you."

My patience thins. "Miles, just tell me everything. Who is Seraphina, and why does she claim our marriage was just a plot for you to exploit me?" The words burst forth, driven by a mix of heartache and a desperate need for the truth.

He looks up, his eyes full of remorse. "Saturn, I promise to explain," he starts, his voice shaking. "But you have to understand; it was never my intention to hurt you."

His assurances don't calm the storm inside me. I'm not looking for reassurance; I need the stark, unvarnished truth. "How did you even know about my powers before I did?" I press on, my voice rising with every word. "Seraphina said you knew. That's why you approached me. Is that true?"

Her accusations echo in my head, casting doubts and questions I can't ignore. Miles lets out a heavy sigh, the weight of the truth-bending him. "Yes, it's true. We knew about your abilities. Our group... we look for people with special talents, for our own gains."

Hearing him confirm my worst fears shatters something inside me. The realization that I've been nothing more than a target to him and his associates is a blow I'm not prepared for. "Why, Miles?" The question barely whispers past my lips. "Why be part of something so... cruel?"

Tears threaten to spill over, the sense of betrayal cutting deeper than anything I've ever felt. Miles reaches for my hand, his touch gentle, trying to bridge the chasm his secrets have created between us. "I was wrong, Saturn. I thought I could use it to make a difference and to help others. But I see now how mistaken I was."

His confession rings in my ears, a bitter reminder of the deceit that has tainted our relationship. I had given him my heart, only to find out he had secrets, hiding his true intentions behind a facade of love and concern. "How could you do this to me, Miles?" Anguish and anger color my words. "How could you betray me like this?"

As my tears finally break free, the overwhelming sense of loss and betrayal engulfs me. I trusted him with everything, only to be deceived. Miles looks down, his expression filled with regret. "I'm so sorry, Saturn. I never wanted to hurt you. I was afraid of losing you, of not having the chance to be together."

His words offer a glimmer of the love that once drew us together, but the damage is done. The betrayal is too deep, the wound too fresh. The trust we built is shattered, leaving us in the ruins of what could have been.

Standing here, amidst the lingering echoes of Miles' revelations, I find myself at the heart of a tale far more intricate and shadowed than any story I have ever heard. The weight of his words settles around us like a thick fog, both chilling and enlightening.

"You know, I guess I always sensed something...magickal about you," I murmur, my voice a mix of wonder and a hint of sadness. It's as if a piece of a puzzle I hadn't known I was assembling falls into place. Miles looks at me, his expression a blend of surprise and relief as if my acceptance has lifted a heavy burden off his shoulders.

"How did you know?" His curiosity is palpable, his gaze searching mine for answers he has long kept buried within the depths of his own secrets.

With a light chuckle, I shrug, "I've always been observant, Miles. You had a way of doing things...it was subtle but unmistakable for someone looking closely." My intuition, it seems, has pieced together the unseen magick that weaves through the fabric of his being.

Miles then delves deeper into his past, his voice a low cadence that speaks of hidden worlds and the heavy legacy of his lineage. "After my parents passed, Lysandra and I were woven into the Conclave of Shadows, a coven as old as the Eridanus coven," he confesses, a hint of sorrow lacing his words. This Conclave, a network of witches and warlocks, has always been a shadow lurking behind the scenes, now brought to light.

"They tasked me with finding you," he continues, regret shadowing his features. "Your powers were a beacon they couldn't resist." The thought sends a shiver down my spine, the idea of being hunted for something I have only recently come to understand myself.

"But, Saturn, my feelings for you, they're real," Miles implores, his eyes locking with mine. "I couldn't let them use you, not when I... when I love you." The sincerity in his voice tugs at my heart, a beacon of truth in a sea of deceit.

"How did they even know about me?" I ask, the question hanging between us like a sword. Miles shakes his head, the weight of the unknown pressing down on him. "It's the boss, whoever that is. They seem to know things...things they shouldn't."

The mention of this "boss," a figure shrouded in mystery and power, only deepens the intrigue and danger of our predicament. It's a reminder of the unseen forces that have set their sights on us, on me.

As our conversation draws to a close, I find myself standing at a crossroads. Miles' tale of hidden covenants, of love entwined with deception, has left its mark. Yet, beneath the layers of secrets and shadows, I see the glimmer of something pure—a love that has defied the darkness surrounding us. "I... I need time, Miles," I say, my voice barely above a whisper. "Time to process this, to understand where we go from here." The path ahead is uncertain, but one thing is clear: the journey we face is one we will have to navigate together, armed with honesty and the fragile hope of mending the fractures that deceit has wrought.

As I look up at the stars, their light seems to pierce the veil of the night, offering a silent promise that even in the darkest of tales, there can be a path leading back to light.

CHAPTER 33

"SHADOWS OF DECEPTION: UNVEILING TRUTHS"

As Saturn recounts her encounter with Seraphina, my heart sinks into the depths of despair and guilt. The thought of Saturn facing Seraphina alone, dealing with revelations that even I struggle to comprehend, fills me with an unbearable sense of regret.

"Who is this 'boss' you mentioned?" Saturn's voice, fragile and laced with uncertainty, forces me to confront the fact that I dragged her into a world filled with shadows and secrecy. "I wish I knew more, Saturn," I admit, my voice barely above a whisper. "He's always been a shadow, orchestrating from afar, his commands echoing through Malachi." The admission feels like confessing to a sin I can't atone for.

Her next question is even harder to bear. "Miles, how did you find out about my pregnancy?" The hurt in her voice is palpable. I look away, unable to meet her gaze. "I... I used my abilities, Saturn. I looked back through time, desperate for any sign of you." The words feel like ash in my mouth, a confession of my betrayal.

Saturn's reaction is a mix of shock and betrayal. It's clear I crossed a line, invading her privacy in the most intimate way. "I'm sorry, Saturn," I stammer, my apology sounding hollow even to my own ears. "I thought I was protecting you, but I see now I was only thinking of myself." Her response is a soft, heart-breaking whisper. "I need time to think." I nod, feeling a chasm opening between us, one that my apologies can't bridge.

Reflecting on Seraphina's encounter with Saturn, I feel a surge of protectiveness and rage. Seraphina has revealed the depth of my deception, unmasking the lie I've lived. "I never wanted to hurt you, Saturn," I say, the weight of my actions crushing me. "Everything I did, I did out of love, even though I now see how twisted my decisions were."

The air around us is charged with tension and unspoken words. Saturn's discovery of my betrayal, coupled with the knowledge that I spied on her, leaves a bitter taste of remorse. "I understand if you can't forgive me," I whisper, my voice breaking. "But know that my love for you was the one true thing in all of this deception."

As Saturn processes everything, the silence between

us grows, a testament to the gulf my actions have created. The pain of knowing I caused her suffering is a heavy burden, one I will carry with me always.

"I just wish things could have been different," I murmur, more to myself than to her. "I wish I could have been the man you deserved, not the one who brought you into this darkness."

The Eridanus mansion, with its magickal, mystical aura, stands as a silent witness to our conversation. The sounds of the night, the rustling leaves, and the distant call of nocturnal creatures seem to underscore the gravity of our situation. Amidst this magickal back-drop, I realize the true cost of my actions—a love that might never heal and a trust that is irrevocably broken.

In the dim light of the Eridanus mansion, I find myself grappling with the weight of revelations that have just come to light. Saturn's encounter with Seraphina has torn open a chasm of deception and betrayal I never intended for her to face. "She didn't hurt you, right?" The concern in my voice is palpable, mirroring the tumultuous storm of worry and appre-hension swirling within me. Saturn's response is a mere whisper, a soft confirmation that no physical harm has come to her, yet her words carry the weight of the emotional turmoil she endures. "No," she breathes out, the simple word echoing like a thunderclap in the quiet of the room.

Her next words send a shiver down my spine. "She just told me that she knew everything about you, about your plans, about your traps." The revelation strikes me with the force of a tempest; my deceit laid bare before the one person I vowed to protect above all else.

"She also mentioned that she has known you for over a decade," Saturn continues, her voice tinged with a mixture of confusion and sorrow. "She seemed to know you better than I do." The admission feels like a dagger to my heart, a painful reminder of the secrets I have kept and the trust I have fractured.

My mind races as Saturn recounts Seraphina's impatience, and her unilateral actions that have propelled her into our lives with a vengeance. The realization that Seraphina has conducted a ritual to sever Saturn's ancestral ties fills me with an overwhelming sense of dread. The very essence of what makes Saturn unique is now under threat, and the blame lies squarely at my feet.

"We're in grave danger, Saturn," I confess, my voice tinged with urgency as I reveal the sinister truth that looms over us. "Seraphina hails from a dark lineage, deeply entrenched in the shadows. She is a formidable adversary, backed by the Conclave of Shadows, a clandestine organization with nefarious intentions." I pause, the weight of my words sinking in as I continue, "The Conclave operates from New York, their reach extending far beyond what most can comprehend. Every time I've traveled for business, I've been drawn into their web, forced to attend meetings where they plot your downfall."

My heart clenches with the knowledge of the danger we're in, and I implore Saturn to understand the gravity of our situation. "We must stand united against them, Saturn. Together, we can defy their darkness and emerge victorious. But we must act swiftly before their machinations consume us both."

In that moment of vulnerability, Saturn shares her inability to wield her powers against Seraphina, a confession that lays bare her fears and insecurities. "I tried, but they didn't work," she admits her voice a fragile thread of sound in the vastness of our challenges.

My frustration at her predicament is quickly over-shadowed by my unwavering belief in her strength and resilience. "You have extraordinary abilities, Saturn. We'll find a way to overcome this together," I assure her, my faith in her unshaken.

As we stand together in the mansion, a bastion against the darkness encroaching upon us, I know that the time has come to share the final piece of the puzzle – my clandestine meeting with Daniel. The revelation looms over me like a shadow, a secret that threatens to widen the gap between us even further. Yet, the truth is a burden too heavy to bear alone, and Saturn deserves to know everything, no matter the cost.

With a heavy heart, I prepare to peel back the last layer of deception, to reveal the depths of the conspiracy that has entangled us. "Saturn, there's something else you need to know..." My voice trails off, a prelude to the storm that is about to break.

CHAPTER 34

"LUNAR REVELATION"

The revelation Miles is about to share sends a ripple of unease through me, my heart hanging on every word. "I want to tell you one more thing, baby," he begins, his voice laden with a heaviness that immediately sets off alarms in my mind.

"What is it, Miles?" The question slips out, laced with a mix of curiosity and apprehension, echoing slightly in the quiet of the room.

His next words are almost a whisper, carrying a weight that seems to press down on the air between us. "I saw someone's shadow in the forest behind Aunt Sage's house when I was checking the place for any traces of you." The words hang in the air, a shadow of their own, dark, and foreboding.

My initial mistrust morphs into shock, my voice barely containing the surge of emotion as I exclaim,

"What? But who could it be? I haven't been there in months, and I certainly haven't sent anyone." The confusion is palpable, swirling around me like a thick fog, obscuring my thoughts.

Miles' expression is grave, his eyes mirroring the seriousness of his discovery. "I know," he concedes, acknowledging the significance of what he's found. "At first, I thought it was a thief, but then it dawned on me that everyone knows the house is empty. A thief wouldn't bother."

My curiosity is piqued, and I press further, seeking clarity in the midst of swirling doubt. "So, who was it, Miles?" The question leaps from my lips, fraught with urgency.

He takes a deep breath, steeling himself for the impact his next words will have. "Daniel Darkwood," he confesses, his tone carrying a mix of regret and determination.

The color drains from my face as the name echoes ominously through my mind. "Daniel?" I stammer; the confusion now tangled with a growing sense of dread. "But why? What does he want?"

Miles' jaw sets firmly, his mind racing to piece together Daniel's motives. "I'm not entirely sure, but his presence at your Aunt's house and his efforts to remain unseen... It all points to something bad—sinister " he explains, the concern in his voice mirroring my own fears.

The thought of Daniel, with his dark ambitions, sends a shiver down my spine. The implications of his actions and perhaps his relentless pursuit of power too, are what seem like a tangled web of impending danger and deceit.

"We must be proactive," Miles declares, his resolve firm. "We can't let them get the upper hand. We need to protect ourselves, and our baby to stay one step ahead."

I nod; a silent agreement forged in the face of shared adversity. Despite the fear, I know we have to face this together. Our history is marked by challenges we have overcome, and this will be no exception. Miles' voice, filled with hope and regret, breaks the silence. He has laid bare his soul, seeking forgiveness and a path forward. "I understand why you did what you did," I admit, my voice soft yet steady. The admission is a balm to the wounds his secrets have inflicted. "But you should have trusted me," I continue, my voice gaining strength. "We could have dealt with this together. Our love deserves that honesty."

The guilt in Miles' eyes is palpable, a testament to the depth of his remorse. He understands the gravity of his mistake and the trust he has fractured.

"I know, Saturn," he replies, his voice thick with emotion. "I was wrong. I let fear guide me, instead of our love."

"I forgive you, Miles, but I swear; this is the last

time," I state, my resolve clear. "We start anew on a foundation of trust, honesty, and openness."

As we face the uncertain future, our commitment to each other is our beacon, guiding us through the darkness. Together, we will navigate the challenges ahead, fortified by the lessons of the past and the strength of our love.

As Miles' relief washes over him like a warm tide, I can almost see the weight lifting from his shoulders. His eyes, a mix of hope and resolve, meet mine as he makes a solemn vow. "I promise, Baby," he declares with a conviction that resonates deeply within me, "to never keep anything from you again. You're not just my wife; you're my best friend, my soul mate, my one true love and there is no one I trust more than you. I swear, I will never keep anything from you again."

His words infuse me with a renewed sense of optimism. Despite the challenges that lay ahead, I believe, more than ever, that together, nothing can stand in our way. Our love is a beacon, guiding us through the darkest nights.

When Miles wraps me in his embrace, it feels like coming home—a place of warmth and safety. His heartbeat, strong and steady against mine, is a testament to the depth of his feelings. For a moment, lost in the comfort of his arms, everything else fades away.

But then, the embrace grows too tight, squeezing the air from my lungs. I gently tap his shoulder, signaling for a little space. He immediately loosens his grip, concern etching his features. "Are you okay, baby?" he asks, his voice soft as silk.

"Yeah," I manage, drawing in a deep breath to fill my lungs with much-needed air. "Just needed to breathe a little."

Understanding flashes in his eyes as he slightly pulls back. "Of course," he murmurs, "I'll be more careful." His care and consideration wrap around me as securely as his arms had moments before.

We linger in each other's company, savoring the silent, shared comfort. His warmth envelops me, his heartbeat a steady drum of reassurance. In his embrace, I find peace.

The calm that settles over us is a balm to my troubled thoughts. Miles' steadfast support is a reminder that I'm not facing the world alone. Together, we can navigate any storm, bound by love and a shared determination.

When the topic of returning to Nightshade Mansion comes up, a knot of anxiety tightens in my stomach. While the mansion offers safety, the allure of the Eridanus Mansion, with its air of mystery and untapped secrets, calls to me. There's something here, a piece of a puzzle I feel compelled to solve.

"Miles," I say, my voice firm yet infused with a sense of longing, "I want to stay here."

His brow furrows with concern, and he counters,

"But it's not safe, Saturn. Without the proper security, what if someone finds you while I'm away?"

I understand his worries, but my gut tells me the answers we need lay within the walls of the Eridanus Mansion. "I'll be safe here," I assure him confidently. "This place is hidden away, shrouded by the forest. Besides, I'm sure I can create a stronger concealment spell that will include you and anyone else we wish to come here."

The conviction in my voice seems to ease some of his apprehension. While he might not fully agree, he understands my need to follow this path. Together, we will face whatever lies ahead, and our love will be a shield against the unknown.

Miles halts, concern evident in his gaze. He begs, "Saturn, if Seraphina confronted you here, they know! Please, let's just head back to Nightshade Mansion. It's not worth the risk."

I softly shake my head. "Miles, I have to stay here. I have a gut feeling that this mansion's library holds the keys to unlocking my abilities. Tomorrow, I'll tidy it up and start looking for any clues or information."

With a sigh, Miles' shoulders lower in surrender. "Okay," he gives in, "I swear, you are the most stubborn person I know. Please promise me you will stay concealed—at all times! In the meantime, I'll make plans for security personnel to keep an eye on you and this entire neighborhood while I'm not around."

Miles grants my request, and I feel a wave of relief. I know staying at Eridanus Mansion is somewhat dangerous, considering the fact that Seraphina was able to find it, but I'm determined to unearth the secrets concealed behind its walls. This old house holds the answers to my powers and maybe my lineage and the future that it holds.

I spend the next day cleaning up the library, changing the dusty, cobweb-infested area into a research-friendly environment. I feel a wave of excitement coming on as I start looking through the enormous library. I have a sense that the answers are there, just waiting to be uncovered from the archives.

I spend hours in the library studying old writings and interpreting mysterious symbols. The quiet and seclusion of the mansion make it the ideal setting for my research. I feel determined and secure, knowing that Miles and our security crew are quietly watching over us.

Over the next few days, my search for answers continues as I dig deeper into Eridanus Mansion's maze-like library, bringing me one step closer to the truth. The enormous library housed inside its walls screams stories of lost wisdom and long-forgotten secrets, with every page offering a possible key to solving the puzzles that beset me.

I go through each book cover to cover, analyzing every word and symbol, looking for anything that will explain why I suddenly lost my abilities. Every book unveils a different aspect of the magickal realm, revealing the subtleties of ceremonies, spells, and the precarious equilibrium between light and evil.

I am particularly interested in a book called "Dance of Luna." The term strikes a chord with me since I feel a strong connection to the moon, which is partly responsible for my powers' unexplained hibernation. I open the book with shaking hands, and an air of old magick fills its pages. As I read through the book, I felt a wave of amazement. It is a grimoire, a collection of lunar knowledge that explains how the moon has a significant impact on magickal skills. The book discloses that every person has a special curse—a restriction intertwined with their abilities—a fine balance that preserves order in the magickal world.

I turn the last page, and my eyes spring wide, a realization that chills my spine. There, in the antique script, is the curse that rules my talents. It says that on the eve of the full moon, my powers will soar to an unprecedented degree, their potency multiplied sevenfold. On moonless nights, however, my powers will be dormant until the sun rises. Furthermore, if the moon's radiance is hidden by clouds, leaving an inky gloom, my powers will revert to dormancy.

I am hit by this realization like a lightning bolt. It explains why I lost my talents on that fateful night - the clouds had obscured the moon, robbing me of its empowering energy. My relationship with the moon becomes clear to me as a basic source of power rather than just something symbolic. With this new understanding, I feel a wave of resolve passes through me. I will no longer be a slave to fate, dependent on the phases of the moon. I'll learn to harness its energy, master its fluctuations, and use my skills with steadfast control.

Miles' face lights up as I reveal my lunar curse to him. He asks, his brow wrinkled in thought, "Why do you think this rule only manifested now?" I think about his question, sorting through the bits of information I have learned. "Perhaps it was always there," I answer, "but since I rarely used my powers beyond practice sessions and never ventured out at night, I never encountered the limitations imposed by the curse." Miles gives a nod of approval. "It makes sense," he says, "Since you never practiced at night, you never experienced the dormancy of your powers during moonless nights."

Then he discloses his relationship to the moon's pull, stating that while his powers peak during the full moon, just like mine do, they continue to function throughout the lunar cycle.

This realization gives me a fresh lease of determination. I refuse to let this fresh curse stop me from achieving my objectives or impede my advancement.

Rather, I will accept it, learn from its rhythm, and apply it to my magickal practice.

Accompanied by Miles, I proceed to examine the subtleties of lunar magick's rise and fall. We try harnessing the moon's energy during its waxing phase, storing its essence within ourselves, and conserving it during its waning phase.

I commit myself to studying lunar cycles after that day, closely monitoring the moon's phases, movements, and relationship to my abilities. I delve into old writings in search of understanding lunar rituals and practices, as well as methods to ramp up my powers during full moons and conserve their energy during moonless nights.

Upon accepting my lunar connection, I experience a renewed sense of self-determination. The curse, which had appeared to be a limitation, has now become a source of strength, a reminder of the delicate balance between light and darkness, between the power of the moon and the tenacity of the human spirit.

CHAPTER 35

"BONDS OF DESTINY"

Since aligning my fate with Miles to safeguard Saturn, my nights have been ensnared in a maelstrom of dreams and visions, each more vivid and enigmatic than the last. It's as if I've been thrust into a realm of perpetual tumult, oscillating between reality and the ethereal, between the clarity of day and the obscurities of night.

In these unsettling dreams, I find myself standing in the ancient halls of Nightshade Mansion, surrounded by shadows that seem to dance and shift with a life of their own. A sense of foreboding hangs heavy in the air as I wander through the complex halls, the whispers of unseen voices echoing in my ears.

Among these nocturnal visions, one theme persistently emerges with striking clarity—the Eridanus constellation and its neighboring star system, Cursa. This celestial fascination, far from being an arbitrary obsession, has its roots in my academic pursuits, a passion for astronomy that blossomed during my years at college.

In those hallowed halls of learning, amidst dusty tomes and ancient artifacts, I found myself drawn to the study of celestial bodies. It was there, under the guidance of my mentors, that I delved into the complexities of the cosmos. Eridanus, with its sprawling expanse and mythological significance, captivated my imagination, becoming a focal point of my scholarly endeavors.

Armed with a telescope that had once belonged to my parents, Heather and Arden Nightshade, I would spend countless nights observing the heavens, charting stars and constellations with meticulous care. Eridanus, in particular, held a special allure, its story intertwined with legends of divine rivers and cosmic journeys. The neighboring star system of Cursa, with its intriguing properties and potential for harboring unseen worlds, only deepened my intrigue.

This academic passion, it turns out, laid the groundwork for understanding the cryptic messages woven into my dreams. The constellation of Eridanus, a symbol of guidance and exploration, and Cursa, a beacon of curiosity and discovery, became harbingers of what was to come. My familiarity with these celestial landmarks provided a key to deciphering the ethereal messages that sought to guide me.

With the vision continuing, I find myself drifting through the depths of space, drawn inexorably towards the neighboring star system of Cursa, I'm greeted by a breathtaking sight – a sprawling network of planets and moons, each one more stunning than the last. The jewel-toned hues of the gas giants, the glittering ice crystals of the frozen moons, and the fiery glow of the sun paint a picture of unparalleled beauty and wonder. In the heart of this celestial paradise, I catch glimpses of my parents, Heather and Arden Nightshade, their presence a beacon of warmth and love amidst the vastness of space.

Heather, with her flowing silver hair and piercing emerald, green eyes, is a vision of grace and wisdom, her gentle smile a balm to the soul. Arden, with his strong and steady presence, radiates a sense of strength and determination, his unwavering gaze a testament to his courage and resolve.

Within the tapestry of my dreams, a scene unfolds that I've never witnessed, yet it resonates with a profound familiarity. Standing amidst a celestial backdrop that seems painted with the strokes of Eridanus and Cursa, two figures emerge, their presence commanding yet serene. One carries the gentle strength of the rivers for which Eridanus is named, while the other holds the mysterious allure of the distant stars.

I've never seen these individuals before, never heard their stories directly from their lips, yet an intrinsic knowing washes over me—these are Saturn's parents, Willow Eridanus and Sebastian Astronaris. It's a realization that arrives without explanation, a certainty born not from memory but from a deeper connection, perhaps woven into the fabric of the very magick that binds us all.

Willow, with her hair that cascades like the river of stars, eyes reflecting the depth of the universe, and Sebastian, whose presence is as steady and enduring as the constellations, stand united. Their bond transcends the physical, rooted in a love as vast as the cosmos itself. In this vision, they are not mere figments of imagination but symbols of resilience, fighting alongside my parents against the dark tide of the Conclave of Shadows.

This knowledge, unbidden yet unshakeable, forms a bridge between the past and the present, linking our families across generations and celestial distances. How I know them to be Willow and Sebastian is a mystery, one that defies logic but speaks to the mystical connections that magick can forge—connections that stretch beyond the realm of the seen and touch the very essence of our beings.

Each dream feels like a piece of a puzzle, a foreboding omen of what's looming on the horizon. I can't shake the feeling that these visions are more than just random threads of my imagination; they're a warning, a glimpse into what could unfold if we don't act swiftly. Recognizing the importance of these nightly messages, I resolve to share my insights with Miles and Saturn tomorrow.

Today, walking into Nightshade Mansion, the home where I grew up, I'm set on sharing my night-time visions. I also promised Miles to bond more with him and to truly connect with Saturn, and today seems like the perfect day to keep that promise. In the family room, bathed in sunlight, I see Miles and Saturn. Their presence instantly soothes the turmoil inside me.

I inhale deeply, a gesture so foreign to me that it feels like stepping into uncharted territory. "So, here's the thing," I begin, my voice unsteady. "Saturn, I need to start by apologizing. At the wedding, I kind of vanished into thin air, didn't I? Miles clued me in on how you might've felt I wasn't exactly thrilled to have you around, which, let me just say, couldn't be further from the truth." I pause, a nervous chuckle escaping me. "It's just, I've been wrestling with my own demons, you know?"

Miles sends me one of his signature looks, a silent "I'm with you" that somehow eases the tension. Saturn caught off guard, raises an eyebrow, clearly not expecting an emotional deep dive with me, of all people.

Miles speaks up, "Lizzy, I've told Saturn all about the Conclave of Shadows and the roles we now reluctantly play in their plans. She now knows and understands what we are coming up against. She's on board with us, facing whatever comes next."

Taking the plunge, I dive headfirst into the depths of my recent experiences. "Right, so, about that. Since we last spoke, Miles, I've been having these... let's call them 'intense dreams.' Not the kind you forget with your morning coffee. These are vivid, almost prophetic visions that have been keeping me up at night." I force a smile, attempting to lighten the mood, but their concerned expressions tell me I've only intrigued—and possibly alarmed—them further.

"The dreams... they've shown me things. Eridanus, Cursa, our parents—yours and mine—standing together against the Conclave. It's like history's trying to tell us something, warn us about what's coming." My voice grows more animated as I share the vivid images that have haunted my sleep.

Saturn's puzzled look deepens. "But you've never met my parents. How could you possibly recognize them?" she asks, skepticism and interest battling within her.

"I know, right? It sounds insane. But in these

dreams, I just...know. Willow and Sebastian, your mom and dad; those are their names, right? It's as if my soul recognizes them," I reply, the words feeling as surreal to say out loud as they do in my head.

Saturn leans closer, her skepticism giving way to intrigue and a little shock. "So, you think these dreams, these visions... they're trying to guide us?" she probes, her voice laced with curiosity and concern.

"More than a sign, Saturn. I think it's a call to action. And that's why I'm here, not just to apologize to you for being a less-than-welcoming sister-in-law but to tell you both that I'm with you. All the way. This thing with the Conclave... we're going to end it, together." My declaration, bold and unwavering, marks a turning point.

Saturn's response is immediate, her warmth enveloping me like a blanket. "Lysandra, that means everything to us. You're family, and knowing we have you on our side... it gives us hope."

The rhythm of our conversation shifts, weaving through plans and fears to moments of unexpected vulnerability and warmth. It's an odd sort of gathering, a trio united not just by blood and marriage but by a shared determination to protect what's most precious. As the room hums with our mingled voices, Miles and Saturn drop a bombshell that brightens the entire space.

"There's something we've been wanting to share

with you," Miles starts, a grin spreading across his face that's so infectious I find myself smiling before I even know the reason.

"Yeah?" I lean in, intrigued. The seriousness of our earlier discussion seems to hang in the balance, waiting to be tipped into lighter realms.

Saturn's eyes are shining, and there's a warmth there that makes the room feel a few degrees cozier. "We're expecting a baby," she says, and the words feel like sunlight breaking through clouds. For a moment, I'm speechless, my heart swelling with a joy so profound it almost aches. "A baby?" I repeat, dumbfounded, as the news sinks in. "You're going to be parents? I'm going to be an aunt?"

The room erupts into laughter at my stunned reaction, but I can't help it. The idea of Miles, my brother, becoming a dad, and Saturn, a woman of such strength and grace, becoming a mom fills me with a sense of hope I hadn't realized I was missing.

"That's incredible!" I finally manage, my voice thick with emotion. "I'm going to be an aunt!" The reality of it, the promise of new life amid our turmoil, brings a lightness to my spirit I hadn't expected to feel.

Miles nods, the pride evident in his smile. "Yeah, Lizzy, you're going to be an aunt."

Saturn reaches over, squeezing my hand. "We couldn't wait to tell you. We wanted you to be one of the first to know."

The significance of their trust and inclusion isn't lost on me. "I'm... I'm so happy for you both. And honored, really. Thank you for sharing this with me." The words feel inadequate to express the whirlwind of emotions inside me, but they're all I have.

As we continue to talk, the atmosphere is lighter, filled with the promise of new beginnings and the strengthening of bonds. The news of the baby, this beacon of hope, reinforces my resolve to protect this family, my family, against whatever challenges lie ahead.

In this moment, within the walls of Nightshade Mansion, we're not just allies in a battle against darkness; we're a family, united by love and the anticipation of the newest member of our clan. And as the night deepens, I'm filled with a sense of purpose and a joy that's both new and deeply familiar.

"So, what's the game plan?" I ask, feeling more like a part of this family than ever before. "How do we take on the Conclave and come out the other side?"

Miles exchanges a glance with Saturn, a silent communication that speaks volumes. "We start by being smarter, more connected than they are. And with you by our side, sister, I think we've got a fighting chance."

The night at Nightshade Mansion ends not with answers but with a commitment to each other and the uncertain path that lies ahead. As I leave the family room, feeling more connected to Miles and Saturn than ever, tears gather in my eyes as I feel the weight of their acceptance. "Thank you," I whisper, feeling a sense of relief wash over me. "I promise to stand by you, by my niece or nephew, and to protect us all from whatever challenges lie ahead."

CHAPTER 36

"ENDURING LOVE'S LEGACY"

In the soft, dim glow of the early evening, where shadows dance like spirits whispering across the walls, I'm ensconced in a whirlwind of thoughts and emotions. These past three months have been a rollercoaster, threading through hope and loss with an unnerving grace. Saturn, the love of my life, with our unborn child cradled within her, shines like a lighthouse amidst the tempest. Her resilience, a stark contrast to the absence of her ancestral wisdom, inspires me. It's not just the love that swells in my heart for her; it's a profound admiration, a sense of awe at her unwavering strength and determination, even when vulnerability nips at her heels. As a partner and a soon-to-be father, she lights up my world in ways I never imagined.

Now, standing shoulder to shoulder with Lysandra,

the scenery around us shifts. The room, once a mere backdrop, pulses with life, charged with the energy of our newfound alliance. Gone is the Lysandra I thought I knew—steadfast and unyielding in her loyalty to the Conclave. In her place stands a comrade, brave enough to voice her longing for liberation from their dark designs.

It's a revelation that could very well cost us everything. Yet, witnessing the blend of raw determination and softness in her gaze, I'm awash with admiration. Her bravery, stepping out from under the oppressive shadow of destiny, kindles a respect in me that burns bright and fierce. Our paths, once parallel, now converge in a joint crusade for freedom from the Conclave's clutches.

Saturn, ever the heart of our trio, extends her warmth and understanding to Lysandra, enveloping her in acceptance and support. This gesture, so pure and genuine, underscores the essence of family—the invisible ties that bind us, even through the bleakest nights.

Their exchange is a symphony of words, a dialogue that stitches the fabric of our collective resolve. Lysandra's dreams and visions, once a source of torment, now beckon with the promise of unlocking ancient secrets and charting a new destiny. With Saturn's steadfast courage and Lysandra's reborn spirit as our ally, I stand firm in the belief that together, we will navigate the storms ahead.

The transformation in Lysandra was palpable from the moment she laid eyes on the ultrasound image of our child; a baby girl. A spark ignited within her, dispelling the shadows of her former self to embrace a purpose reborn. The tiny heartbeat flickering on the screen, a beacon of life and potential, stirred something profound within her—a maternal instinct, fierce and unyielding.

Watching Lysandra evolve is a revelation. Freed from the chains of duty and obligation that once bound her to the Conclave, she now stands with us, a sentinel poised to face any threat. Her loyalty, once shackled, now flourishes, fueled by a relentless drive to safeguard our growing family.

Reflecting on our shared history, I marvel at the journey we've undertaken. Lysandra's metamorphosis from a loyal sister to a formidable guardian is nothing short of miraculous. Her dedication, once dictated by command, now guided by love, reshapes every facet of her being. She's not just changed; she's reborn, stronger and more determined, a guardian in every sense of the word.

Yet, amidst this awe, a twinge of regret laces my thoughts. Regret overlooking the signs of her transformation, for letting past conflicts cloud my recognition of the incredible woman she's become. But with this regret comes gratitude—a profound appreciation for witnessing her rebirth and for the unbreakable bond that unites us.

In the quiet of the evening, with only the gentle hum of life around us, a sense of peace envelops me. It's a peace born from the knowledge that together, there's no storm we can't weather. Lysandra's loyalty and resolve are beacons that light our way, reminders that our family, bound by love, is a force to be reckoned with. In this moment, I'm reminded of the power of love to shape our destinies, a power that guides us, steadfast and true, into the unknown.

The twilight embraces us in its gentle grasp as we stand on the training grounds, the wind murmuring secrets through the trees around us, hinting at the magick that saturates the very air we breathe. Tonight, under the watchful gaze of a full moon, its silver light cloaks everything in an ethereal glow, weaving a spell of mysticism over the scene. In this sacred space, I feel a profound connection and a sense of belonging that both empowers and humbles me.

Returning to Nightshade Mansion, the decision was fraught with complexity for Saturn and me. Her curse, a bond with the lunar cycle, makes her powers ebb and flow with the moon's phases. On nights like this, she's unparalleled in her strength, a force of nature. Yet, in the new moon's darkness, she becomes vulnerable, stripped of her magick. This curse, a double-edged sword, presents us with challenges and gifts in equal measure.

Our training under the full moon is more than preparation; it's a rite of passage. The Conclave's potential to harness lunar power as we do makes them a formidable foe. Yet, our resolve is crystal clear. Bound by love, blood, and a destiny to protect what we hold dear, we press on.

Lysandra, bathed in moonlight, her olive skin glowing, her hair a cascade of shadows and light, her green eyes a reflection of the lunar brilliance, stands as a testament to transformation. Once ensnared by duty's shadows, she now stands as a sentinel beside us, her loyalty unwavering, her purpose reborn in the forge of family.

As the moon climbs higher, anticipation crackles in the air, electric and alive. Our plans, intricate and well-conceived, lay before us. We've woven a tapestry of signals, ready to adapt to the capricious whims of weather, ensuring Saturn's strength remains our ace in the hole.

Facing the Conclave of Shadows, a defiant fire burns within me. They shrouded in mystery, seek to unravel the enigma that is Saturn, only to find themselves up against a united front. Lysandra and I, together, are more than just allies; we are the embodiment of resilience, a testament to the strength of our familial bonds. The Conclave, with its cryptic motives and elusive presence, presents a silent challenge. Their silence, a gauntlet thrown in the hush of night. But we stand ready, our determination unwavering, our spirit indomitable. Gazing up at the moon, its calm light a balm to the tempest within, I find a moment of peace. The path that has led us here, through trials and revelations, has prepared us for this moment. Standing with Saturn and Lysandra, our bond is unyielding, forged in adversity's fire. The love I bear for my sister, the devotion I hold for Saturn, and our collective protective instinct are our greatest assets. Together, we are an unstoppable force, a beacon in the darkness, ready to face the shadows and emerge triumphant. Our story is one of resilience, love, and the unwavering power of family, standing united against the tide, ready to illuminate the night.

Lysandra steps away as Saturn and I discuss our plans under the luminous gaze of the moon, Saturn voices a yearning that resonates deeply within me. "I wish we knew more about the Conclave of Shadows and their history with my ancestors and Eridanus," she muses, her voice tinged with curiosity and concern.

A spark of inspiration ignites within me, fueling a determination to unravel the secrets veiled by the passage of time. "What if we could journey back through time?" I find myself suggesting, the idea coming to life with a newfound zeal. "We could seek answers from your parents and ancestors directly," I propose, envisioning not just a voyage through the temporal folds but also an expedition to Eridanus. The thought of consulting Saturn's lineage for guidance lights up a pathway not only across the epochs but also across the cosmos, where the wisdom of ages past may reveal the truths we yearn to uncover.

The idea of time travel sends a thrill coursing through me, the possibilities unfurling like the pages of an ancient tome. "Time travel," I echo, the notion both exhilarating and daunting.

Saturn's gaze meets mine, a silent plea for understanding passing between us. "In the Book of Shadows," she explains, her voice brimming with resolve, "there's a spell—a spell of time travel. By combining it with your time loop ability, we could journey back to Eridanus."

The prospect of unraveling the mysteries surrounding Saturn's lineage and the Conclave's vendetta against her family fuels our determination. "Let's do it," I declare, my voice resolute. "Let's uncover the truth about your lineage, your ancestors, and the Conclave's motives."

With a shared nod, we embark on the meticulous preparations for our journey. Saturn devotes herself to rewriting the spell in the Book of Shadows, weaving in the intricate ties to my time manipulation abilities. Meanwhile, I gather the herbs, crystals, and talismans necessary to anchor our spell and ensure a safe passage.

As we stand in the midst of our preparations, the

weight of our impending journey pressing upon us, Saturn turns to me with a determined gleam in her eye. "It's time," she declares, her voice ringing with resolve.

I nod in agreement, the gravity of our mission settling over us like a cloak. "But first, we need to tell Lysandra," I reply, knowing that her support and understanding are crucial to our success.

We make our way to where Lysandra is, her presence a comforting anchor amidst the storm of uncertainty. "Lysandra," Saturn begins, her voice steady despite the turmoil swirling within her, "we have a plan."

Lysandra regards us with a knowing smile, her eyes betraying a hint of mischief. "I'm listening," she says, her tone playful yet attentive.

Saturn outlines our plans, explaining our decision to journey to Eridanus in search of answers. Lysandra listens intently, her expression shifting from amusement to concern as the gravity of our undertaking becomes clear.

"I'll stay behind," Lysandra says, her voice filled with determination. "I'll keep the Conclave of Shadows busy and ensure they remain none the wiser."

A sense of relief washes over us, knowing that Lysandra will watch over our backs even as we venture into the unknown. "Thank you, Lysandra," Saturn says, gratitude lacing her words.

Saturn and I catch Lysandra's worried look, concern

etched deep into her features. But Saturn, ever the beacon of optimism, reassures her with a wink and a smile, "Don't worry, Sis. We'll be back before you know it with all the answers we need." Her words fill me with renewed determination to protect her at all costs.

Lysandra returns our smiles, her eyes sparkling with warmth and affection, saying, "Just make sure you guys make it back in one piece," she teases, a hint of seriousness underlying her words. "I've got a niece to train, after all."

As we share a lighthearted moment with Lysandra, the weight of our impending journey lifts, if only for a fleeting moment. With a final exchange of farewells, we turn our attention back to the task at hand, our resolve strengthened by the knowledge that we have each other's backs.

Intertwined and hearts beating as one, Saturn and I find ourselves standing within a sacred fire ring nestled deep within the enchanting forest behind Nightshade Mansion. The verdant canopy overhead filters the moonlight, casting dappled shadows that dance upon the forest floor, adding to the mystique of our surroundings. Around us, the air hums with the energy of nature, alive and vibrant.

In the center of the fire ring, a delicate arrangement of herbs, crystals, and talismans lies poised, each imbued with its own unique energy, ready to enhance our magickal workings. The flickering light of countless flameless candles bathes the area in an ethereal glow, illuminating our makeshift altar and lending an air of otherworldly beauty to the scene. With our preparations complete, Saturn and I stand side by side, our hands clasped tightly together as we begin to chant the ancient incantation. The words flow from our lips like a melody, resonating with the very essence of the forest itself. Around us, the spirits of the woodland seem to stir, drawn by the power of our spellcasting.

As our voices rise and fall in perfect harmony, a sudden gust of wind sweeps through the forest, stirring the leaves and sending them swirling around us in a wild dance. Loose strands of hair whip about our faces, adding to the sense of exhilaration and magick that fills the air. Sparks of light ignite in the darkness, casting a mesmerizing display of colors that paint the trees and foliage with an iridescent glow. In perfect synchronicity, we place sigils at the cardinal points—north, east, south, and west—anchoring our ritual in the elemental energies of the earth. Each symbol pulses with its own unique power, connecting us to the primal forces of nature and channeling their strength into our spell work.

As we continue to chant, the very fabric of reality seems to shimmer and warp around us, the boundary between the mundane world and the realm of magick growing increasingly thin. With each passing moment, we can feel the energy building, crackling like electricity in the air, as we prepare to unleash the full force of our combined will upon the universe. With each verse of the incantation, the energy grows more intense, building like a crescendo in a symphony. I can feel the power of the spell coursing through my veins, a potent blend of magick and determination. Our voices reach a crescendo as we speak the final words of the incantation, "By the power of the stars, by the light of the moon, through the threads of time, we shall commune. Eridanus, ancient and wise, open your gates, reveal the ties." And at that moment, time seems to stand still. Saturn's eyes meet mine, and I see a spark of excitement mirrored in her gaze—a silent understanding passing between us.

And then, with a sudden rush of energy, the circle erupts in a dazzling display of light and sound. A portal begins to materialize before us, swirling with colors and patterns that seem to dance and shift with a life of their own. With a shared glance and a nod of determination, Saturn and I step forward, our hands clasped tightly together. As we cross the threshold of the portal, a sense of exhilaration washes over me, mingling with the anticipation of what lies beyond. And then, with a final burst of energy, we are swept away into the vast expanse of the universe, our hearts filled with wonder and awe at the boundless possibilities that await us.

As we disappear into the portal, I can't help but turn to Saturn with a grin. "Well, baby, looks like we're off to explore the universe!" I quip, my voice filled with a mix of excitement and humor. Saturn chuckles, her eyes sparkling with mischief. "Just another Tuesday night for us," she replies, her tone playful and lighthearted. And with that, we vanish into the swirling vortex of time and space, ready to embark on our next great adventure together.

To Be Continued...